The Burnt Lotus

CATH WEEKS

Copyright © 2013 Cath Weeks

All rights reserved.

ISBN-10:1492887331
ISBN-13:978-1492887331

ACKNOWLEDGEMENTS

Cover image by Leele. Author image by P. Gettins

Heartfelt thanks to John Carey for the mentoring and inspiration; to Marc Riley for his help in the eleventh hour; to Natali Juste and Ali Carter for allowing me to disappear for 2013; to Karis Christie for tea at 3pm; to Mum for the trail of my business cards that you have left across the southern hemisphere; and to dearest Nick, Wilfie and Alex for their love and support.

Dedicated to
Mrs Murray, for saying at parent's evening that
I would achieve whatever I set my heart upon
And to
Mum, for dashing home to tell me

A vision is not a cloudy vapour or a nothing. It is organised and minutely articulated beyond all that the mortal and perishing nature can produce. I assert that all my visions appear to me infinitely more perfect and more organized than anything seen by the mortal eye.

William Blake

The first child

Aaron Deakin turned fifty-five years old on Valentine's Day. He marked the occasion by dining at the Chop Suey Bar with Belinda, a divorcee whom he was dating. He wore his habitual tweed jacket, which was patched on the elbows through necessity and not fashion, and opted for the sweet and sour king prawn, as he was prone to do. The next morning he woke with the strong desire to tell Belinda that he didn't care for her teenage daughters and their neuroses, but instead he lit a cigarette and pecked Belinda a kiss before hurrying off to the homeless shelter. He had been managing the shelter for seven years and knew that the moment he crossed the threshold all thoughts of Belinda and her daughters would dissolve.

Sometimes late at night when Aaron couldn't sleep, he scrolled through dating websites, viewing profiles of ladies who liked to bake blondies, who ate egg-white omelettes, who had always wanted to go to Venice; and he tried to imagine what it would feel like to be in love.

ONE

They were stood inside the Sacré-Couer in Paris on a cold evening in April when Beth first saw the child with the missing front teeth.

Beth had one hand on her guide book and one hand on top of Brett's head to lock him into place, as they gazed at the mosaic of Jesus glowing on the ceiling. "It's the largest mosaic in the world," she said. "Look – the Virgin Mary, Joan of Arc, and Saint Michael the Archangel."

"Angewell," echoed Brett.

"Churches are cool," said Erland, folding his arms and nodding appreciatively. "Why aren't we religious again, Mum?"

"You're such a geek," said Danny

"He's not a geek. And to answer your question…" Beth lowered her voice. "I'm not sure about all this stuff."

"What stuff?" said Erland, blinking.

Beth glanced at him, wondering whether he was toying with her. Aged twelve, he was now the same height as Beth and had taken this literally, levelling with her about everything: *do you think God supports a Premiership team or*

1

Hartlepool? "Roast chestnut?" he said, offering her a crumpled bag. He had just bought the chestnuts from a peddler on the steps outside.

"Could you be more naff?" said Danny. "Who eats chestnuts? Why don't you get yourself a knitted jumper to go with it – one with snowflakes on?"

"Stop it you two," said Beth. "People are praying." She pointed to the pews, at the hunched forms of tourists whose heads were bent in prayer, their backs clad in a colourful array of spring raingear from around the world. Viewed from the air, their forms would have made a splendid mosaic of their own.

"Mama," said Brett, jigging his leg and tugging at Beth's arm. "I need wee wee."

"Okay, poppet," she said, her heart sinking. There were few public toilets in Paris. No wonder the French drank from tiny espresso cups and not mugs of tea. "Can you hang on for me?" She doubted it; Brett was tired. He had managed to climb the two hundred and twenty-five steps to the church on the promise of a treat at the top. Sacré-Couer wasn't the ice-cream shop he was expecting.

She was about to leave, when Danny nudged her. "Look, Mum," he said.

A noiseless line of nuns in white habits was flowing into the alter area. There was a flutter of excited murmurs from the tourists, who rushed to sit in the pews, pulling out their phones to film the revered Benedictine sisters.

A man with a thin moustache dashed forward. "No film," he said, wagging his index finger and clicking his tongue.

The sisters came to a halt as one, their eyes fixed ahead at a shared vision, and began to sing. It was impossible to move once the music began. The sound rooted everyone present – not only to the ground, but to each other. Everyone within the church at that moment was at once human, united and yet removed to elsewhere.

Either side of the choir, framing them, were the thousands of charity candles flickering in the gloom – each flame a prayer to be answered.

Beth swallowed, tears appearing in her eyes without any accompanying sadness. She reached for Brett, scooping him up, holding him close to her.

When she looked again at the Benedictine sisters, the child had appeared.

Beth felt her legs stiffen, her skin prickle. Had Danny and Erland noticed? No. Their attention had been stolen by three teenage schoolgirls in cerise berets and sweaters that said *Berlin Brandenburg International*.

Beth stared at the child in incomprehension. The little girl was standing right next to the singing nuns – almost part of the choir, swaying as she stared upwards at the mosaic, twiddling her fingers absently. What on earth was she doing there? Beth looked about the church for a chatting parent, a frustrated nanny, a bored older sibling, but there was no such guardian. The child looked as though she had run away from school. She wearing a green cheesecloth dress, the sort that girls wore as summer uniform. Her hair was lank and unbrushed, her skin was sallow. Where was the man with the moustache? Why wasn't he shooing her away?

"Why are they letting her stand there like that?" said Beth.

"Who?" said Danny.

"That girl."

"What girl?"

At that moment the child turned to look directly at Beth, as though she knew they were talking about her. And then, over the heads of the praying tourists, above the sound of the singing sisters, she delivered a wide smile straight to Beth – a smile that exposed her missing front teeth.

Beth gasped, feeling inexplicably panicked. She

reached for Danny and Erland, pulling their attention away from their cerise-bereted girls. "We need to go," she said, ushering them out of the church.

"But what about the nuns?" said Erland.

Outside, Beth stood looking blankly about her, trying to see beyond the crowds. A man was playing an Irish jig on a violin; a teenager was performing tricks with a football – kneeing it, spinning it on his finger.

"Ice keem," said Brett, who was still in her arms, pushing his fingers experimentally into her face as though he could mould it like plasticine.

"We need to find a toilet before ice cream," Beth said. "I'm not sure where the nearest toilet is."

"How about there?" said Danny, pointing to a man who was urinating in an alley way.

"Oh, for goodness sake," said Beth, leading the boys away.

They stopped before a low wall with all of Paris before them. It was a murky evening and the grey of the city ran to a smudgy horizon. The Eiffel Tower was to their right, not yet illuminated for the evening. Rain was dotting the sky. There was a vague pause in the air, before nightfall.

Beth turned to look back at Sacré-Couer, at the hundreds of tourists amassed at the top of the steps. Skinny peddlers with hungry eyes were weaving through the crowds – flashing open cases, unravelling magic carpets, everything fast and temporary, ready to be snapped up if the police appeared. A homeless man approached through the throngs of designer anoraks, making his way to the church entrance where he lay down on the top step, his hands clasped underneath his face like a child in slumber. The tourists stepped over him, occasionally looking down distractedly to see what it was that had tripped them.

Beth led the boys down the side of the hill to the Place du Tertre in Montmartre – the square where artists gathered to paint portraits for tourists. It was early for an evening meal, so the restaurants were quiet and they found a table quickly.

"Listen to this," said Erland, studying the guide book. "There was this bloke called Saint Denis who was decapitated. So he carried his head under his arm to the site where Sacré-Couer now stands. How cool is that?"

No one replied. They were too hungry and tired.

"The druids used to worship at Sacré-Couer," said Erland.

"Really?" said Danny, looking up instantly from his steak.

"Now you've got his interest," said Beth.

At the age of fourteen, Danny wasn't becoming less interested in supernatural forces but more so. The world around him was hardening – his school friends were shrugging, slouching, eye-rolling – and yet Danny was holding firm to his notion that life was a magical journey.

"You may jest," Danny said, laying down his knife and fork, "but there are approximately ten thousand druids in England today. In fact, Winston Churchill was a druid. Bet you didn't know that."

"You seem very knowledgeable on the subject," said Beth.

Danny flushed and looked away. He wasn't normally bashful about his beliefs, which made her wonder what new little nerve she had touched.

"Anyhow," she said, "not even Churchill could convince me to believe in something invisible."

"Oh? And why's that?" Danny said, despite having had this conversation many times before.

She always gave the same reply. "Because spiritual things aren't tangible. They aren't reliable enough...Maybe I've just been through too much," she added.

"Odd," said Danny. "Because when people experience pain, they often turn to magic to add more control to their lives." He shot her a funny look before turning back to his steak.

They ate the remainder of their meals in silence. And then Brett announced that he had wet his pants. They were in such a rush to eat, no one had remembered about the toilet.

They were staying in a family room in a small hotel, a ten minute walk from Sacré-Couer. It was quiet in the hotel and utterly black at night once the shutters were pulled. The drinks machine was broken and there were no tea facilities, so they bought bottles of water which were scattered about the floor. The boys had fallen asleep as soon as they kicked off their trainers.

Beth couldn't sleep. "Dan?" she whispered.

"Yeah?"

He was awake. She was glad.

"There's something I want to tell you." She paused. How to say it? "Next Saturday...."

"You've got a date."

"Yes," she said. "How did you–?"

"Heard you arrange it on the phone."

"Oh." She stared into the darkness, wishing there were more light in the room. "And you're okay with that?"

There was the sound of the bed sheets lifting and dropping as Danny shrugged.

"I don't know if I like him," she said. "It's just a date. Do you understand?"

"Course," he said, a little too quickly.

They fell back into the hush of the room.

"Danny?"

"Yup."

"Did you really not see that child in the church?"

"I really didn't."

She waited until Danny seemed asleep before she sat up in bed, reaching through the darkness for her bag and stepping forward with her arms outstretched. She made it to the bathroom, where the light set off a loud fan. She glanced back into the bedroom, but no one stirred.

She closed the door and perched on the edge of the bath. From inside her purse she prised a small photograph that was hidden in a secret panel.

She sat with the photograph in her palm, as though holding a rare fragile butterfly.

Gently, tenderly, she kissed the photograph – the lightest kiss she could render. She had read once that butterflies only lived for a day. The photograph was equally time-restricted. One day, her kisses would rub him away and he would be no more. It was the only photograph of him that she had.

She slipped back into the dark bedroom, following the sound of Brett's snoring to find her place back with him in bed. And within a short while, she found sleep.

The best thing about their new home, aside from having a canal and palm trees at the bottom of the garden, was that Danny had his own bedroom. After years of sharing with Erland and wondering whether his brother was still alive, due to his ability to lie so still, Danny now lay alone in his attic bedroom wondering whether everyone below him was still alive because he couldn't hear a thing up there.

It had been snowing on the January morning that the removals van stalled outside Lilyvale, its tyres spinning through the drifts. The removal men had cursed as their legs grew soggy and numb, struggling with boxes over snow. Yet it was the best possible start for the Trelawneys. Snow was magical, with its shape-shifting abilities and power to transform wherever it fell. So although the bottom fell out of the box marked *fragile*, the snow caught the china plates and no harm was done. January had been magical, spiritual. He had spent the first few weeks forcing open the attic window to breathe in the frosty air and watch the ice drifting down the canal.

Snow went with Lilyvale, suited the exotic garden, the proximity to water, the freshness of the new life that they needed. They moved in scarred and bruised by the past, and the snow soothed them. The drifts lasted several weeks, after which point the world was washed new. It was a baptism of sorts. They all felt it. Even his mum.

And now it was spring and they were all feeling good. Thanks to the snow and to Lilyvale, their silent keeper.

The only sad thing – Danny had noticed that there always had to be one flaw, even on a masterpiece painting – was that snow reminded him of his dad. He knew it would always be that way, that his mission was to live with the sadness – not by trying to flap it away as though it were a huge buzzing fly but by accepting it, the same way that everyone had to accept things like illness, death, England losing at penalties.

The last time he saw his dad was over a year ago, back at the old house, back in the old plot, back in the depressing scenes. His dad had lifted those scenes, had set light to them with the power of a blow torch, just by standing there. He had appeared out of nowhere because Danny's snow spell had worked. It was a miracle, one which Danny thought would change his life forever. But then the torch got turned off with a dismal *flughhhh* sound and everything went back to its saggy state. His mum and Jacko sat there on the couch, Erland sulked in his room, and their dad retreated outside, saying something about getting on back to London before the next snow fall.

Danny had wanted to tell his dad to stay longer, to tell him to ignore Jacko's noiseless threats, to ignore his mum's cold greeting, Erland's immaturity, but the damage was done.

As he stood there on the doorstep, watching his

dad walk back along the road with frail snowflakes tumbling around him, Danny willed him to turn around one more time, before turning the corner.

Please, *please*, *Dad*.

And then his dad turned to look at Danny and raised his hand to wave goodbye, before disappearing out of sight.

They promised to stay in touch, but Danny knew it was difficult for his dad to call because of his wife and kids. Sometimes, love wasn't enough. God knows why people wrote songs suggesting otherwise.

Since the trip to Paris, Beth had been thinking about the Sacré-Couer child obsessively. She couldn't rid the vision from her mind. When she thought about that smile, seemingly aimed only at her – about the hollow gaps where teeth should have been, she closed her eyes and shook her head to dispel the thought. The vision dissipated, only to reassemble minutes later. She couldn't think of anything to do but wait for time to sort the matter out. In a few weeks, the memory would be too thin to resurrect.

She was having trouble sleeping, wondering why she hadn't noticed before now how painfully silent and ethereal Lilyvale was, with the deep canal lying coiled at its feet. She found herself rising in the small hours to sit by her bedroom window, watching the clouds rush by, her thoughts moving with them as though they were hurrying her across the sky back to Sacré-Couer.

Had she seen the child outside the church? Could she remember seeing her anywhere but next to the singing nuns? Had there really been no guardian present – no other children in the same uniform? If only she had pursued the matter at the time, but how much could she do with her toddler in her arms and two teenage boys at her side? And what was there to pursue anyway?

It was just a silly kid playing truant from school, playing a daft game by locking eyes with someone to unnerve them.

She had chosen the wrong person to lock eyes with then.

In January, the week they moved into Lilyvale as it happened, Beth was signed off from her parenting programme. No more therapists, courses, procedures, specialists prodding her around. She was officially a Good Parent. Case over.

At least, it had felt like case over, until Sacré-Couer – until that child had appeared.

She thought of Danny's words in the Place du Tertre restaurant. They hadn't spoken of the past since moving to Lilyvale, having decided – without discussion – that it was healthier that way. But then he had said at dinner that people turned to magic to help them through pain, and had given her that funny look.

What was behind that look of her son's – Danny, whom she used to be able to read so well – whom everyone used to be able to read so well? He had changed more than any of them – had concluded somewhere along the way that transparency was weak, a betrayal of secrets.

He had been so pleased about Beth being signed off. He went around the house whistling for a few weeks. It was the start of their new life, he said. But then little by little, subtly, she felt him pull away. He was spending more time in his attic room than with them downstairs. It was probably his age. She hoped it was his age.

She was sat at her usual spot at the bedroom window. She glanced at Brett's form underneath the blankets. He slept in a small bed next to her double one. At some point she would move him to the spare room, but not yet. She liked to have him near, to hear him breathing.

She rose and stood watching him sleep, moving the sheets away from his face. He was snoring softly. There was a whiff of medicine in the air. She placed her hand on his forehead; he was running a temperature with his cold.

She returned to the window. There were flecks of rain on the glass. The window was open slightly, a night breeze touching her brow. She could hear the rustle of the palm trees at the bottom of the garden.

A sudden gust of wind prompted her to close the window. Back in bed, she drew the sheets up high. The window was shut but it felt as though the cold air was still upon her, as though the palm trees were still rustling, brushing against her hair, whispering the secret.

You were the only one that saw her.

It was the semi-final of the South-West Premier Cup. It was one of those mornings when the clouds wouldn't let the sun through, so all was grey aside from the trees at the end of the pitch which were tinged with light, as though a painter had been too heavy with the yellow. Danny breathed in deeply, calming his nerves. He felt like those trees: highlighted, set aside from the rest, lit up with expectation.

Everyone watched him when he played – eyes followed his form around the pitch: spectators, talent scouts. Who knew where an outstanding performance today could lead? He was now Bath Under 16's top striker – a position which he sustained with the petrol of his imagination. His team mates teased him for being a dreamer: *hey, Trelawney, got yer lucky pants on?* One of these days he would let them know that it was actually his dreams that were scoring all the goals.

Danny's game was entrenched with ritual and superstition. Before a match, at every stage of his preparation he projected success. As he pulled on his team strip, he was scoring the winning goal for Chelsea in the F.A Cup final; as he laced his boots, he was skidding across the grass on his knees, landing in front of his mum and dad in the V.I.P. box, shaking his fists in the air. With his first step onto the pitch, he thanked the universe for his outstanding performance to come.

Today, the imaginary crowd's cheers were faint in his ears, the glory was fragile. He stood squinting in the sunshine, eyeing the Exeter Colts, who seemed long-legged and much older. Fitter, stronger – young male horses basically. He had a bad feeling. For the first time none of his family were here to support him, as Brett had a temperature. He had mentioned to Erland that he might like to check out the game, but Erland muttered something about a flat tyre – even though he only ever skateboarded. Danny couldn't be bothered to point out the indiscretion.

He sensed that he was going to have to make an impression quickly against the colts. The whistle blew and he was off, feeling like an ant scurrying across the pitch, hoping not to get crushed. A herd of tanned thighs came at him and he crossed his heart and made an ambitious tackle, similar to the one that he often made at the F.A. Cup final moments before scoring.

He didn't feel the pop of his bone right away. The sound and the pain arrived a few seconds later, colliding to create a colossal blow to his system. And then he passed out.

Beth was trying to coax Brett into eating a mouthful of medicine when the phone rang, causing her to pour it onto his lap. Brett laughed, slapping the red liquid on his legs to make it splash. "Blood!" he said, delighted.

It was Danny's coach on the phone. Danny was being taken to Bath Central hospital by ambulance with a fractured knee. Could she come immediately?

When they arrived at the hospital, Danny was lying in the emergency ward, his face twisted with agony.

Beth stifled the temptation to cry. "Oh, Danny," she said, perching on the edge of his bed. "What can I do for you?"

Danny looked at her and shook his head, tears appearing in his eyes.

A nurse swept back the curtain. There was a man in green overalls with her, who kicked the brakes off the bed. "X-ray time," the nurse said. "Won't be long."

Beth and Erland stood waiting in the cubicle. Brett had fallen asleep in the car journey over. He was still running a temperature. Beth leaned against the counter to bear his weight, perspiration prickling her forehead from the heat of holding him.

They were back in hospital – back here again, worrying about what lay ahead. Except that this time it was just a football injury. Nothing to really worry about; nothing they couldn't handle. There was no getting away from hospitals when you had children…So Beth's inner dialogue went, whilst Erland slouched against the counter, idly poking through the boxes of gauzes and plastic gloves.

When Danny returned, a doctor was accompanying him. "It's not as bad as we thought," the doctor said.

"Oh, thank God!" said Beth. She beamed at Danny, gripping his hand. Danny smiled at her, squeezing her hand back.

The doctor glanced from mother to son as though disconcerted by their behaviour. "Danny has fractured his patella," he said. "He'll need a cast for six weeks." He turned to Danny. "How's the pain?"

"Not enough to justify missing the semi-final."

"Don't worry," said the doctor. "You'll be back for the start of next season."

Danny groaned. The doctor left them.

"We'll do some fun things this summer to distract you," said Beth.

"Right," said Danny, his voice full of disbelief.

"I can teach you chess," Erland offered. Danny groaned again.

Beth smiled. She felt almost euphoric. He was going to be all right. They could deal with this.

That was the thing with single parenting: she was always assessing her ability to cope with each situation – an eternal check list of *can I do this? Yes I can!*

"Hey, Mum," said Danny, propping himself up on his elbows. "You still going on your date tonight?"

"Oh, gosh!" said Beth. "I'd forgotten… No." She shook her head.

Danny flopped back down onto his pillow, a smile flickering onto his lips.

On Monday morning, the house was in a state of hushed respect as they crept around the kitchen swapping marmalade and orange juice, despite the fact that Danny was on the third floor and couldn't possibly hear them.

When the phone rang at eight o'clock, Beth snatched it up in annoyance.

"Hello?" she said, perching the receiver under her chin whilst cellophaning sandwiches. There didn't appear to be anyone at the other end of the phone. "Hello?"

There came the sound of heavy breathing – an odd rasping noise dotted with loud clicks. She was about to hang up, when someone spoke.

"Beth Trelawney?" He had a polite, calm voice.

"Yes?" Beth said

"Can I take the last Mini Cheddars?" said Erland, dangling a packet in front of her.

"Yes," she said, batting him away. "Hello?"

The speaker cleared his throat. "My name is Reverend Trist."

Beth scanned her memory for the name. They had been involved with social workers, police offers, lawyers, but never the clergy – aside from the time that a missionary knocked on the door to tell her he was praying for her soul.

"I'm calling from H.M. West Marsh."

"Digestive biscuits?" said Erland, holding the tin out speculatively, his head cocked. Beth frowned at him. From upstairs there came the distant sound of a bell tinkling. It was Danny ringing from the attic for her.

"I'm assisting Pamela Lazenby," said the reverend. "Pamela tells me that she was your foster mother. She'd like a word with you, if you wouldn't mind. I'll put her back on."

"What?" said Beth.

Brett entered the room, pushing a red train along a ridge in the tiled floor. "Choo choo." He was still in his pyjamas, his hair frizzy from a sticky night's sleep.

There came the sound of the heavy breathing again. "Princess? Is that you?"

Beth sat down heavily at the kitchen table in shock.

There was a series of wheezes. "It's okay," the reverend was saying in the background. "Take it nice and slow."

Then the clicking – some sort of apparatus. A ventilator?

"Forgive me, Princess..."

"That's enough for now," Beth heard the reverend say. Then to Beth: "Would it be possible–?"

From upstairs, came the tinkling of the bell again.

"Why is she calling?" said Beth. "What does she want?"

"Your forgiveness." He said it so forthrightly and civilly, as though requesting the return of a borrowed handkerchief.

"I don't understand. Why does she want my forgiveness? Is she dying?"

He cleared his throat again – a small action that belied his intention to give his words weight. "Yes."

"I see...And now she's trying to buy a ticket to heaven?"

"No," said the reverend. "She wants to give you

the chance to buy *yours* – a chance for you to find happiness."

Beth laughed in surprise. "Then I guess we're both going to hell then," she said. "Good day to you, Reverend." She hung up and stood staring at the phone in amazement.

When she turned, still holding the cellophaned sandwiches in her hand, Brett was running his train over her feet. "Was that Daddy?" he said.

"No, poppet," she said. "It was no one."

She ran back through the conversation in her mind. She had been ungracious, damning. Good!

No, not good.

"Trouble at mill?" said Erland. Everything he said seemed steeped in sarcasm and mirth. Sometimes she thought he was watching her life as though it were a tedious family sit-com.

She picked up the phone. The last number that rang wasn't available because it was a private listing. What was the name of the place? Marsh Field? Marsh Wing?

Danny rang his bell again. "Erland, could you please see what Danny wants?" she said, dashing through to her study to start up the laptop.

"But I'll be late for school!" Erland shouted after her.

"Come on," she murmured to the computer, drumming her fingers.

As she waited, she heard Erland sighing sadly to himself as he climbed the stairs.

What was she thinking? He would be late for school. Danny needed his pain relief. Brett was due at preschool any moment.

Pammy couldn't come into her life out of nowhere and set everything off balance. They had a rhythm, a way of living together that was synchronised, like clay spinning on a potter's wheel. A finger – a pointing finger – could easily cause the clay to collapse. She had to protect their life – put it back on straight, set it spinning smoothly again.

She went out to the hallway. "I'll see to Dan," she said to Erland. "You go off to school."

Erland shuffled back down the stairs, his satchel bouncing on his back. "Righty-ho," he said.

"Have a good day," she said, pressing a kiss onto his cheek. "I love you."

She moved back into the study to turn off the computer. She felt calm, her priorities back in order. It was a normal Monday morning in the Trelawney household again.

As the laptop stopped its whirring noise and blacked out, the room fell into darkness. It was a west-facing room that she had chosen for her study as the sun didn't stream in until late afternoon. It was a peaceful place – perfect for her work.

"Brett?" she called out, glancing at her watch. They would have to go now. Where were his Wellingtons? He would need them today, to walk along the potholed canal path.

She was closing the study door, when something stirred in the corner by the curtains. She stopped and frowned.

The curtain was moving. She felt her heart turn over, her breath stop.

Maybe it was the wind. Had she left the window open? Maybe it was a cat. Or a…

Her thoughts were stopped. Because the curtain had lifted to reveal the intruder.

There, in the study, with her hands wrapped shyly in Beth's raspberry velvet curtains, was the Sacré-Couer child: the same sallow-skinned child in the cheesecloth dress.

"Oh, God." Beth glanced about her in panic. How had the child got in? How had she even got here?

How was it possible? "What do you want?"

"Mummy?" The door pushed open. Brett was stood there wearing his stripy anorak, ready for preschool.

When Beth looked back at the curtains, the child in the cheesecloth dress was gone.

TWO

With Brett at preschool and Danny medicated and asleep in the attic, Beth crept through to the study to examine the raspberry curtains.

There was nothing there. No trace of anything untoward.

She opened the window, tied back the curtains and stood surveying the garden. It was a fine spring morning, the sunshine brilliant after a sudden downpour. The rhododendron bush lining the fence was beginning to bloom, its thick leaves iridescent with raindrops.

It wasn't possible for the child to have followed them all the way from Paris. It wasn't possible at all.

If the child hadn't followed them, then she didn't exist. She was an illusion, a fantasy of Beth's own creation. But why? Everything was going well. She was working on a challenging commission, writing a paper on the metaphysical poets for Florence University. Perhaps she had been working too hard. With Danny home sick, she could afford to take time off to keep him company. It might even bring them closer again.

She could always mention the child to her therapist. She didn't have to go to therapy any more; it was voluntary. She went whenever she felt the need to talk, over Italian filter coffee. Her therapist wore exquisite nail varnishes; Beth scribbled down the shades – *Bubblepop, Mermaid Dreams*. She preferred to see the therapist's as a sort of beauty salon – a holistic retreat, not a padded sanatorium.

It didn't feel like a retreat any more, but a complication – a threat. She wouldn't be able to talk openly. Much would be made of the child; much would be made of Beth's seeing things. Not enough time had lapsed for her to be tossing around words like *fantasy* and *illusion* in the therapist's office without provoking concern.

It was best not to say anything. She would cancel her next session, using Danny's leg as an excuse. Then she would forget to rearrange

She was climbing the stairs to wake Danny, when the phone rang. She guessed who it would be. She was half-expecting the call.

"I think you should come and see her for yourself," the reverend said. "Please don't lose this opportunity to do the right thing. I cannot stress how important this is."

Beth closed her eyes to stop herself from reacting. *She* was supposed to do the right thing?

The reverend cleared his throat. "Life is short, Miss Trelawney. Life is precious. Don't regret–"

"Okay," Beth said, surprising herself with her acquiescence. "I'll come. Is tomorrow all right?"

The reverend sounded surprised too. He exhaled

in relief. "That is wonderful news. Pamela will be thrilled. Thank you. Thank you."

Pamela will be thrilled? Beth hung up. Was that the same scraggy old Pammy who had raised her – who had scuffed about in slippers with the soles hanging out and a cigarette permanently stuck to her lip like a birthmark?

Perhaps people could change. Or perhaps people changed in front of ministers right before they died.

Beth had always assumed that Pammy was serving time in Cornwall, not far from the town of Pengilly where they had lived. Having played a part in bringing justice to Pammy, it had suited Beth to compartmentalise the past, popping her foster mother into a faraway venue that had little to do with present life. So it came as a surprise to discover that there were no prisons in Cornwall, and that Pammy had been nearby all along – in South Gloucestershire.

H.M. West Marsh was a forty minute drive from Bath.

The next morning, she left Danny in bed with a pile of snacks and the cordless phone. He was groggy so didn't enquire as to where she was going, thank goodness; she was a terrible liar.

She didn't have long. She would drive there, stay an hour and drive back. She had to pick Brett up from preschool at one o'clock. It was the perfect excuse to not linger.

She was bustling Brett out the door, when the phone rang.

It was Jacko. He often rang in the morning to

speak to Brett, even though she had told him it was the most inconvenient time. Normally, she ignored the call but today something made her pick up: the sudden desire to hear a voice that she knew.

She told him, again, that Brett had started preschool.

"Really?" he said. She could hear the windscreen wipers moping across his car window. "So what you up to today?"

She hesitated. "I…" It was tempting to tell him about Pammy, to obtain advice, even just a good luck wish. But Jacko wasn't capable of it; he couldn't be supportive. It would be like trying to make an ostrich fly. Instead she said, "Nothing. Just work."

She grabbed Brett's hand and headed on out.

It had to be raining; she expected nothing less. Angry, stabbing raindrops, to make this difficult journey even more arduous.

She dropped Brett off. He ran into preschool, looking like any other normal kid – a status that hadn't been easy to obtain, but had been achieved nonetheless.

And so Beth set off to West Marsh, the rain lashing down heavily as she crossed the hilly outskirts of Bath and made for the Cotswolds.

The problem was, she thought as she drove, that the tables had turned. It had been clear before, easy to apportion the blame: she was the victim.

But now frail, being kept alive by breathing apparatus, a reverend by her side, Pammy had morphed from offender to sufferer. She wanted Beth to find peace – to find forgiveness and happiness. Somehow Beth had become the one that needed fixing.

The thought had infuriated her yesterday. Yet as the day wore on, she witnessed a transformation within herself – a morphing of her own. By nightfall, her anger had melted to immeasurable sadness.

She squinted at the windscreen. It wasn't rain – it was hailstones. She turned the windscreen wipers on faster and sat forward in her seat, gripping the wheel, watching the hail bouncing on the road ahead.

She passed a sign post. It was five miles to West Marsh.

Danny had given up trying to converse with Erland on the subject. Erland didn't want a dad because he had his cyber chess friends. EdinburghBoy had been outmanoeuvring Erland for years; it didn't get any deeper than that as far as his relationships went.

But Danny thought about his dad more and more. He was impatient by nature, so his imagination only served him so far before he began to strain to see things in the flesh.

There was only one way to gain control of one's destiny, to manifest those whom you missed: by using magic.

The attic at Lilyvale was the ideal place for spell-making. It was quiet and private, with enough light to illuminate and enough shadow to hide. There was even a secret nook underneath the floorboards, where he hid his Magic Compendium.

The compendium had been his companion for the past five years. It was a large notebook that contained his thoughts, findings and research. It was the place he turned to when he needed to make sense of the universe – whether it was about his goal strategy, his maths homework or his mother's dating plans.

It was the latter that was occupying his thoughts of late – the disturbing idea that a man could enter their lives again and destroy the harmony, just like Jacko had. He had known all along that Jacko was wrong for his mum, for them all, but would she listen? It had been disastrous.

He wasn't going to let it happen again, not whilst he was living here. Mind you, it wasn't as though he was some sad teenager who had nothing to do with his time but arrange his mother's love life. *Au contraire*, he was a football legend. But he was the man about the house and it was his job to make sure that everything worked properly. His mum could read feminist poetry and listen to *Women's Hour* as much as she wanted. He knew the reality: blokes fixed things.

And so, in his wisdom, he had concluded that the only way for the Trelawneys to be happy was with his dad, Peter, living with them. Peter: a man with a steady income, a twelve-piece spanner set, and a love of Chelsea Football Club.

There was only one big problem that he could see: neither of his parents knew anything about Peter moving in. (The other problem was that Peter lived in London with his new family, but Danny hadn't noted this in his compendium thus it didn't exist.)

His parents' ignorance wasn't an issue because they could be kept in the dark to the last minute, leaving him to work his magic unhindered. The real problem lay in the fact that magic wasn't to be used to make people do things against their will, nor for personal gain. And since Danny was the only one who desired his father's presence at Lilyvale, this was rather a stumbling block.

Danny had pretended to be asleep this morning, but as soon as he heard his mum's car reversing down the driveway – where was she going in such a hurry? – he eased himself onto the floor and pulled up the floorboard.

He sat for a while with his leg stretched out in its cast on the floor, studying his compendium. It took him two hours, twenty minutes and a bumper bag of M&M's to solve his problem.

He would use a disclaimer. Just like his mum had signed a form at Bath Central saying that if his leg exploded during the blood draining then it wasn't the doctor's fault, so Danny would use small print to cover off damages.

The answer had been right in front of him. Years ago, he had written *if it be for the Greater Good* on the front page of the compendium. He hadn't a clue what the words meant at the time, but he liked the sound of them. And now he had realised why the words were there, the purpose they served: they were his disclaimer.

The moment he finished the spell to summon his father, he would utter these words and release himself from any ill intent or consequence.

Besides, he was doing it to help his mum. He overheard her conversation with their neighbour last night. The neighbour was a single parent too. She wore flares and sweaters that said things like *Peace* and *Hope*, and she laughed too loudly, as though pretending that she was having a much better time than she really was. She was the type of person who laughed all night, then sobbed herself to sleep. Danny wasn't sure how he knew that, but there was someone on *Home and Away* who did the same so he just put two and two together.

He had no idea what his mum and *Peace* had to talk about, but they did a lot of it. They talked on and on, the bottles clinking in the recycling bin. Then they started talking more loudly because they had drunk too much wine and Danny distinctly heard his mum say, *it's just so damned lonely!*

One day his mum would thank him. When his vision manifested, she wouldn't be lonely any more.

He packed away his compendium and eased himself over to the window. He liked looking out at the canal below. On a sunny day, he could follow the line of water to the horizon; a silver string threading through the countryside.

Lilyvale was on the east side of Bath, south of the canal. It was hard to describe an area of Bath as being posh, since the majority of the city was that way inclined, but if there was one area where statues of lions and griffons liked to congregate then this was it. Danny and Erland were the only children along their road who attended the comprehensive school; the others were strapped into black cars and whizzed off to boarding school every season change.

Still, the lack of community suited them. Their neighbours were too self-absorbed to wonder whether the Trelawneys had a dodgy past. All they saw was a pretty woman who was a big deal in academia – big enough to afford Lilyvale. That was all they needed to know.

It was raining heavily. The canal looked turbulent. He wondered what his mum was doing.

His knee began to throb. He took more pain relief and sank back into bed.

He was ready. Tonight, he would cast his magic candle spell.

H.M. West Marsh lay on the edge of the Cotswold village of Fairton; such a picturesque area, the prison seemed incongruously placed.

Beth turned onto an avenue with a church at its head. The avenue soon divided: the right lane into the real world, the left into a well-groomed road with a lodge at the entrance, reminiscent of the gateway to a country estate.

She pulled over and sat with her eyes closed. The rain had stopped and the sun was throbbing down. She was parked next to iron railings and a shroud of trees. Amongst the leaves, hidden in the folds on an oak tree, was the prison sign.

"Damn it!" she said. She was losing her nerve. She pulled her mobile phone from her handbag.

Her therapist answered immediately. "I don't know what to do," Beth said, unwinding the window for air.

"Where are you, Beth?"
"West Marsh."
"West what?"
"Pammy's prison. In the Cotswolds."
There was a pause. "Why are you there?"
"Because she called me."
"And?"

"She's dying. I've…" Beth reached into her jacket pocket and pulled out a tatty matchbox. "I've got the mood ring with me. I want to give it back to her."

Her therapist exhaled. She was trying to keep her cool, Beth could tell. "Has anyone seen you yet?"

"No. I'm in my car."

"Then drive away now. Take it nice and slow."

Take it nice and slow. That was what the reverend had said to Pammy yesterday on the phone.

"You should have called me first, Beth."

Beth didn't reply.

The therapist sighed. "No harm done. Just come on home. Come on home to who you are now – not who you were then. You've done so well. Don't undo it all with a rash decision."

What was it the reverend had said? They all sounded like each other: instructive, persuasive. *Don't lose this opportunity to do the right thing. I cannot stress how important this is…Life is short…Life is precious...*

"Beth? You're leaving, yes?"

"Yes," said Beth, turning the keys in the ignition.

"Good. Good…Call me as soon as you get home."

"Okay."

Beth hung up and slipped the phone back into her bag. She sat looking in the rear view mirror at the way she had come, at the road back to Bath. And then she drove past the lodge, straight ahead down the avenue.

She had to leave the mood ring at the Family and Friends Centre. She was reluctant to do so, but the staff assured her that Mrs Lazenby would receive it. As she was half an hour early, she was told to make herself at home in the centre.

She stored her handbag and coat in the locker as instructed, leaving herself with loose change, her passport and her visiting order. There was no one else around. The room was quiet and cool, adorned with paradise palm plants and apple green walls.

Her mouth was dry so she got a coffee from the vending machine and walked up and down, scanning the posters on the walls: *Inside Poetry Book Volume 4 now available! Email a Prisoner – new service; Jail mate greetings cards – because other cards just don't say it.*

She paused and looked out the window at the fields opposite. Normal life was just there, within reach. It was peculiar to see cows chewing grass, unaware of what was going on here. She had no idea of what went on at West Marsh either – whether the prisoners' lives were unbearable, whether the dominant feeling was hope or despair.

She rinsed her face in the bathroom, staring into the mirror at her frightened eyes. She looked gaunt underneath the artificial lighting.

It was time to go.

At the gate, Beth's passport was checked and her visiting order taken. She stood with her arms out whilst a female guard patted her down and a dog walked in circles around her.

"Come with me, please, ma'am," said the guard. "Mrs Lazenby is waiting for you." She led Beth forward a few yards to a door on the right. "This is the visits room. Visitors sit on the red seats."

Beth entered the room and looked about her. It was like an odd café. Tables were set about the room, each with three red chairs and one black. There were a couple of children in the play area, several people punching numbers into the vending machines, and everyone else was seated. There was one woman in burgundy uniform sat on the black chair at each table.

She couldn't see Pammy. She sat down nervously at the only empty table in the room, a bead of sweat trickling down the side of her body.

A guard was at her side in a moment. There had to be a woman in burgundy at the table for Beth to be able to sit down. She had broken the rules. "Who you here to see?" said the guard.

"Pamela Lazenby," she said, her voice sounding as though it had shrunk.

"But…" The guard frowned in confusion.

At that moment, the door opened and in came a very small man wearing a clerical collar. He whispered a word to the guard, who pointed at Beth.

She watched, her heart pounding. There seemed to be a problem. The guard was staring down at his boots. The reverend was shaking his head.

The reverend approached her, looking anxious. "Miss Trelawney?" he said. "I'm Reverend Trist."

They shook hands. His hand felt light and little in hers.

"I'm terribly sorry," he said. He took a deep breath. "Pamela has passed away."

She stared at him in a stupor. "But…"

"Yes, I know. They told you she was waiting for

you." He glanced with annoyance at the guard. "Tsk, tsk."

"Why would they do that?"

He leaned forward to reply discreetly. He was still standing, but wasn't that much taller than Beth in her seat. "Force of habit," he said. "The visitors arrive, the prisoners are seated waiting for them. It's like clockwork. The wheels turn without contemplation."

He sat down in a red chair next to her. They both gazed at the empty black chair where Pammy would have sat.

The reverend was distracted, smoothing his hands like applying imaginary hand cream. Whether it was the clerical attire or whether he would have appeared the same in a baseball cap and shorts, when he finally fixed his eyes upon her he conveyed an air of authority mixed with humanity. His eyes were watery green, as though his tears were always available. He seemed the sort of man who bore the world's grief upon him, to the point where it had stunted his growth.

"Did…" Beth throat tightened. "Did she know I was coming?"

"I'm afraid not. I was worried you might change your mind so I didn't mention it."

"Oh." She blinked away tears. She was too late. She felt something fall inside her, as hope ebbed and faded away. Hope for what? What could she have hoped to gain from this meeting? She lowered her head in despair, feeling the sadness of last night pressing upon her breastbone once more.

"I'm glad you came," the reverend said, patting her hand consolingly. "She talked about you a great deal."

Beth gazed about her, at the children playing, at the machine chugging out coffee, at the dark-eyed prisoners in burgundy uniforms who looked as though there was little reason still to breathe. She knew nothing of Pammy, of her old life, of her new one here; whether she often sat in a black chair with guests or whether no one but the reverend had visited her. She couldn't grieve someone whom she had despised, nor could she celebrate their demise – for a life was a life, no matter how rusty the vessel it had dwelt in.

"She wanted you to have this," the reverend said, pulling a Polaroid photograph from his pocket and handing it to her. It was taken over thirty years ago in the garden of Yew Tree Cottage, Pengilly. Pammy was stood with her arm around Beth's waist. Beth was stood straight, her hands slapped to her side, her A-line dress stiff. She wondered who had taken the picture. The colours were unrealistically yellow and sunburnt now.

She flicked the photograph over. She recognised the handwriting, although it was shaky. *Forgive me, Princess*, Pammy had written.

"For goodness sake," said Beth. "Could she be any more manipulative?"

The reverend didn't reply. She handed the Polaroid back to him. "I don't want it," she said. "Throw it away."

"As you wish," he said, keeping the photograph on the table between them. "Can I get you a coffee?"

Beth nodded. She watched the reverend searching his pockets for coins at the coffee machine. He seemed utterly out of place in this room – a serene spiritual man, plunged into an absurd world of colour-coded chairs, guards with batons, burgundy-clad criminals. Humans seemed to like juxtaposing nature's gentlest against the worst that mankind could offer: priests at confessions, nuns on death row. The reverend was so out of his depth, he was struggling to reach up high enough to put the money in the slot.

He handed her a cup of coffee. She sat with it cradled in her hands, blowing the steam away.

"So what did she die of?"

He sighed. "Lung cancer...Very unpleasant business. She was in pain for a long time."

"I'm not surprised. She was quite a smoker."

"Yes, we pay for our vices in this world." He paused for a moment, sipping his filmy tea. "Her doctor estimated that she smoked over half a million cigarettes in her lifetime. A slow form of suicide, wouldn't you say?"

Beth shrugged. "I wouldn't know."

He laid his hands out flat on the table and cleared his throat. "I'll be frank with you," he said. "Pamela wanted your forgiveness. She wanted it more than anything else. She isn't here with us now, but that's not to say that you cannot fulfil her wish."

Beth opened her mouth to reply, but found that she didn't know what to say.

A little girl wearing a nurse's hat appeared at the reverend's side to serve him a toy cup of tea and a plastic hot dog. "Bless you," he said, smiling gratefully. Beth watched the child moving around the room, pushing a pram as a makeshift trolley, handing out plastic tea. With each offering the girl waited for the reaction, her eyebrows raised, her palms pressed, before basking in the praise.

Perhaps the visitors here were so depressed that it felt like being offered soup in a war zone.

"Reverend…" Beth turned back to him, remembering something the guard had said at the gate. "Was Pamela ever married? The guard referred to her as 'Mrs'."

He smiled. "I'm glad you care enough to be curious," he said. "Yes. She was married a long time ago. He walked out on her in the early seventies. Broke her heart."

Beth tried to picture Pammy being married, having a broken heart, possessing anything fragile enough to be breakable. She used to cry at sad films and then jump up, snap the television off and whistle a happy tune. If some people retained emotions like sponges, Pammy shed them like unwanted skin.

"She told me about your nickname: Princess." Beth watched the reverend's lips as he spoke, feeling slightly enchanted. His voice had a slight impediment, a lisp that made him sound as though he had a mouthful of toffees. He had a funny sing-song way of speaking – up and down – lilting. "It was a play on the princess and the pea," he said. "P was for Pammy, and you were the princess. Apparently, you demanded that she called you that."

"Oh," said Beth. "I don't remember. I always thought she made up the name."

"No, it was all you." He laughed, his eyes twinkling warmly. Beth felt a rumble of irritation in her stomach. He was winning her over – reminiscing about her foster mother as though she were a kind soul.

"You seem to have a different opinion of her than

I have," she said. "She isn't someone whom I'm going to remember fondly, Reverend."

"I see." Displeasure clouded his eyes. He put down his cup of tea as though the fun were over.

"Did she tell you what she did to me?" she said.

He closed his eyes slowly, affirmatively.

"Did she tell you why she wanted to hurt me?"

The reverend looked confused. "She *didn't* want to hurt you," he said.

"She didn't?" said Beth. "Well, she would say that. And I don't suppose you pressed the issue?"

"No, Miss Trelawney," he said, firmly. "She was dying. I did *not*."

"Then our business here is done."

"Some day you may see things differently," he said. "And I pray that you do."

"Please don't pray for me, Reverend," she said, scraping back her chair to stand up.

"If you don't forgive her, you'll never find love. You'll always be alone."

Beth stared down at him, incredulous. He was still seated, his hands placed piously before him as though not a moment could be lost before praying for her soul.

"How can you possibly say that?" she said. "You know nothing about me – nothing at all."

"I know emptiness when I see it," he said.

She jolted slightly – an imperceptible motion that looked like nothing on the outside. "I must go," she said, turning away.

"I've offended you," he said. He rose swiftly, extending his hand to her. "Let's not part like this. Please accept my deepest apologies."

"I'm not offended," she said. "I need to go and collect my son."

They looked at each other. No one had won. Conversations like this couldn't be won.

Disappointment filled the old man's eyes. "There's an old saying about anger, Miss Trelawney: that holding on to it is like holding on to a hot coal. It only hurts you."

"I'm not holding any hot coals," she replied.

"Aren't you?" he said, looking at her wistfully. "Anyhow let's let the matter drop…Would you care to take my details?" He pressed his business card into her hand.

She studied the card. "You're the reverend of Pengilly Methodist in Cornwall?" she said, surprised. "The church on the quay?"

"The very same. Pamela's local parish. I took over there shortly after you left, I believe. Two ships that passed in the night."

She felt her shoulders fall; she hadn't realised how rigidly she was holding them. Somehow his being from Pengilly changed things – made him less alien, more on her side. "I didn't realise you were from there," she said, suddenly wanting to cry but resisting.

She wished he had said sooner. And she wished they hadn't passed like ships. She would have liked to have known him back then – to have known that there were people like him in the world, people whose eyes were awash with compassion.

"Did you ever attend chapel?" he asked. He had correctly gauged her lack of faith. Perhaps he was prodding to see how far back her godlessness went.

It went all the way.

"No," she replied. "There was little point."

"Oh?" He rocked on his feet, like a skittle that had been knocked, except that this was a lulling movement as though comforting himself. She had never considered before how hard it must be for a clergyman, facing daily objections to your life's purpose.

"I could see your church from my bedroom," she said. "I thought it was part of a secret world that I wasn't allowed entry to...And I was right. Because I never found my way in."

"Are we still talking about the chapel?" he said. "Because you are more than welcome to—"

"No. Not the chapel," she said.

"Then what?"

She looked away. "I thought you said you know emptiness when you see it."

There was an awful silence. Everyone in the café went quiet at the same time, as though they had all reached the same heart-wrenching point together. There was a lull and then voices began to murmur. The jaded prison heart began to beat again.

"I lost the only man I ever loved because I was frightened to be close to anyone," she said, setting her eyes upon him.

"Ah!" he said, as though everything about her now made sense. "The father of your children?"

"One of them," she said. "There are two."

"I see." There was no judgement in his eyes.

"My two oldest sons have the same father: Peter."

"The man you loved?"

"Yes."

"What became of him?"

"Married," she said. "To the wrong woman." She tried to smile.

"Evidently," he replied, nodding solemnly. "And if that is so, then it will manifest accordingly. If you love him and he loves–"

"I didn't say–"

"You didn't have to," he said. "And what of the second father?"

"Moron," she said. "We're separated."

"Oh." He shook his head, rubbing his hands together, lost in thought. "Miss Trelawney, would you take my help if I offered it?"

"Your help?" she replied. "With what?"

"Healing you, of course," he said, holding out his hands to her as though saying *Welcome to Disneyland!*

"Healing," she echoed. *Healing.*

Throughout all the therapy she had received, the parenting programmes she had endured, the life coaches, social workers and consultants she had met, no one had ever mentioned that word. She had been treated as if she were broken and they needed to fix her. She was a problem and they were solving it. There was no mention of healing. Healing was gentle, tender; it was chicken broth and ointments.

And at that moment she suddenly wanted it desperately.

"What do I need to do?" she said.

He didn't hesitate. "Forgive her."

"I thought you'd say that." She looked down at

her feet. "I don't know if I can."

"It won't be easy," he replied. "Especially without God. But it's not impossible."

She thought for a moment. "I'd like to find the others."

"The others?"

"The other foster children. She fostered others, didn't she?"

"Yes, but I don't see how–"

"I want to find out how she treated them – what she did to them. If I know the whole story, I can forgive her."

"I don't like the sound of this…" he said, scratching his head. "Why do you need to involve anyone? Isn't it safer to keep it personal? What if you hear something you don't like?"

She shrugged. She had made up her mind.

"Okay," he said. "I'll see what I can dig up for you." But he was tutting and his face was crumpled with disapproval.

Beth glanced about the room, having forgotten momentarily where they were. The guard was watching them, a combination of scorn and curiosity upon his face. One of the prisoners was saying goodbye to her family, crying noiselessly into the back of a little girl's hair. When the girl broke away, Beth saw that it was the same child who had offered cups of sympathy around the room.

"Come," said the reverend. "Let me see you out."

I can leave. I'm a red chair, not a black chair, Beth found herself thinking. For the rest of her life she would grateful for this small matter of chairs.

They made their way out of the visits room, back to the gate. The female guard moved forward quickly, like a startled spider, until she spied the reverend and retreated to her post. The guard's dog was slumped with his head between his paws awaiting instruction.

"I will help you, but I must offer a word of warning," said the reverend, as Beth turned to go. "Tread carefully."

She frowned. "Oh? Why?"

"Because sometimes when you start a witch hunt, you become the hunted."

What a strange thing to say, Beth thought.

But as the guard and the dog escorted Beth wordlessly back to the centre, she glanced back at West Marsh and her stomach fluttered ominously, as though the hunt had just begun.

THE BURNT LOTUS

How to perform a love spell using Hoodoo candle magic

You will need:
one green candle
extra virgin olive oil
a small sharp knife

1) Find somewhere peaceful. Using the knife, carve an X at the bottom end of the candle. This symbol is the rune of Gyfu (old English) meaning love and forgiveness.

2) Breathe deeply. Imagine that love is filling your body and the air around you.

3) Rub the candle with oil, starting at the middle and working towards each end, continuing to think about love.

4) Light the candle, saying: "May my life be filled with eternal love. May love radiate through me for all the days of my life, from each sun rise to each sun set."

5) Leave the candle to burn, until it is one seventh of its length. As you extinguish the flame, say: "Thus it shall be."

6) Repeat the spell from step four for the next six days until the candle is no more.

THREE

Pamela Lazenby had run a 'safe house' at Yew Tree Cottage in Pengilly, harbouring children who needed urgent, temporary refuge. Beth was the only foster child in Pammy's care at the time, but she could remember children arriving in the small hours of the morning. She would wake to the sound of voices rumbling beneath her room, to doors creaking open and sea gales slamming them closed again. There would be an army of people accompanying the child, traipsing around the cottage before leaving again – a slow-worm of car lights sliding up the hill out of Pengilly in the darkness. At breakfast the new child would be sat bug-eyed, spooning cereal. Beth would swagger about, whistling, helping herself to juice, until Pammy came in and clipped her on the back of her head. When Pammy turned her back, Beth would do a V sign with her knife and fork, prompting the first sound from the new child: a startled laugh.

The new arrivals never stayed long – not long

enough to earn a nickname, a place at the table, a plastic cup of their own. They wet the bed during their sojourn, had nightmares, called for parents who hadn't realised that their child had left days ago. Beth felt nothing for these children though. She was too embroiled in her own misery to care a hoot about someone whom she would never see again.

But since becoming a parent, she had found herself thinking of those children – of how she could have been kinder to them during their brief acquaintance. A little boy with a broken arm had sleepwalked into her bed one night, calling her mama and holding out his good arm to hug her, so Beth had poured a cup of water over him to wake him up.

It was reassuring for adults to believe they were born kind. But Beth knew that children were born neutral and remained so, until the world showed them what to expect. It wasn't until she grew much older that she realised it was possible to comfort others when they were hurt.

Beth looked back at her time in Pengilly with unreserved regret, wishing she had met more benign people so that their ways might have rubbed off on her like a soothing balm that helped her sleep. Instead, she slept fitfully and spent her childhood viewing the world through nervous eyes that had been trained to stay alert to fend off attack.

She had never met any of the other foster children – the other children who had sat in her chair at the kitchen table, had slept in her bed, who had dreaded each approach from their guardian. Like the reverend, they had missed each other, their sense of timing off. Yet she had wondered about them; about how many of them there had been; how they had fared in the world after Pammy altered their courses and sent them off kilter.

And now their names were in front of her – a list from the reverend: the four foster children who had grown up at Yew Tree Cottage.

Aaron Deakin
Teresa Close
April Morgan
Rowan Grimshaw

She stared at the names as though the written word could tell her their secrets.

What did Pammy do to you?

She was lost in thought when the phone rang.

"I've managed to get their occupations and home towns," the reverend said, animatedly. He had a friend in children's services who was willing to pass on some information, given his position in the church. "It was all rather hush-hush," he said. "I'll send a bottle of Claret over."

Aaron Deakin, charity worker, Brighton.
Teresa Close, housewife, Truro.
April Morgan, animal carer, Southampton.
Rowan Grimshaw, D.J., Poole.

Odd that they were all based by the sea, Beth noted – still connected through the earth's elements to Pengilly. Even the canal at the bottom of her garden, lazy and innocuous though it appeared, would eventually merge with a river and find its way there.

"Now what?" she said.

"A quick search online will provide us with addresses, I'm sure."

"And what then?"

He cleared his throat. "I'll contact them," he said. "We'll invite them to the funeral."

"What makes you think they'll come?"

"You'll be surprised," he said.

The funeral was at Pengilly Methodist in a week's time. It would be a burial, Beth guessed; a grim, depressing burial.

"I wouldn't have thought there would be anyone there for Pamela Lazenby but the guy with the shovel," she said.

She hung up and was staring at the list again, when she became aware of something moving in the kitchen doorway. She tensed, expecting to see the child again, before realising that it was only Danny.

"Why are you getting involved with Pammy?" he said, his cheeks burning.

"She's dead," she said. "How involved can I get?"

"I don't know, Mum," he said. "You tell me." And he turned and left the room, his crutches creaking.

"How can I tell you when you're always walking away?" she shouted after him. She heard him creaking down the hallway to the lounge. A few moments later there was the soft murmur of voices on the television.

She made a tray of tea and went out to the back garden. It was unseasonably warm for April. She sat quietly at the patio table, watching a group of teenagers make their way along the canal path chattering in what she guessed was Italian. She envied their freedom of movement – the way they walked loose-limbed, uninhibited, unguarded.

"Okay, so tell me about it," said Danny. He was stood in the open doorway, leaning on his crutch. She tried to disguise her pleasure by turning her face away as he approached.

He sat down with some difficulty. "Here," she said, drawing another chair towards him to prop his leg upon.

He listened quietly to her account, his arms folded. His jaw bone was nudging inside his cheek – the only sign that he was perturbed. He had learnt to control the main culprit – his tongue – but not its companions.

"This is about healing," she said.

"Healing," he said.

"I thought you'd be pleased."

"Why, because you're raking up all that bad stuff? What's there to be pleased about?"

"I…" She felt herself blush and put a hand to her cheek defensively. "I need to do this, Danny. I want to heal. It's time."

He was expressionless. Even his jaw bone had rested.

Two sparrows landed on the lawn, tapping away at the hard grass with their beaks. She felt like this with Danny: pecking at him furtively for information and responses. Like the sparrows, most days she gave up and went hungry.

"Why aren't you saying anything?" she said. "You have no opinion?"

He shrugged. "You don't need my permission."

"Don't I?" she said. "I don't want you fighting me

on this, Danny. It'll be hard enough."

"Then why do it?" he said. "I thought we were trying to have a fresh start."

"We are. And that's why I've got to do this."

"Then do it," he said, heatedly.

She looked down at her feet. He caught her sad expression, and his own mask immediately altered. He was multi-layered now, but his kind soul was still within. And it was never that far out of reach.

"I'm not trying to be an ass," he said. He reached out and tapped her knee. "I just don't know how to deal with all that Pammy stuff. I can't…" He shook his head.

He had never asked her what happened in Pengilly, not even during the court case. It was a dark place that he couldn't visit – one that didn't exist in his colourful world. "It's up to you how you deal with it."

She surveyed his eyes, his jaw bone, his straight back. Everything was perfectly aligned. He was telling the truth.

She glanced at her watch. "Okay. Well, I'd better go and get changed so I can pick up Brett," she said. "Thanks for the chat."

As she turned to leave, he grabbed her hand. "Just promise me," he said, looking up at her with eyes that seemed suddenly more childish. "If things go wrong, you'll pull out."

She nodded. "Promise," she said.

"Good. Now I can get back to *Cash in the Attic*," he said.

Stepping back into the house, she felt soothed. Lilyvale had a funny vague smell: a smell of nothingness, as though it scooped up the day's events into a cloudy bundle of laundry and tossed it out the window whilst they slept.

She had felt it at her first viewing of the property: its openness to possibilities. The front of Lilyvale was the façade, the face that they presented to a street that valued evergreen topiary, electric gates, the smooth crunch of tyres on gravel. But the back was wild – a portal to adventure: palm trees, overgrown grass, mooring platforms with boats bobbing expectantly; a canal waiting to slip them away. At Lilyvale, she felt both rooted and free.

Their belongings hadn't taken over the house. They hadn't descended with all their possessions and smothered the building – despite the amount of football merchandise and wooden train components. The house still breathed around them, still encouraged them to find new ways of doing things and not to become stuck in grooves. It was the height of the ceilings, the emptiness of the tall walls. There was no need to redecorate – the previous owners had only just done so. Everything was pale cream, mink, French grey. A blank palette.

Her favourite room was the kitchen because it epitomised new beginnings, new possibilities. It was here that Erland had unveiled his passion for cuisine. He was so keen to experiment that once a week she allowed him to do so, seating herself nearby with a glass of wine and an amused look. He liked to cook with celeriac, kale – things that she couldn't identify. When she asked what was for dinner, he would shrug and begin chopping root ginger, whistling. And the results were extraordinary. Erland was one of those enigmatic boys who was going to blossom into something altogether more enigmatic as a man. The world was his oyster, marinated or otherwise.

She went upstairs to her bedroom to change, enjoying the sound of her feet slapping the bare wood. Her room overlooked the back garden. The floorboards were sandblasted, the walls were the colour of dusted fondant. It was a feminine, yet unadorned room.

She sighed. The house felt sleepy today, heady. She was sure that the canal had a lulling effect, lying at the edge of their lawn. She was feeling more settled for having spoken to Danny. It had gone as well as it could in the circumstances.

As she looked for a T-shirt, she glanced out of habit in the direction of the mood ring which she kept buried at the back of the wardrobe under a pile of jumpers.

Damn. She had left the ring at West Marsh. She would mention it to the reverend.

No. She would leave it.

It was apt: Pammy's ring abandoned in the place of her punishment, carelessly tossed down a waste disposal unit, lying in a pit of the prison's rubbish.

It was the first step forward. She was right to pursue this path. It was going to be all right.

She was pulling on her T-shirt, humming happily, when suddenly she felt the hair on her arms spike.

The child was in the room with her.

Beth spun on her heel to see the girl stood right behind her, smiling. It wasn't the missing front teeth that made Beth scream; it was the drop of blood sneaking from the child's mouth.

Danny thought instantly that he was back at their

old house.

Wincing, he eased himself onto his crutches and made his way down the hallway. "Mum?" he shouted, sweat breaking onto his forehead. "Mum?"

Nothing.

He stopped in the kitchen, leaning on the counter. He needed his painkillers. His knee felt like it was going to fall off or burst open. "Don't make me come up there!"

He stared at the ceiling. Still nothing.

Then there was the sound of her bedroom door slamming and footsteps on the stairs. His mum breezed into the kitchen wearing a T-shirt and jeans.

"Why did you scream?" he said.

"Hey?" she said, stopping in front of the mirror to fix her hair.

He wobbled towards her. "You screamed."

"Don't be daft," she said, applying gloss and smacking her lips together. "You're imagining things. Maybe we need to ease up on those pills."

"I haven't had any today," he said.

"Then maybe you should," she said, snatching up her keys. "I'm off to get Brett."

"What's happened?" he said. "A minute ago we're having a nice chat. Next thing, you're acting all weird. What's changed in five minutes?"

"Nothing," she said.

"So you expect me to be honest, but it's okay for you to be mysterious, going round the house screaming and then acting like nothing happened?"

She raised her shoulders and dropped them. "It was a spider," she said. "I was embarrassed to tell you…Happy now?"

He followed her to the back door. "I'm coming with you."

"You're not," she said. "You're not well enough."

"I need the exercise."

She waited patiently whilst he put his trainer on his good foot. She didn't offer to help, which she might have done in the circumstances. Instead she whistled a nothing song that was going nowhere – a sure sign that something was up. She wasn't musical in the slightest. For her, singing or whistling was mental distraction, a hands-free way of pummelling a stress ball.

The journey was probably going to kill him, but he wasn't going to let her wriggle off. He needed to pursue the matter, not let it get brushed away with all the other daily administrative debris.

The preschool was only ten minutes from their house. The air alongside the canal was stifling, still. His mum was on edge, jangling her keys. It could have been because he was walking so slowly and they were running late, but it was more likely that it was because of whatever had made her scream.

"I know it wasn't a spider," he said, panting for breath.

"Oh, for goodness sake, Danny," she said. "Why would I lie?" She stepped up the pace, probably deliberately to stop him from speaking.

"You've been jumpy lately – twitchy. I've been wanting to ask you about it, but I didn't want to upset you. Was that why you screamed? Are you on medication? Because you can tell me if you are. I can–"

"Enough, Danny, please! Not now!"

"Not now?" he said, stopping and holding his crutch out in front of her to bar her way. "Because it seems to me that this can't wait. What's going on?"

"No, Danny," she said, curling her lip. "I'm not discussing this here. Not now." She pushed the crutch away and marched on. "I won't let Brett down," she shouted over her shoulder.

The preschool sign was in sight. Sometimes it flapped in the wind like a lonely pub sign, but today it was still.

"You already have," he called after her.

It was harsh. He knew it would wound her, but he didn't know how else to reach her.

His tactic hadn't worked. She was propelling away from him. He wiped the sweat from his forehead, watching her walking away.

She couldn't see that it was already happening, that she had started something that was gathering momentum. She had just promised that she would pull out if things got bad, yet she wouldn't be able to apply the brakes now even if she tried. She was driving a ropey old vehicle by herself because the only friend that she'd had in the world was him and she'd just dumped him out the passenger seat.

Jesus, Mum. It's happening again.

She was freefalling, a fluffy wisp unaware of the danger – a dandelion clock floating towards the sea. He couldn't save her. The wind was too strong, the elements too powerful. The wind had snatched her up higher, taking her beyond his reach.

She thought he was judging her. Since the court

case, she was paranoid about judgement. But he wasn't judging. He had meant what he said about it being her choice. Who was he to say how she should deal with Pammy? No one could decide that but her.

No. What was really bothering him was the fact that he had spent the last three nights waving candles and oil about the attic.

Who knew what spirits his spell had released, what powers he had awoken, who or what would come creeping to their door as a result?

The Hoodoo spells were potent. If he had known what his mum was dabbling in – that she was meddling with redemption, an evil soul, death and a wise old reverend – then he wouldn't have called to the spirits for their help. Because if there was one thing he had learned about the supernatural, it was that the spirits had a way of tangling their arms when they all rushed forward at once.

"Everything go okay?" said Beth, ruffling Brett's hair. He curled himself around her leg and began to sing *London Bridge is falling down*.

"We've been singing, haven't we, sweetheart?" said the nursery manager. She was young, but robust. Normally, she was pleasant. But today she was looking at Beth as though the latter had a fly on her nose.

"Can I have a word?" she said.

Something in the way she said it made Beth's stomach flip.

"Of course," said Beth. Danny had just arrived, his T-shirt dark with perspiration. Beth turned to him. "I don't suppose you could show Brett the lambs?" she said, as though they hadn't just argued, causing her to abandon him along the canal path with his broken leg. Danny muttered agreement.

The manager waited for the boys to cross the road to the field opposite. She moved closer to Beth and lowered her voice. "There was this man hanging about by the farm gate earlier," she said.

Beth nodded, unclear how it concerned her.

"He wanted to know which one was Brett," the manager said.

Beth opened her mouth in astonishment.

"Do you know anyone who might do that? Someone with a grudge maybe?"

"No," said Beth, shaking her head adamantly. "No one."

"Well, it's just that some of the other parents…"

"Some of them what?" said Beth.

"Well…" The manager blushed a deep red. "They're concerned, because of Brett's history…"

"Brett's history? How do you know about that?"

The manager averted her gaze. "People talk."

Beth looked at her shoes, wishing that she hadn't argued with Danny. "What do you want me to do?" she said.

"Check with your ex-husband. And have a think if there's anyone else who might be involved. I'd prefer Brett to stay home until things are resolved."

Beth hadn't expected this. "Oh, no," she said. "Don't do that. He's settled in here so—"

The manager held up her hand. "It's only for a short while," she said, smiling a rigid smile that closed the subject.

Beth could barely breathe on the walk home. "So much for healing," Danny muttered.

"I beg your pardon?" she said.

"Nothing."

She would have argued with him, but he was clearly in too much pain. The walk had been too much for him. He was shaking, his face contorted.

She put an arm supportively on his elbow, whilst hanging on to Brett's hand. "So Brett's banned?" he said.

"Keep your voice down," she hissed. "And no, he's not banned. Concentrate your efforts on walking home. It's not far now."

"Yep, not far to the edge of that cliff," he replied.

She used every cell of good will within her at the moment to prevent herself from dropping his elbow and letting him struggle home alone. But he was her son and bleak though things currently looked, they wouldn't look the same way tomorrow. And yet he would still be there looking at her, asking her to account for her every action. So she wouldn't make this a bad action. She wouldn't give him something else to add to the tally.

She tightened her grip on Brett's hand. He seemed happier than ever today. He was wearing his red trousers and pirate jumper – scuffing at stones, stopping to pick up dead beetles and sticks, singing softly to himself: *London bridge is falling down, falling down, falling down.*

Elias opened his eyes with a start. It was pitch black in his room. He thought for a moment about what had woken him. He listened. Ruby, his red setter, was snoring at the foot of his bed.

He flicked back the curtain at the tiny window. Adept at reading the sky, he saw that the time was half past three in the morning.

He pulled on his cloak and moved quietly to the adjourning room, opening the door a fraction to peek through. The girls were sleeping, the toadstool nightlight glowing upon their faces. He had told them before that embracing the solace of darkness was the only way to sleep, but they were both too neurotic to welcome night. For his own ability to sleep like a baby, he was utterly grateful.

Returning to his room, he lit a purple candle and knelt upon his star-embossed rug in the middle of a stone circle – just small enough to accommodate him. He was not a large man, although his feet were uncommonly long. Clown-like. Yet nature had not intended him for comedy.

Ruby woke momentarily, lifted her nose, twitched at the smell of the candle burning, before flopping back down. It wasn't the first time her master had woken her at an ungodly hour. She fell back asleep, moaning.

Elias stroked his beard, enticing himself into a meditative state. It didn't take long, particularly in the small hours of the morning when the day was young.

He uttered the words: *Dear Universe, illuminate my mind with knowledge so that my soul may forever be true*, then reached out of the circle for seven oak leaves which he laid before him within the circle, like a pack of cards.

He fell silent, gazing into the centre of the candle's flame.

Then he selected one of the leaves.

"Ah," he said, softly, examining the grooves in the leave. "So it is the salmon. I knew you would come for me."

He gave Ruby a kiss on her head, blew out the candle and eased himself back into bed.

As the darkness descended, he closed his eyes and could see the candle still burning in his eyes.

He knew what had woken him earlier. He had heard others in the Order talk of it: a sharp blow to the stomach in the early hours of the morning. It was impossible to sleep through. It wasn't painful; merely concentrated, deep – a feeling of connection where your umbilical cord had once existed. It felt sore for days afterwards, the belly button throbbing and tender as though newly cut from its cord.

He hadn't needed the oak leaves to tell him that it was the salmon jumping. He had already known. The salmon always returned to the place of its birth.

So too was Elias to return – to go upstream against the flow of everything he had achieved so far, of everywhere he had travelled, to turn against the rhythms of the life he had made, and return to himself.

He had known all along that this day would come.

He got back out of bed and went through to the girls' room, snapping on the light. They both jumped up, screaming, clutching their blankets to their chins before realising that it was only Elias and relaxing again. They would have to go their separate ways soon. He couldn't abide company for long, but he couldn't abandon them yet. They would sicken and ail without him. He would let them travel with him a little longer until they could survive on their own, and then he would let them down, gently, onto land.

"Get dressed, please," he said. "We need to get going. Something has occurred."

"Occurred?"

"No need for hysteria," he said. "Not yet anyway."

With a flick of his cloak behind him, he went to wake up Ruby, and to get the bacon and sausages started. They would need a full English this morning.

FOUR

As soon as Danny's door slammed shut upstairs, Beth picked up the phone. Since the incident in her bedroom, she was having trouble controlling her shaking hands. Her head was throbbing so badly she was struggling to think. She needed help, but from whom? One word and the social services would descend upon her like locusts.

There was only one person who might understand. Even so, she sensed that discretion and caution was in order.

She dialled Reverend Trist's number.

"What do you know about visions?" she asked.

"Visions?" he laughed in surprise. When she didn't elaborate, he continued, more seriously. "Well, as a man of the cloth I would say they are the pathway to God."

"The pathway to God?"

"Why, yes. God said, *I will pour out my Holy Spirit upon all mankind, and your sons and daughters shall prophesy, and your young men shall see visions, and your old men dream dreams.*"

Your old men dream dreams. She liked that. It sounded Shakespearian.

Brett appeared in the study doorway, dragging his toy box behind him. She smiled at him, wishing that he hadn't entered at that moment. He plonked down at her feet and began assembling his train track. "The red twain wan up the twack…The blue twain went down the twack and smashed into him…"

She lowered her voice into the phone. "What if you didn't believe in God?" she asked. She had to watch what she said. Brett would repeat her words like a parakeet.

"All the more reason to experience a vision," the reverend replied.

She paused, absorbing his words.

"Why are you asking?"

"Just curious," she said. "Do you really believe that people can have visions, Reverend?"

"Yes, I do."

"So what does it mean?"

"Is this about you?" he said, softly.

She didn't reply.

"All right…Well, the standard opinion, Beth, is that there are three reasons why one sees visions: if one is mentally ill, haunted by ghosts, or seeking God. The trick is determining which reason applies."

"I see."

"And if this is about you, I urge you to either confide in me or in a healthcare professional. Do you know any therapists?" he said.

"Oh, yes," she said, wondering how much he actually knew about her.

She hung up, deep in thought. The phone rang immediately. "Beth?" It was the reverend. "If you're the one experiencing visions, then it's vital that you work out whether the vision is of a holy or an unholy nature. Do you understand?"

Once more, she didn't reply for fear of implicating herself. "If it's of an unholy nature then it's imperative that you don't talk to it. Walk away, turn away. *Reject it.*"

Beth shuddered, thinking of the trail of blood coming from the child's mouth. "Thank you for the information," she said, as neutrally as she could. "Speak to you soon."

"Mama?" said Brett, touching her arm. "Which one do you want to win? The red twain or the blue twain?" His blonde curls were flat at the back from a heavy night's sleep. She kissed him and patted his bottom.

"The red train," she said. He beamed. She had answered correctly. He plonked back down onto the floor and continued with his train story.

She wished that her life was a simple choice of red or blue. Perhaps it was. Good or bad. Holy or unholy. Insane or haunted.

She went out to the hallway to listen for Danny, to check that he was still upstairs, and then returned to her computer.

She eyed her work uneasily. She hadn't looked at the metaphysical poets paper for Florence University for over a week. Her commissioners never chased her, under the impression that rushing her work would decrease its merit, but she didn't want to squander her privileges.

That said, the metaphysical poets were going to

have to wait. As would Sixteenth Century Female Authors for Lisbon University, and the Influence of the Renaissance on English Literature for Florida International.

She pushed her paperwork to one side, took a deep breath and typed *visions*.

The reverend appeared to be correct: mental illness, ghosts and God. They were all jostling for first place in the search engines online.

My girlfriend says I'm crazy because I keep seeing a woman in a black cloak. I do suffer from seizures though. Am I going insane?

My dad keeps seeing ghosts in our bathroom. Is it haunted?

You can see visions too! In the bible, Daniel simply said I looked *and he saw.*

She was least interested in the mental illness and the hauntings, and more drawn to the religious opinions since they were of a more serious nature. She was skimming through a website about religious visions, when a passage about *Sacré-Couer* caught her eye:

Marguerite-Marie Alacoque, a nun of the Visitation Monastery, experienced visions of Jesus from 1673 to 1675, in which He revealed the marvels of His love and the unexplainable secrets of His Sacred Heart.

Beth was disturbed by the phone ringing again. She answered the call, still reading the screen. It was Jacko. He was in a fluster because the police were trying to get hold of him. "What have you been up to this time?" he said.

She was so annoyed, she hung up and continued reading.

The sister's visitations were sometimes disturbing, but a

Jesuit priest was drawn to Marguerite-Marie's message, declaring that the king must build a chapel in honour of the Sacred Heart. Hence the Sacré-Couer in Paris was created.

He called back. "I didn't mean it like that," he said to the answer machine. "Come on...Pick up...I want to arrange Brett's next visit."

Brett looked up when he heard his name. When he realised it was his father's voice, he abandoned his train and trotted to the phone to pick it up, his face lit with expectation.

She prised the receiver gently from him. Exhaling, she continued their conversation. Mentioning Brett's next visit was merely bait. In truth, Jacko wasn't able to see Brett for a few weeks. He had a meeting in Frankfurt, then Gibraltar. And he was taking his girlfriend to Paris for her birthday. "Eighteenth?" asked Beth.

The girlfriend had popped into existence a few months ago, growing shockingly quickly, like a weed in summer. She was Spanish, which didn't seem right to Beth because she was called Valerie. But she did exist because Brett had met her on one of his weekend visits, referring to her afterwards as Wah-ler-wee. Or Wally, as Erland called her.

Beth played with the phone cord, twirling it round her finger. She watched Brett pushing his red and blue train around the track on the carpet, round and round he went. The same thing over and again. Just like his father.

"Shall we pencil something in for a month's time?" she said, quietly furious.

"Yeah, pencil it."

He had been easier to deal with when he was lying

in bed next to her every night. She could ask him questions and watch his face whilst he invented lies, as she tried to gauge the extent of the fib. Over the phone like this, it was impossible. He was evasive, non-committal. He drove her crazy.

He had changed his job and was rarely home now. Their visiting arrangements were beginning to unravel, become sloppy. There was nothing she could do about it except watch and wait. Thing were either going to improve, or fall apart irreparably. Rather like Jacko himself.

It wasn't entirely his fault. Things hadn't gone well for him since the separation. His company had folded for a start. She had felt sorry for him at the time. He rang on Christmas Eve to tell her the news, crying, whisky bottle sloshing, begging to see Brett. He resurfaced sheepishly on Boxing Day, clutching an unwrapped train set. She told him he could spend the day with them if he would acknowledge her eldest sons, but he refused. He had ignored Danny and Erland from the moment he moved out last year, citing them as the reason for the breakdown of their marriage.

As if the lads were to blame. As if anyone was to blame for the breakdown of a marriage but the two people involved. Multiple reasons were always given from a cast of thousands, but in truth it was just the couple that were broken. Nothing and no one else.

He hadn't stayed low for long; he found a job as a pharmaceutical salesman. He was nothing if not resourceful.

The one thing they agreed on was not to rush into divorce. Not because they sensed a reconciliation, but because they were managing to sustain a working relationship for now. Wah-ler-wee would change things the moment she wanted to, Beth was certain.

The doorbell rang. Brett went running down the hallway to the front door. "Mummy, Mummy! Police, police!" he was shouting.

The police were wasting their time talking to Jacko, Danny knew. It was hard enough to get that loser to see Brett on the weekends. There was no way that he would be hanging around the preschool.

It made him sad to hear his mum on the phone to Jacko – the way she screwed her eyes shut, pinched the top of her nose, anything to control her temper. If she said the wrong thing, she could topple Jacko over the edge, out of Brett's life. It would be no loss that Danny could see, but it seemed to matter to her. And Brett liked his dad, which was odd since no one else did.

Whenever she spoke to Jacko, she was quiet for the rest of the day – snippy, curt. She walked around bearing guilt on her shoulders all the time, like an African woman wearing a fruit bowl hat, except that she wasn't singing native songs and smiling about her load; she was pressed down by it as though she was about to snap. It was to do with the way she and Peter had split up. When women got beaten up or cheated on by men, it was okay to split the family up by leaving. But when you just decided that you wanted to go it alone and left your bloke, taking the kids with you, it was different.

Danny knew this because it was on the Ricki Lake show. He was currently reliant upon television, until he got a girlfriend or grew close to his mum again – whichever happened first. Females and television were useful sources of information for personal growth. He could have gone his whole life without having heard the term *passive aggressive* if it weren't for Ricki. No one mentioned it at school or football training.

A strange thought was nestling into the back of his mind. It arrived yesterday and he batted it away as a silly thought. But it was still there. When his thoughts hung around he tended to give them some attention, whether they were strange or not.

The thought was this: he had performed a potent Hoodoo spell to summon their father and then suddenly a strange man was hanging out at the preschool asking for Brett. Wasn't that too much of a coincidence to ignore?

Despite his spiritual beliefs, Danny knew that there came a point in a man's life when he had to snuff out the candles, stop the chants, and pick up the phone.

So when the police arrived, he waited for his mother to usher them through to the lounge before sneaking through to the study.

His mum's address book was kept on the shelf above the desk, amongst her literary bibles. It was the thinnest, tiniest book possible. She only needed to enter about three people's names in the book: Rosie, their grandma of sorts; Jacko, their step dad of sorts; Peter, their father of sorts. And that was it. Sometimes a Post-it note fluttered in optimistically, before it was ripped out again like pulling off a plaster. His mum didn't believe in hoarding things – not china, knitwear or friends. The only exception to the rule was her books, of which she had plenty. Her books, she said, had been her salvation – her way out of a muddle. Listeners would think a muddle meant that she had lost her pencil case. She had a knack of making light of adversity – a knack that he admired and mistrusted.

Looking under F for Freeman, he felt slightly panicked when he discovered that his father's name wasn't there. He looked under P for Peter, but it wasn't there either. He thought for a moment. Where would she put Peter? He turned to the last page of the book and there he was: an appendage that she didn't want to look at in the normal run of things. Why was that, Danny wondered?

He glanced guiltily down at the papers scattered on her desk. He felt bad sneaking around her room, but he reminded himself of *The Greater Good*. He looked at the title of the paper; she was writing something about metaphysical poets. Because she was so dismissive, it was easy to dismiss her. Yet here in this little room lay the evidence of how clever she was. He didn't understand what she wrote, but other people did and paid a fortune for it.

Her rise to glory happened out of nowhere, in the best magic trick Danny had witnessed. Professor Moss wasn't able to persuade her to return to her old job at the university, so he assigned her some research papers to write from home instead. One of her papers, *What's wrong with Hamlet?* broke new territory and was bought for thousands of dollars by a university in Massachusetts, who commissioned her to write a dozen more at double the price. Other universities around the globe followed suit. Now she was contacted on a weekly basis with commissions – some which she accepted, some she didn't. It was bizarre, she said, because she hadn't given the

Hamlet paper much thought and it wasn't even in her specialist area.

And that was their mum: nonchalant about earning thousands of pounds; defeated by a spider in the bath tub. She was unfathomably deep and puddle-kickingly shallow; and it was this quality – this duality – Danny was certain, which made her papers valuable.

What Danny wanted to know was: was it what was wrong with Hamlet, the character, or Hamlet, the play? He asked his mum, but she shrugged and said, *I never really said.*

Whoever it was, Danny wasn't complaining. They had an awesome new house and were only a bike ride from their old school. Except that Erland wouldn't bike it. He skateboarded it, with his hair gelled flat on his forehead, his school jumper pulled over his fingers. Everything about Erland sagged, as though there was a giant magnet inside him dragging everything down.

But enough about Erland. If he thought about him, Danny wouldn't do what he was about to do. It was new territory, but his mum needed help – a thicker address book, metaphorically speaking. And so he picked up the phone and did what he did, with no regrets.

Clare had just hung up from the educational specialist when the phone rang again immediately. She hated that. She had been on the phone for at least twenty minutes, so whoever it was ringing was one of those impatient types who pressed *redial redial redial* like a four-year-old until their call was taken. So she let the phone ring and ring, without picking up. She was too upset to speak.

Her husband hated it when she cried, so she had got into the habit of crying on her day off on Fridays when he wasn't home. Today it was about Sasha. Last Friday it was when a currant bun got wedged in the toaster then set alight, tripping the fuses. The week before it was when she found a dead sparrow in the garden. She kept meaning to look up what Crying on Demand signified, but didn't do so for fear of what she might discover.

The specialist had confirmed that Sasha was dyslexic. It wasn't exactly life threatening, but still Clare cried until her eyes stung. She had always imagined that the twins would follow her example and study at Cambridge. Dyslexia didn't rule out Sasha being able to excel academically, the specialist said. It just made it more of a challenge.

Clare didn't want a challenge. She had enough of a challenge getting her seven-year-olds up of a morning. Sasha wasn't too bad, but Sarah refused to leave her duvet and Floppy Bear. Clare shouted at them to eat their cereal – to stop trying to make a face with the Cheerios, to stop worrying whether Floppy Bear was sitting comfortably.

Her husband had no sense of urgency either. He sauntered around with a dot of shaving foam on his chin, consulting his Ipad, tickling the kids as though they weren't all due to leave in five minutes. At this point, Clare would go mental that the childminder was late, and then the door would slam and in would walk Bernice in her skinny jeans and pastel pink pumps, smiling *hello*.

Some days Clare felt like she was doing everything on her own, that she was the only grown-up with access to a clock. It had taken her eleven years to work her way to

HR Director, but most days she was on the verge of throwing it in. What would that leave her with? Tears at home every day of the week. Singed currants. Dead sparrows.

Just this morning she had discovered that her upper eyelids were sinking into her eyes. Soon she wouldn't be able to see. She discovered ghastly things every time she gazed into the mirror, which she did after Bernice shimmied the girls to school, and silence fell upon the house. Fridays were supposed to give her time to catch up with chores, but they had a cleaner in twice a week so there was little left for Clare to do. It was clear that she would have to return to work on Fridays. But for now she enjoyed sitting at the kitchen table with the magnified mirror, examining her pores, her wrinkles, her fading beauty.

The one consolation was that she hadn't ever been beautiful. She was attractive in an Irish blonde hair, green eyes, freckly sort of way. But her sharp cheekbones – beautiful on any other – were too angular on her face; her lips were too thin, her eyes too narrow. Her overall look was one of sparseness, as though God had run out of assets when handing them out.

Overall, the outlook was not good.

A man had moved in next door. He was a banker or a criminal, or both, to be able to afford a three-storey semi-detached in Bounds Green on his own.

He was rather attractive. She glanced at him on her way to work and he returned her glances. Sometimes she wanted to push the issue, to find out whether he liked her. It was so difficult to gauge these things once you had children. Not that she would act upon it. Certainly not with the man next door.

Some Fridays, if it was pouring with rain, or a currant bun had set alight, or a sparrow dropped dead, she thought about *her*. The woman whose name she couldn't bear to say out loud.

Beth Trelawney.

These were not healthy thoughts. They were dark, nagging thoughts that constricted her breathing. She thought about how beautiful and dark *she* was. Dark meant enigma, intrigue, mystique. And – on this occasion – fertility. *She* had popped out children for him, and probably carried them casually about in one of those baby slings, one hand in her back jean pocket. *She* was like Bernice. Too cool.

She would sack Bernice, as soon as she could find a replacement. But she couldn't sack *her*.

Getting him to forget about her had been like the limpets she had played with on Malahide beach as a girl. You only had one shot at getting a limpet off a rock. If you fiddled, if you tried to do it in stages, the moment the limpet realised what you were about to do, it clamped down with an iron will that nothing could move – and certainly not the wet hands of a bucked teeth nine-year-old. The only way to do it was with one powerful blow, using the element of surprise.

He would never have given up the love of his life, if Clare hadn't dealt him the awful blow that she was pregnant. It was immoral, clichéd, beneath her, but it got the limpet off the rock. He asked Clare to move in with him. A few weeks later, she informed him that the pregnancy had gone away. She feigned sadness. And so did he.

It took several years for the repercussions to manifest, just like she knew they would.

She had manipulated fate, and fate responded by dealing her a limpet-removing blow of its own: that she was reproductively challenged.

Yet the fertility treatment had worked, and now she had her girls.

She just didn't know if she had her husband any more.

The phone rang again. It would be the insistent *redial redial redial* person.

She wiped her eyes. "Yes?" she said, with obvious irritation.

"Uh…Peter?"

"It's clearly not Peter."

"Oh, yes…Course not…Do you have any idea where he is?"

"At work. Who is this?" she said, a nasty suspicion beginning to stir in her.

"It's no one…Sorry to have bothered you."

And then the line went dead.

It didn't take long to work out who it was. It would take a little longer to work out what to do about them though.

Beth could see the yellow and blue check of the police car outside. It was a familiar sight eighteen months ago, but not now at their new home. She hoped none of her neighbours were in.

The two police officers were female, kind in appearance. They perched on the edge of the sofa, admiring Brett's string of toys that he presented them with.

"So you're separated from Brett's father, Jacko Best?" said the first officer.

"Correct," said Beth.

There was a noise from the hallway – the sound of crutches clattering.

"Someone else lives here?"

"My two older sons."

"Their father –?"

"Peter Freeman. Lives in London."

"And you last heard from him?"

"Oh, goodness….Twelve months ago?"

"Is there anyone else linked to Brett? Someone who has a problem with you?"

Danny coughed. He had entered the room and was leaning on his crutch by the door. The cough meant nothing to the police, nor did they notice the invisible smile that Beth gave in response – that she knew Danny was there if she needed him.

"Go get your train, poppet," she said to Brett. She watched him totter from the room. "Who wouldn't have a problem with me?" she said. "I was accused of abusing Brett. The court found me innocent, but people judge."

The officers stood up. "Just start Brett back at preschool Monday. We'll send some cover down to keep an eye. And in the meantime, if you need anything…"

"There is one thing…" said Beth.

Brett had returned with his red train, holding it out to the police officers, his face full of joy. "I don't think we're welcome there any more," she said, her hands over Brett's ears like muffs.

"Miss Trelawney," said the first police officer, firmly. "They'll welcome you with open arms. Got it?"

"Got it," she said, trying to control the urge to laugh or cry or both. "Thank you for your kindness." She followed them down the hallway. "God bless."

God bless? She closed the door behind them. Where had that come from?

"God bless?" said Danny, wrinkling his nose.

"Don't start." She went through to the kitchen to put the kettle on, Danny's crutches squeaking behind her. "It's the reverend. I've been spending too much time talking to him."

"I like it," said Danny. "It's better than nothing."

"Well, don't get used to it," she said. "It's temporary. I'll be back to nothing before you know it."

He smiled. For a moment, it felt like it used to be between them, and then the moment passed and his smile went with it. He muttered something about television and squeaked off out of the room.

She was so relieved that the police ordeal was over. They had understood the matter perfectly. She would liked to have believed that they had sent over the two kindest police officers in the area for this most delicate of missions, but knew from experience that it was merely good fortune. Yet that was fine; she would take good fortune by the handful. Discovering that a positive outcome hadn't been engineered by humans seemed such a let down, until one realised that it was far better to have the universe on one's side than the people who lived in it.

Perhaps this was a sign that things were going to be all right. Slowly the past was dissolving, until it ran clear.

She stood at the window, listening to the kettle sighing to boiling point, watching the cherry blossom trees swaying in the front garden. The clouds were racing across the sky. It was a windy day. Spring was making the most of its time, before summer blanched it away.

That was it – of course. Why she had said God bless. It was Pammy. Pammy always used to say God bless in place of goodbye.

The second child

On Teresa Close's forty-second birthday, her four children presented her with homemade cards stuck with pasta shapes, glitter and carpet hair, and a shop-bought cake. Teresa found shop-bought cakes tasteless, but she didn't say so. Instead she smiled as she opened her presents: a hairbrush, a porcelain gorilla, and a Transformers postcard upon which her youngest child had written *Dear Mummy, did you know that carrots can be purple?* Her husband apologised – the gorilla was his idea. He would take her out for a meal after pay day. He had to go to work, but would drop the children off to school to save her doing so. She should have a great day; go to town, buy a coffee.

Teresa sat sucking air through her teeth. She had a gap between her front teeth, where she liked to poke her tongue; an old habit from childhood.

She was perfectly content. There was so much to be thankful for.

An hour later, she found herself climbing into bed, where she laid her head underneath the soft cool sheets and wept. For it was this very day, forty-two years ago, that her mother had given her up.

FIVE

Elias Underwood hadn't chosen his course in life; it was as predestined and natural as a starling coming in to roost at dusk. Druidism was in the Underwood blood. He was born a druid and would die one. And yet he had broken away to forge a different future from that of his forefathers – an achievement which he was mightily proud of, happiness being a birthright that few people actually acquired.

The Order that his father and uncle were sworn into was of a different nature to Elias'. His father, a solicitor and local councillor, moved in elite social circles in Sussex. A Fraternal Druid, he wore a personalised blazer and used fountain pens to sign cheques of charitable donations that he raised through the fraternity. Elias was in awe of the Order, but its secrecy frustrated him. An only child whose mother had died years before, he was profoundly lonely. He spent his childhood gazing at locked doors, straining to hear hushed voices, locked out of the enigmatic world that his father dwelt in.

When Mr Underwood Senior suddenly passed away in 1971, Elias ran away from home to join the Ancient Druid Order. Living underneath a bridge by a weir in Norfolk, an enigmatic man who called himself Malachi – 'my messenger' in Hebrew – taught Elias about animals, herbs, trees and cloud formations – the mysterious skill of *neldoracht*. Elias, eighteen, greedy for solidarity and kinsmanship, lapped up Malachi's words, transcribing them into his own personal *grimoire*: a magical manual. With Malachi, amongst the druids, under that bridge, he had found home. He learned that he belonged not only there, but everywhere. The world had no limits. He was part of everything. All was connected. No bars. No passwords. No locked doors.

Druids were druids, however – whether fraternal or ancient. Elias' Order, like his father's, was well-organised and highly structured. The Order was divided into three groups: Bards, Druids and Ovates. The Druids were the highest rank: supervisors, judges, advisers and teachers. The Bards were the orators and musicians, purveyors of myth and legend who told stories around the camp fires. And the Ovates were the healers, the visionaries and mystics, of whom Elias was one.

His grimoire, full of Malachi's teachings, still existed – outliving its source. Because Malachi, like so many in the Order at the time, was malnourished. Living in damp conditions, rarely eating warm food, surviving on alcohol and hallucinogenic plant compounds, Malachi's health waned. Morphine, mescaline, potent cider; these were found in the snow next to Malachi's body on the night that he died of hyperthermia.

With two fathers lost to him, Elias – still a child in essence – set off south, as far south as he could go. He didn't know where he was going. He was hungry, lost, reeling from grief. He just did what Malachi had told him to do: he followed the clouds.

All this was a long time ago.

Elias stroked his beard, lost in thought.

Sometimes it felt so long ago, so indistinct, so unreachable, it was as though it hadn't happened to him – as though his father were someone else's father, as though Malachi had been someone else's mentor. Perhaps they were someone else's after all. Not his to keep.

These losses were undoubtedly why he had vowed to live his life alone, with no ties, no earthly responsibilities. He didn't live a nomadic life through a sense of bitterness or brokenness. He simply couldn't open that part of his soul again. Or rather, his soul had become a different type, evolving into a more plant-like state that didn't require emotional connection to others. The more he studied nature, the more he felt connected to the earth, rather than to people. What was the use in personal attachment? The earth would never die, at least not in his lifetime.

He had kept nothing of his father, aside from a silver watch on a chain that had stopped the night he died. Of Malachi, nothing but his grimoire. Elias had stolen both the watch and the grimoire; no one knew that he had taken either.

Wherever he went, the watch, his own grimoire, Malachi's grimoire and the grimoire of one other lost soul travelled with him. The three grimoires rarely emerged from the cloth sack where they lay, but he slept with the sack curled next to him each night, as one might embrace a spouse.

The girls had gone to bed early. They had little stamina. They barely saw daylight, emerging to squint, stretch their arms, flop about before retiring indoors. They hadn't even asked where they were headed for. They didn't seem to care. He wondered when to let them go off on their own, whether they would ever be ready. They barely ate. At least they were cheap to feed.

Ruby was curled at his feet. She was old. He had made the mistake of loving her, knowing that she would leave him. But he knew that she would do everything to resist, would put the day off until Elias could bear it. They spoke about it late at night. It was all agreed. No sudden accidents or deaths, on either part.

He was heading south again. It was a long time since he had done so.

He must do as the salmon bid, yet it felt unnatural to his core to be travelling against the flow. The path ahead was not smooth. It was laced with danger.

He fixed his eyes upon the horizon and comforted himself with the thought that his father – if not Malachi – would be proud if he could see the course that his son was now travelling.

There was every possibility that his father was watching. The watch might stop, but the spirit was never still.

It was all set for the funeral tomorrow. Beth would

be away overnight. Jacko's mum, Rosie, was going to look after the boys. Danny wanted to go too. He was fed up with being stuck at home. Beth objected. Funerals weren't enjoyable, she stressed. Besides, this wasn't a sentimental venture but a fact-finding mission. She wasn't sure that the facts would be age-appropriate…

Danny hated that phrase. They were about to launch into a discussion about political correctness and funerals, when he found the photograph. And that changed everything.

She was changing the bed sheets. Danny was lying on the floor, his head propped against her wardrobe. As she pulled the pillows off the bed and shook them, the photograph fluttered onto his lap.

She didn't see it immediately. She was wrestling the mattress protector off the bed.

"Who's this?" Danny was frowning.

She glanced down.

Oh no.

"No one," she said, reaching down to pluck the picture from him, but he held it firmly.

"It's Dad, isn't it?" he said, looking at her as though she had betrayed him.

She went to the window, still hugging the bed sheets, her heart racing. How could she have been so clumsy?

"Why have you got that picture in your bed?" he asked. "Do you still love him?"

He was behind her. She felt his breath on her hair. Before, he would have placed a hand on her shoulder, forced her to face him. But he wouldn't touch her now, because his governing feeling was not one of compassion any more.

"I don't want to talk about this," she said in a low voice.

"He told me that he still loves you," he said. Her body stiffened around the sheets that she was hugging. "Bet you didn't know that." He sounded almost triumphant.

"When?" she said.

"That night he visited… He came all that way to see you and you did nothing about it. You let him come and then go, like you always do. Just like I knew you would."

"Who the hell do you think you are?" she said, turning rapidly to confront him. He took a step back defensively, his eyes full of mistrust. "Give me back my picture!" She snatched it from him.

"Why are you so angry?" he said.

"Why? You know why!" She stormed over to the wash basket, dropping the sheets into it and fixing the basket upon her hip. "It doesn't matter about all the good things I do, does it – that I stand on the sideline every week in the wind and the rain cheering you on? None of that matters. Because you've made up your mind that I'm wrong and now all you do is pick at me all day long."

His Adam's apple wobbled. His fringe was heavy with sweat. "I didn't–"

"I don't know you any more." Her voice trembled. She wasn't going to cry; he expected her to be emotional. She turned away, heading for the door. "I don't know whose side you're on any more."

"Wait!" He struggled towards her. "Are you in love with Dad?"

"Who cares?" she said.

"I do," he said.

She laughed. "Yes, and I know why. Because you don't trust me any more. You want him here – *anyone* here – to take over the reins."

"So what if I do?" he shouted, his cheeks reddening. "Who knows when you'll try to top yourself again?"

"Ha!" she said, pointing at him. "So there we go! *That's* what I'm talking about!"

He set his jaw hard. "I'd be stupid not to have someone lined up. You always have a bench with substitutes on. Every fool knows that."

"If between now and tomorrow you're on my side again, then there's a space for you in my car," she said, quietly. "But you and I both know that's not going to happen."

She didn't cry until she was downstairs in the laundry room, with the door closed behind her. She was still clutching the picture. She forced it angrily into her jean's pocket and pressed her knuckles to her eyes. Don't cry, don't cry. Damn it!

Stupid photograph. What was the point in carrying it round with her? It was as meaningless as cutting out an idol from a magazine and hoping to marry him some day. She would destroy the picture immediately. The last one of him…

But as she pushed the laundry into the machine, feeling the soft sheets at her fingertips, she thought about how she liked to sleep on top of the photograph, its love radiating through the pillow. It was *The Princess and the Pea* for grown-ups; the idea that something so small could make a difference through all those padded layers.

It was her favourite fairy tale, the only one she could remember reading. She had found the story in the cosy corner at primary school. The notion of any corner being cosy was new to her, so she sat there for hours after school with the fairy tale on her lap, until the buzz of the hoover told her that the cleaners were approaching and she would be asked to leave.

Her mother never came to collect her like the other mums. Beth always passed her way through the school gate on her own, ignoring the expectant faces of the parents, the hugs, hair ruffling, kisses and other gestures of happiness. No one's eyes lit up for her. She made her way home mechanically through the village of Pentruthen, like a feelingless marble rolling along the pavement. People were used to seeing her, with her straggly hair and holey socks. No one bothered her.

The only thing worse than being bothered with, was not being bothered with at all.

She had borrowed the book from the cosy corner to take home. She kept the book under her pillow. She had wanted to be like that princess. So delicate and regal that no one dared try to hurt her.

She stopped loading the machine, realisation halting her progress.

Pammy had been telling the truth: she had called herself Princess. She had demanded it upon her first day of arrival – a misguided attempt at self-defence; a word of caution to her new carer, that this wasn't just anyone arriving but someone who was to be treated well. Like royalty, in fact.

It was the worst thing she could have done in a place like Yew Tree Cottage.

Danny sat down on the bed. She was right: he didn't trust her any more, but it was hardly surprising. It wasn't so long ago that she tried to take her own life. How was he supposed to deal with that? No end of promises would make him feel as though it was going to be any different in the future.

It was unbelievable. His dad was in London living with a wife and kids, still in love with his mum. And she was here, sleeping with that photo under her pillow.

It was a good photo though. It looked nothing like Peter now. Danny only knew it was his dad because it looked just like himself. The eyes gave it away: full of dreams.

He had no dad, a brother who never wanted to speak to him, a little half-brother who could barely speak, a mum whom he didn't trust, an attic full of crappy spells that didn't work, and a broken leg.

He put his head in his hands and cried. It was the pain of his leg, and the fact that he was still a kid. A big hairy kid who didn't know how to keep it in like a man.

He heard a creaking at the door. It was his mum.

"You can come with me tomorrow if you really want to," she said. "It might even help us to..." She trailed off.

"I'll go if you tell me why you screamed the other

day."

"Hey?"

"You want me to trust you, but I know you're hiding something."

"It was a spider," she said.

"Oh, Jeez," he said. "Then you're right. I can't take a place in your car tomorrow."

He didn't know if he was going to be able to take that place ever again.

She turned away, disappointed. Something was sticking out of her jeans pocket. It was the photograph. And it brought him an idea.

Beth left as soon as Rose arrived in the morning. It was early. The boys weren't awake yet. She reversed quietly and eased away underneath the orange sky.

The drive took her three and a half hours. By the time she pulled into Pengilly and parked outside Yew Tree Cottage, school had started, the villagers were at work. There was no one about.

She took a walk, her legs wobbly from the journey. The village smelt as it always had – damp, chilled, no matter the time of year. The post office hadn't changed. The same rusty ice-cream sign, the same fierce heating system inside. Beth remembered standing in the same spot on errands for Pammy, flapping the back of her dress to keep cool.

The old lady still ran the store. She frightened Beth then, and did now. Beth made for the fridges, leaning through the plastic flaps for a bottle of water. Except that the shop was so warm and the fridges so old, nothing was chilled.

"That all?"

"Yes," said Beth. She could have felt differently – could have felt like a smelly child with grubby hands, but she had come prepared. Her hair was in a ponytail, her lipstick was red, as were her nails – one of her therapist's recommended shades, *Florida Kissin'*. She was wearing a black fitted top tucked in to black trousers with a tan belt, and red high heels. She felt polished and in control. Nothing of the six-year-old orphan remained.

The woman begged to differ, eyeing the flashes of red with disapproval. "Here for the funeral?"

"That's right," said Beth.

"There'll be a big crowd, I 'spect."

Beth was surprised. She had expected just herself, the reverend and the other four, if they bothered to come. Plus a few others who wanted to make sure she really was dead.

"Lovely woman," said the old lady, pressing the change into Beth's hand and glaring at her through her horn-rimmed spectacles, which made her eyes look devilish. The lenses looked as though they had been smeared with fish oil.

"Who?" said Beth.

"Pammy!" said the woman, tutting. "Whoever else? How d'you know her anyhows?"

"I was one of her foster children," said Beth.

"Oh," said the woman, blankly. Clearly being one of Pammy's foster children didn't warrant any reaction.

Beth turned on her heel and left. The shop was as hot as hell.

She walked along the seafront, deliberately not looking at Yew Tree Cottage as she passed by. There was nothing there for her, now that Pammy was gone. No questions could be answered, no more information handed over. Her only hope lay in that chapel, within whoever came forward to her today with testimonies.

She sat down on a bench on the seafront, her ankles crossed.

She sipped the water and stared ahead of her at the horizon, watching the white horses in the bay, waiting for the chapel bell to ring twelve.

Peter was in the habit of walking to Soho Square of a lunch time. There was an Italian delicatessen en route where he picked up a ham, mozzarella and basil panini from a saucer-eyed girl called Margherita, who sometimes threw in an amaretti biscotti for free. He liked to sit at his bench underneath an elm tree that sheltered him from drizzle, but allowed the sun to reach him on sunny days. By good fortune, no one else was ever seated at it. He arranged for it this way. He believed in the manifestation of things through positive thought. As he walked, he said to himself *it's great that no one is sat at my bench today*.

Today, he must have been distracted by the prospect of free biscotti because when he arrived at the bench there was a lady sat there. He had to try harder, focus more. And then something great happened: the lady got up and left.

He took his usual place, got out his phone and plugged in his earpiece for a spot of Radio Five Live.

Chelsea were in the final of the Champions League against Barcelona on Sunday. He would have to find a way to sneak out to watch it. Clare wouldn't know that it was on. Even if she did, she wouldn't let him watch it. She would say that he didn't see enough of the girls – that he didn't seem to want to be a part of this family, that he should have married Chelsea instead.

Was there a way to do that? Because if there was...

If he'd had sons, they would have been watching the match with him on Sunday at the pub. Hell, they'd be at home taking over the whole lounge watching it on a huge television with a crate of beer and a barbecue firing up in the garden for half time.

He did have sons though.

He thought of his eldest son every Chelsea game. He suffered the team's highs and lows, taking comfort in the knowledge that his son was suffering them too. It was like looking up at the moon, knowing that whoever you were separated from could see it too – that the world was a small, if rather sad, place.

He had thought about Danny a lot since the night he had visited Bath – almost a year and a half ago now. He hadn't known at the time that he wouldn't see the boys again. Beth had phoned him a few days later, asking him to make up his mind whether he was going to be in the boys' lives as a permanent fixture, in which case they would draw up a regular plan; or to forget it and leave them alone. It had to be all or nothing. It wasn't fair to mess the lads around, she said. When he confessed that it would have to be nothing then, she went quiet. Just before she hung up she asked him never to mention this phone conversation to Danny. He would blame her, she said.

Every male went through a phase in their teens of blaming their mothers. In their early twenties, the blame shifted to the government. By their thirties, it was Man United. And by the time they retired, it was their mothers again – for not having told them that life was one long exhausting disappointment.

Clare had gone crazy when he returned from Bath. He hadn't known such anger was possible. No horror film could have prepared him for that night.

She couldn't abide the thought of his other family – of Beth. Her green eyes flashed angrily, she ground her teeth and pounded her fists on the kitchen counter. He had sneaked off without telling her! He had gone behind her back! Behind the girls' backs! How could he do this to his girls?

She covered the girls' ears as she screamed insults at him, before rushing them upstairs to the safety of their beds. But it wasn't safe, as it turned out. The girls could still hear the argument. All of Bounds Green could hear the argument. Sasha was struggling at school – they discovered since that she was dyslexic – meaning that she had become sensitive and highly strung. That night she lay in bed crying so hard that she wet herself, soaking the sheets through to the mattress. Sarah self-induced a chronic asthma attack. Clare cut herself on a broken glass that she hurled at Peter. It was like a scene from E.R.

And Peter just stood there, watching it as though it *were* a television scene and nothing to do with his real life. Because, in truth, it was nothing to do with him. It hadn't been about him for a very long time.

He told Clare he was going to bed. He left her to deal with the girls. It would look bad on him, but it was exactly the way she wanted it to be. She would want to brush the girls' hair, soothe them, tell them it was okay – that mummy loved them, hush now, hush now.

So he wasn't able to get in touch with Danny. Neither of the women in charge had allowed him to.

He was surprised that Danny hadn't called him though. He had seemed so keen to stay in touch. Still, what was the point? Peter couldn't have offered him anything. Not unless he wanted to lose Clare and the girls.

Was it even about losing Clare any more? Perhaps not. Perhaps it was just the girls.

But ah, the girls were all about *Hello Kitty*, so uninterested in football or any sport. Made in their mother's image, they sat there at the breakfast bar on high stools next to her and ate cereal with a universal rhythm, carefully spooning food past their hair, one hand holding their locks away from their mouths. Their mother did the same thing. Just tie the damn stuff back, Peter wanted to say. Or cut it off.

But he didn't say anything. They couldn't help the way they were. They had no intention of meeting him halfway on sport or on anything else. He spent cup finals hanging out the bathroom window listening to a crackly radio in a rainstorm, his shirt getting soaked, whilst they cosied up with popcorn in the lounge watching X-Factor in surround sound.

He had become of those clichéd men who drifted in and out of their homes like polite ghosts, paying the mortgage, answering with stock phrases, only half-listening. No one was interested in anything that he had to say, yet they chastised him the moment he didn't respond when asked for an opinion on their new hair cut, their new shoes, their silly war with a woman at the check out. Whatever the inane conversation, he had to force his eyes to light up. Failure to do so resulted in chaos.

He had become so automated, he was barely living.

His affliction was such a common problem for men his age, it should have had a title: Robot Disease; Self-Respect Decline; Softening of the Spine. Many men decided at this point to boost their self-esteem by having an affair. Like that was going to help.

And they wondered why Radio Five Live was so appealing.

So yes, if he could have married Chelsea...

He finished his panini, shaking the wrapper onto the pavement for the pigeons, who began to peck at the crumbs. Silly birds, he thought.

When had he become so critical? So sad? So alone.

He kept a small photograph in his wallet, hidden in a panel of broken lining at the back. No one knew it was there, but him. He looked at it most days when seated here, in the solace of his own company, with the sun blessing his thoughts.

It was a photograph of Beth – Beth as he had first seen her at university. Not taken literally upon first meeting her, but several months after he had managed to get her to agree to a date. In the picture she was sat cross-legged in a field, her head to one side, looking happy. He had taken her off campus on a small road trip. They had kissed in that field, in the long grass.

He had thought of her constantly since his visit last year. She had looked remarkably good, although strained with Jacko sat next to her, his arm around her in a ridiculously territorial pose. Peter had wanted to prise that huge paw off and run away with her, back to the sunny day of the photograph – to the kissing field.

It had been simpler then. Or had it?

There had always been a barrier with her. It was there from the start: a sense that she would never give herself wholly to him. He hadn't known whether it was just him, or whether anyone else would have stood a chance. Looking at the man she had married, he supposed not. There was no way that she had ever given herself fully to that beef cake.

She had understood sport. She hadn't at first. She had recoiled from any notion of activity with disdain. But she had set about trying to interpret football – Peter's interest in it – as a matter of analysis, trying to work out why an otherwise intelligent student such as himself would be so interested in that silly little ball and the men kicking it about.

It hadn't taken her long.

They were stood in a pub watching an England world cup qualifier, when Gazza scored and the place erupted. People were going crazy – jumping up onto the bar, singing The Fog on the Tyne, doing that daft dance. Up to this point, she had been holding his hand deep inside his jean pocket. She liked to stand like this. She seemed small when she did this, child-like. He liked this aspect of her personality more than anything else – the need to be cared for. It gave him a sense of strength, of masculinity. He wanted to tell Clare that she didn't have to be so angular, so tough all the time; that she could be gentle sometimes and give him a damned chance at being the man.

So England scored and he was jumping up and down, slopping his cider, when he realised that she was stood still amongst the ear-splitting noise, looking up at him triumphantly.

She grabbed him and pulled him outside onto the street, where he stood blinking dumbly. *I get it!* she said. *You're the players. You're them! When they score, you score. When they lose, you lose. It's your highs and lows – it's your successes. I get it!*

He felt overcome. It was the cider, the summer rays, the Gazza goal. *I love you, Beth Trelawney,* he said. *Marry me.*

She turned and left. She actually walked off and left him there on the pavement, with the goal celebrations still going on inside.

That was all a long time ago. No use thinking about it any more.

He checked around him for onlookers, then pressed the photograph to his lips and kissed it, before returning it to the hidden panel of his wallet.

SIX

The bell began to toll languidly at midday in a fashion befitting the occasion. Beth watched discreetly from beyond her sunglasses as cars pulled up, parking skew-whiff around the village, and mourners trailed in a constant black stream through the chapel doors.

She had imagined the four foster children and herself standing out, not only because there would be so few attendees but because they would look out of place with their ambivalent expressions. But there was no telling who Aaron, Teresa, April and Rowan were. The whole crowd looked to be in mourning. Even the crows on the telegraph wires were hanging their heads, the wind howling miserably around the litter bins.

How could Pamela Lazenby, that warped old woman, have summoned such a gathering in her honour?

Beth waited until the doors were about to be closed before slipping into the chapel, like a little wisp of smoke that no one detected. She sat down at the back, her shaking hands clasped on her lap. There was a hush as the doors opened and the coffin bearers entered.

She didn't think about who was lying inside the coffin. She thought about how this was only the second time she had ever set foot in the chapel, about how there had been such a tranquil place with its visiting book, flower arrangements, carved pews and ancient pulpit just metres from her home. Perhaps some of the congregation were the same girls who used to attend here with ribboned hair. Now they were all grown up and there were no ribbons, but there were invisible strings that were pulled the moment that they entered this space and were greeted with warmth and respect. The same warmth and respect that Pammy was evidently evoking because there were handkerchiefs being dabbed to eyes. It was astonishing and disconcerting.

"Pamela Lazenby," began Reverend Trist from the pulpit, "lived her entire adult life in Pengilly. People came and went, but she remained devoted to the village. And the large attendance today is testimony to this devotion."

Beth looked away, unable to buy into the mood of the occasion. There was actually the sound of sobbing near the front of the chapel.

She shouldn't have come, she could see that now. She couldn't even wish the woman well now that she was no more.

Pammy had been incarcerated. Did no one pay heed to that any more – about what she done to be put behind bars?

No one noticed Beth rise and leave – the wisp of smoke. She slipped out as easily as she had entered and resumed her place on the bench outside.

It was true: when you felt unpleasant unkind thoughts, you thought them alone. The next half an hour was one of the most uncomfortable of her life.

When the doors finally opened, Beth watched the black trail as it snaked around the side of the church to the graveyard. Pammy had a prime spot in sacred ground. And why shouldn't she? What was Beth expecting – for her body to be dumped over the cliff?

She sat with her lips pursed, watching the burial from afar. As the reverend scattered the earth, something made him look across to her. Despite the distance, she knew he was looking straight at her, wondering why she was sat apart.

A man began to shovel earth back over the grave. The funeral party slowly made its way out of the chapel grounds and past Beth, who stayed seated erect on her bench, aware of how ridiculous she looked, clad in funeral gear.

The wake was in The Old Duke. Everyone had gone there and suddenly the road was quiet again – just the empty cars, their windscreens shimmering in the sun.

The reverend was the last to pass by. He lifted an eyebrow to her.

"Well, I came, didn't I?" she said. "That's got to stand for something."

He patted her on the arm. "The people who you want to see are over there." He gestured to the pub.

"They all came?"

"I think so. There are four people whom I don't recognise."

So this was it.

She was finally going to find out what Pammy had done – not just to her, but to all of them.

Danny got Rosie to drop him at Bath Spa station for the nine o'clock train. It was an hour and a half to Paddington. From there, he would take a cab to the West End. His dad worked for Travel News. He looked it up online. It was on Greek Street in Soho. He had just known that his dad would work somewhere cool.

It seemed mad doing it on crutches, but he would be sat down most of the day travelling. He told Rosie to pick him up from the station at four thirty. She was the sort of subservient older woman who did whatever anyone asked her to do. Danny didn't want to take advantage, but it served his purpose to do so. He asked her not to mention his journey to anyone, especially not his mum if she rang.

He travelled light as he was only going to be gone a few hours. To his embarrassment, he fell asleep and woke with a jolt when everyone got off at Paddington. It was the painkillers – they knocked him out.

London was humid, awash at this hour with hurrying suits and beeping horns. The cab fought its way through the morning traffic to Greek Street, dropping Danny right outside Enterprise Titles.

He steadied himself for a moment against the bustle around him and then entered the building. The receptionist, the most beautiful woman he had ever seen, was wearing a headset and holding out her hand before her to admire her nails. "That's right," she was saying. "Uh huh."

He gazed at the board of publications, saw that Travel News was at the top, and stepped into the lift.

The doors closed. An automated voice said *going up*. And sure enough with a lurch the lift ascended, making Danny's tummy churn in a manner that didn't seem entirely due to the motion.

The pub was too small for that many people. They were all squashed around the bar, whilst the flustered barman pumped beer as though his life depended on it.

Beth had no idea where to start, who to talk to. The reverend was tied up in conversation. She glanced around her warily.

"How did you know her?" said a chunky man, with a ginger moustache that was coated in froth from his ale.

"Foster child," Beth replied.

"Ah. That'll be right. She was a good sort. Fostered her whole life, she did." He smacked his lips around his drink again. Evidently he was thirsty. "I used to do her plumbin'," he said.

"Then you'll know how rat infested her property was," said Beth, before moving away.

She knew it was bad form – that you shouldn't speak ill of the dead, but this funeral was a charade. It was taking things too far.

She felt a tap on her shoulder. The man had followed her to the entrance of the ladies. He looked aggrieved.

"Everyone here knew," he said, pointing his finger at her, "that that charge was a disgrace. She gave her life up for you brats – churning foster kids in and out, giving them a safe place, a home, with never any thought for herself. She didn't have time to organise the upkeep. We all knew she had let the cottage go, but that's all it was."

"You'm on about Pammy?" said another man, turning to join in. "Bloody disgrace that was. What a way to thank her for all them years help she gave. They wanted her quickly enough when they were looking for bleedin' homes for them kids, didn't they?"

The ginger man took a step forward towards Beth in a manner that she didn't like. "That prison killed her. Sure as I'm a day old."

"That and the chain-smoking," she replied.

"Come this way, Beth," said a voice beside her. It was the reverend. He led her by the arm through a narrow hallway, out to the back garden.

"They defend her so fiercely," she said. "I don't understand it."

"Yes, well, the Cornish are a loyal lot," he replied. "They stick together in times of strife."

"I value loyalty as much as the next person," she said. "But they forget that Pammy was charged with–"

She broke off. It had suddenly gone quiet. They were stood in a sun-kissed rose garden with a view of the Atlantic. She never would have guessed such a pretty haven existed out the back of The Old Duke. Her voice had startled the guests, who had turned to look at her.

"Meet your friends," the reverend said.

On a table in the middle of the garden – the only people in the garden on this beautiful day – were four people.

She cast her eye over them. They were a

mishmash, a hotchpotch of identities – young, old, red-haired, grey-haired, studded, tattooed; a mini circus in a beer garden. Nothing appeared to bind them together, and yet everything did. The sunlight hung over them; the wind didn't reach this sheltered place. Everything was still, frozen in time. It could have been a portrait entitled The Lost Ones.

"Everyone, this is Beth Trelawney," said the reverend. "She was one of Pammy's foster children. Just like you."

This cleared the air. The four of them dropped their enquiring glances. They could relax. This was someone as beaten up, as unimportant as they were. Another damned orphan. One of the women rose to buy peanuts. She hadn't eaten since St Austell, she said.

"Aaron Deakin." The man sat nearest to Beth stood politely to greet her. He held his hand out straight as a ruler, oddly tucked in to his side as if he didn't like to extend too much of himself too soon. He was unshaven, red-eyed, but kindly-looking.

"Nice to meet you, Aaron," she said. "I've been thinking about you, wondering what you were like."

"You have?" he said, bashfully. "Well, I hope you're not disappointed."

"Not in the slightest," she said, thinking how disappointing it was to meet someone from the same background as her who was so grateful for attention. Was this how she came across: self-effacing, hungry for love?

She appreciated his welcome, however, as it prompted the others to do the same.

"April Morgan," the young woman said. She was

at least ten years younger than the others. She wore a tooth brace and a heavy Henna-dyed fringe. She looked bored, angry almost, and was sucking on a stud in her tongue. Around her neck on silver chains were various symbols: a Buddha, a cross, a Russian doll, a skull. "I'm into Japanese fashion," she said.

"Oh," said Beth. "That's nice."

"And I'm Rowan Grimshaw." Rowan patted the bench next to him for her to join him, raising his eyebrows at her. He was wearing a muscle vest and camouflage trousers. Obviously he wasn't bothered about paying his respects. He was tattooed all up his bulging arms, and wore a hoop on his eyebrow. His chest appeared to be waxed and he was generous with his aftershave.

Beth sat down next to him. "What's that, love?" he said, pointing to the back of her neck. "Your label's showing."

"Oh?" said Beth.

"Yeah, it says *made in heaven*." He raised his eyebrows again.

This clown was no threat. Like the others, he was too aware of his own inadequacies. Like a clown, his mouth smiled but his eyes betrayed him. And it was this flaw, Beth realised, that formed the common thread between them. They were patchwork kids; not only because of their colourful tapestry childhoods going from one home to another, but because they had all been broken and sewn back together again. Patchwork kids with botched seams that could unravel at any moment.

She felt suddenly nervous. When Rowan offered to buy her a glass of wine, she accepted enthusiastically.

Teresa Close came back from the bar, clutching a bag of peanuts which she pecked away at. She wore her hair in a frizzy grey perm. Her teeth seemed too big for her mouth, so she kept her lips quite firmly around them. She carried a baby changing bag as her handbag and her car keys were festooned with photograph keyrings of children. She wore one of those necklaces where children's fingerprints were captured in silver. She looked beaten down by something, maybe motherhood. It looked like it was years since she had had any fun.

It was all very well scrutinising everyone, but Beth was reasonable enough to realise that they would be judging her too. She wondered what they saw when they looked at her. A sophisticated woman in black and red, or someone who had overdressed so much for a village funeral in Cornwall that it came across as desperate? She hid her hands between her legs, wishing that she hadn't painted them *Florida Kissin'*.

The wine helped. It helped all of them. They began to talk – the men mainly. Beth was quite a hit, overdressed or not. Aaron and Rowan were both talking to her animatedly, trying to win her favour with the funniest line, the most charming anecdote. She could tell that they thought she was attractive. It was flattering, but it didn't do much for her relationship with the two women. April looked as though she about to walk into the ocean. Teresa looked as though she would do well to find it.

Beth could drink whatever she wanted, since she was staying upstairs at The Old Duke. They were all staying upstairs, aside from Teresa who was catching the coach back to Truro, being the only one who lived near enough to return the same day. There was nowhere else to stay within five miles of Pengilly.

Someone suggested a jug of Pimms. The sun was still warm in the garden. It seemed like a very good idea.

Two jugs later, Aaron had taken off his tweed jacket and Rowan was asking her to *feel his guns*, flexing his muscles.

"So…" said April, turning her dark eyes upon them, sucking on her tongue stud. "Who's got the best memory about Pammy?"

"I once slipped on horse poo in the kitchen!" said Rowan.

"I found her asleep with two lit fags in her mouth!" said Aaron.

"I really liked her," said Teresa, quietly. "She was the only mum I ever had."

A ripple of respect moved around the table, bowing their heads. Aside from Beth, who remained upright, indignant.

"I vote we cut the crap," she said, "and talk about what that monster really did."

They stared at her. Teresa had a mouthful of peanuts. One toppled out.

"Well?" said Beth, looking at each of them accusingly.

"Well, what?" said Aaron, shrugging.

A silence so strong buzzed into Beth's ears, ringing. No one said a word.

"I have to go to the bathroom," she said.

As she crossed the garden, she glanced back. The four of them were leaning across the bench towards each other, heads bent forward in private chat. She was being discussed. What were they saying? What could they say to each other that they couldn't say in front of her?

She felt disappointment squeeze her chest, mixed with resentment. Why was she the odd one out? Had they met up before without her? Had they met prior to today? Why did it feel as though they were a team, a family, and she wasn't a member?

Not again...Always on the outside.

In the quiet of the ladies toilets, she leant tipsily with her back against the cubicle door, her chest rising and falling.

Whatever was happening, whatever they were about to tell her, she had to go back and face it.

The other mourners had left. The pub was quiet, empty. The bar staff were clearing up for the next wave of evening business – clinking glasses, running taps.

It was just the five of them now.

She could smell the salt of the sea as she crossed the garden, could taste it in the air. A seagull was circling above her, crying.

Give me strength, she thought. Let them be gentle with me.

"If there's something you need to say, say it now," said Aaron, firmly, glancing round at the others in a gesture that said he was speaking for all of them.

"Me say something?" she said. "I thought it was the other way round."

"Nope. We've got nothing to say. We just want to know what your agenda is. 'Cos it's clear to us that you've got one."

"Us?" she said. "Why does it feel as though there's a divide here – that it's the four of you on one side and me on the other?"

"Because you have a different story from the rest of us," he replied. "So let's hear it. Why are you here?"

Beth laid her hands out flat in front of her, her stupidly red varnished nails gleaming. What a fool. She would throw the bottle in the bin as soon as she got home.

"Why did you ask the reverend to contact us?" said Rowan.

She stared at him. The reverend had told them her intention? He wasn't supposed to have done that. He wasn't supposed to mention her at all. He was just supposed to invite them to the funeral. What had he said?

"She abused me," said Beth.

She didn't look at any of them. She looked at her hands, at her silly nails. Her skin was ageing, beginning to get crepey. Self-loathing filled her. The seagull continued to cry above. "She... she used to put her cigarettes out on me."

Rowan laughed. "I'm surprised at that, love!" he said. "The one thing Pammy weren't short on was ashtrays!"

The others laughed, in varying degrees.

"Are you saying I'm lying?" said Beth.

"I wouldn't go that far," said Aaron, holding up his hands in peace. "It just sounds...far-fetched, that's all."

And it was then that the truth finally hit Beth.

The gull stopped crying. She could hear the waves crashing onto Pengilly beach, out of view but never out of earshot. Always the sea, churning over.

"She didn't hurt any of you," she said, as though stating it to herself.

"That's right," said Aaron.

"She didn't," said Teresa.

"Not me." April and Rowan shook their heads.

Beth's throat tightened. "So it was just me…I'm never going to be able to prove it now."

"Prove it?" said Aaron. "You wanted to prove it?"

Beth gazed at him. "Not exactly. Just…" She trailed off.

"She served her time, Beth," Aaron said. He fixed his red eyes upon her solemnly. It struck her that he was all at sea, adrift with woes of his own. He may have sent up his own distress flare years ago, but no one had ever seen it, paid heed to it.

"Seems to me that you're just looking for someone to blame," he said. "I think I'm right in saying that in all our cases, the damage was already done well before Pammy came on the scene."

There were sounds of agreement around the table.

"My mum couldn't cope with me," said April, dreamily, as though talking about her favourite film scene. "Couldn't have cared less whether I was dead or alive."

"I've no idea who my mum was," said Teresa. "All I know is that she didn't want me. But…Aaron's right," she said, reaching out her hand to Beth. "What about your real parents? It's their fault, if anyone's. Pammy wasn't perfect but then she *was* a foster parent. Not our real mum."

"That's no excuse!" said Beth. "Even more reason to care for us properly!"

"Aye, but she had kids going in and out there all the time. I was just grateful for a bed to be honest," said Rowan.

"Well, you know what?" Beth said. "I might have been too, had it not been a stinking wet bed, and if my arms hadn't have been weeping."

"Let it go, Beth," Aaron said. "Blame's a mug's game. Get you nowhere, but an early grave. Or the mental institute."

"But that's just it," said Beth. "I was here on a path towards healing."

"Well, it's not really worked out for you, has it, love?" said Teresa, in an inanely benevolent tone.

"Go home," said Aaron. "There's nothing more for you here."

He wasn't being mean. He was just drawing things to a dignified close.

Beth stood up. There was nothing more to say. They were four, she was one. She couldn't confirm her story. She couldn't convince them that she was telling the truth, because no one thought it mattered. Perhaps it didn't. But where did it leave her regards forgiving Pammy?

The past had never felt so murky, and yet so inconsequential.

She drifted quietly away from them, feeling as she had felt her entire life: unseen.

She knew she would never see any of them again.

When she looked back, they were chatting together as though she hadn't existed. Only Teresa was gazing after her ponderingly.

Upstairs, she wished she hadn't had anything to

drink. She wished that she could think straight, that she could drive out of Pengilly, never to return. She didn't want to be doing any of this any more.

She lay down, wrapping herself in the sheets, too numb to cry.

Healing was a fantastical place that she had glimpsed in her imagination at West Marsh. It wasn't real. It was as elusive as all the pretty corners of Pengilly had been during her time here.

She felt something stir in the room.

There, on the pillow beside her, was the child.

Beth's skin rippled with goosebumps, but she didn't scream this time. She didn't push the child or run away. She merely lay still and looked at her – at her tangled hair, at the deep creases in the cheesecloth dress.

And then Beth smiled at her, because there was nothing else left to do.

She couldn't tell whether the child was holy or unholy. She didn't want to reject her, as the reverend had instructed her to do. Because she was tired of living in a world where children were rejected.

The little girl smiled back, revealing her missing front teeth and held out her hand.

Beth accepted the child's hand. "Who are you?" she whispered.

But the child was asleep. Which was fine with Beth. She was just glad not to be sleeping alone any more.

Travel News at Enterprise Titles was the coolest place on earth. There were blonde girls swishing around in tight skirts, Otis Redding was playing and there was a chocolate machine *and* a pool table.

In the centre of the office, swivelling around in his chair like Captain Kirk at the helm of the Enterprise, was his dad. He was even wearing a fitted T-shirt, although not mustard colour. He looked as though he'd been working out a lot, or maybe he was naturally lean. Danny would have to ask. It mattered, since he needed to make notes for his own future.

Peter was handsome. It was hard to rate these things, but his female colleagues seemed to like hanging around him. There was some flirting going on – on their part, not his. He was the editor and too professional for that – dignified, in charge. Not like Captain Kirk, getting off with aliens all the time.

All this Danny took in whilst leaning on a filing cabinet, until a lady asked if she could help him. She led him to his dad – he didn't tell her it was his dad, but she didn't seem to care either way. She looked Swedish, not interested in English family trees.

"Thanks Brigitte," said his dad. She could have been Brigitte Bardot, this guy was so cool. Until now Danny had him down as a loser oversharing sort of person, which just went to show that you never knew how someone behaved at work.

"Danny," Peter said, swivelling round in his chair. "You've broken your leg."

"It appears so."

"Football injury?"

"Yep," said Danny.

"Prediction for Sunday?"

"Chelsea, two; Barcelona, two. Chelsea win on

penalties."

"But what about Messi?" said Peter.

"Don't worry about Messi. They've got to worry about Hazard and Mata."

"Take a seat," his dad said, pulling up a chair on wheels.

He was playing it faultlessly, not reacting to Danny's arrival. It was peculiar, until Danny realised that there were eyes on them, and that maybe no one knew about him. Or maybe they played squash with his wife and would tell her about his visit…

"So what brings you here?" said Peter, in a low voice. "You could have phoned."

Danny felt his cheeks redden. Here it was: the reaction.

"You…you never returned any of my calls," Danny said.

Peter had been tossing a ball made of elastic bands into the air and catching it, but he stopped, clasping the ball in his hand. "Hey?"

"I called your house a few times. Spoke to what's her name."

"Oh?" said Peter.

"She didn't tell you."

"No."

"And how about you?" said Danny. "You don't like using the phone?"

Peter put the ball down and wheeled his chair closer to Danny's. "This isn't the place to be having this conversation, son."

Danny felt his face flush again, this time with pride.

Did his dad just call him *son*?

Peter glanced at his watch. "I normally take a stroll round about now. Can you manage it?"

"Yep," said Danny, rising.

"Come on then. Let me buy you a panini."

A panini? What was that? It sounded like a type of poodle.

Danny liked the delicatessen, the Italian lady called Margherita, the walk to Soho Square, and he especially liked the bench where his dad sat of a lunchtime. If he had nothing else to take away with him, he would have this: a snapshot of his dad's daily life. Sat on the bench, the sun came down through the tree's leaves, splashing their arms. Danny thought the panini was the best thing he had ever eaten.

"How's your mum?" asked Peter.

"She's fine…In fact," said Danny, "I'm here because I've got a secret to tell you. It's not the sort of thing I could leave on your answerphone…"

"A secret?"

"Mum's in love with you."

His dad jolted.

Here, on this bench, he was the dad that Danny had glimpsed before, that he was related to. He had a crumb of bread on his chin, his eyes were full of expression, there was no guard, no guise.

"You've got a bit of…" said Danny, flicking the bread from his father's chin.

"She said that?"

"Yep," said Danny.

"She actually used those words."

"Well…not as such…"

"Knew it." Peter sat back and continued eating his panini.

Danny wasn't going to lose. "She sleeps with your photo in her bed," he said, quickly.

The chewing stopped again. "She does?"

This was fun, like turning a robot off and on. "Yep."

"Oh." Chewing again. Thoughtfully.

"By the way, you weren't hanging around Brett's preschool the other day, were you?"

"I don't think so," said Peter.

"Good. Because if we've got a stalker then I'd rather it wasn't you."

"Thanks," his dad said.

"That's okay."

They didn't say anything else until they were on desserts. Peter drank an Americano coffee and they shared a bag of chocolate-coated Amaretti, which they got free from the nice lady because of the crutches.

"So why are you here?" said Peter.

Danny shook his Orangina robustly. He took a long drink, then wiped his mouth. "I'll admit there's some other reasons."

"Which are?" Peter sat back with his arm around the bench, one leg crossed over the other. Danny liked the way his dad moved – the way he was relaxed, the way he relaxed others. Did he do yoga? He didn't seem like the yoga type. He was naturally chilled out. It boded well. A chilled out man around the house. Their house.

"I'm worried about Mum. Her foster mum died

and she's obsessed with forgiving her and healing."

"Sounds healthy to me," said his dad.

"Well, it's not," said Danny. "It's dodgy as anything."

"Oh?"

Danny glanced at his dad. Was he to be trusted? He always seemed such a nice bloke – a good bloke, on their side. But he never acted as such. He never phoned or sought them out. "I heard her screaming the other day. I think she might be going…mental again."

Peter put his hand on Danny's knee. "If there's one thing I know about your mum, it's that she's not mental. Far from it. I'm sure it's all under control."

"It wasn't before," Danny said.

"No." Peter nodded. "I know you went through a rough patch. I'm sorry that I couldn't do more for you. But your mum's still here, and so are you. And you look pretty good to me."

"But I can't trust her any more."

"You can't?" Peter put his hand out, counting off on his fingers as he spoke. "She keeps you warm, right? Fed? Clothed? On top of school work? Bet you're a straight A's kid…And she drives you to football? You're Bath's top striker, right? And she supports your matches?"

Danny was nodding, rather indeterminably. It sounded much like the speech his mum had given him yesterday. Either they were conspiring, or they had a point.

"Then she's doing a good job." Peter took a long drink of coffee. "I know it's tough, but it's your age. You just need to remember that your mum loves you. She's a good person and she's not had the privileges that you've had. Maybe cut her some slack, eh?"

Danny hung his head. It felt horrible hearing it out loud.

"If you want me to help in any way…" Peter trailed off, as though already regretting the offer.

Danny sat up instantly. "I thought you'd never ask! So when would you like to visit?"

"Visit?"

"Yeah, to chat to Mum. And to…well, you know…explore any feelings…How about on her birthday? I bet you still know the date."

His dad's eyes were looking misty. "You don't know how much I'd like to do that." He shook his head. "But it's impossible."

"Why?"

"Are you kidding? If I visit you again, my wife will divorce me."

"So?"

"Danny, you can't just walk out on a marriage."

"Jacko did."

"He did?" The robot stopped again.

Danny smiled to himself, despite the fact that he didn't like the way things were going. Erland had attempted the trip to London a year ago at the height of their turmoil and had got nowhere. Danny thought that with his own superior conversational skills, he had a real shot at success. He couldn't be the second Trelawney boy to take that doomed train journey home in tears.

"They split up last year," he said.

"Oh," said Peter.

"So does that make things better?"

"No! It makes them worse. If my wife finds out that Beth's single and I'm visiting her, she'll hit the roof."

Suddenly, the tearful train journey loomed before Danny as reality. He could see that all the candle spells in the world weren't going to bring his dad back to them.

"I did Hoodoo for you two," he said, sadly.

"Sorry? Is that some kind of poem?"

"Forget it."

Danny got to his feet, pain returning to his knee. The pain did that – rushed in all at once, throbbing, searing.

"I've wasted my time," he said. "And my pocket money."

They walked together in silence, as silent as it could get on the busy lunchtime streets. Danny felt that it was the sorriest, saddest, most painful walk of his life.

"You can hail a cab easily from here," his dad said, hands shoved hard in his pockets.

Sure enough, a black cab arrived.

"Paddington station," his dad said, handing the driver a wad of notes. "Keep the change. Please can you see that he's okay at the other end? He's on crutches."

Danny got into the cab and wound down the window.

"I liked your bench, Dad," he said, trying to smile. "Thanks for showing it to me."

His dad blinked rapidly, turning his face away.

"And thanks for the panini."

And that was it. Just those words set Danny off.

He began to cry. Like Erland. They were both a bunch of sorry losers whom nobody wanted. Like all the Trelawneys. Even his mum's mother had given her away.

She had a foster mum because no one else wanted her. They were so tragic. If it weren't for the Champion's League final on Sunday to look forward to…

His dad leaned forward through the window. "Don't cry, please, son," he said. "I can't bear it."

Son!

Now that Danny had started, he couldn't stop. He hated himself – hated his inability to control his emotions. Just when he thought he was growing up, he took a giant step backwards by crying. And the pathetic thing was that he was always going to be this way. Age wouldn't make any difference. He could feel it in his bones.

Damn it damn it damn it. And damn the pain of his leg!

And then somewhere amongst the tears, above the sound of the rumbling cab engine, above the noise of the traffic around them, he heard his dad saying those magic words. "I'll come. Sod it – I'll come!"

"You will?" said Danny, brushing away his tears. "Dad, that's brilliant! That's absolutely brilliant!"

"Can we leave now?" said the cabbie, gruffly.

And so Captain Kirk went back to the Enterprise, and the triumphant Trelawney boy took the glorious train journey home, knowing that Chelsea would win Sunday, and that his Hoodoo candle spell had finally worked.

SEVEN

Beth was up the next morning with her belongings packed, her bill paid and on her way to the rectory before the first soul stepped outside in Pengilly.

She rapped on the door impatiently. She heard footsteps approaching on the other side. "What did you tell them about me?" she said, as soon as the reverend opened the door.

He looked bleary-eyed, dressed in his gown and slippers, a stray hair hanging down the wrong side of his bald patch. In ordinary clothes, he seemed older, mortal. "Come in, Beth," he said, wearily.

He showed her into a room in the conservatory – a study with walls adorned with leather-bound books. Three cats were stretched out in the morning sunshine. He motioned for Beth to sit down and took a seat besides her in a well-worn armchair.

"You didn't do what we agreed," she said.

"I don't recall any agreement…"

"I want to know what you told them."

He sighed. "I merely mentioned that you were looking for answers."

"I thought you said you would just invite them to the funeral. Why did you have to say anything? They were set against me from the start."

"I doubt that," he said. "And besides, none of them would have come. I had to give them a reason. They weren't bothered about attending."

"But if they loved Pammy so much–?"

"Love?" he said. "I don't think any of them mentioned loving Pamela, did they? Do you have to make everything so black and white?"

"Me, black and white? You're the one that talks about holy or unholy. You can't get much more black and white than that!"

He sighed again, more deeply this time. A clock was ticking loudly. Beth looked around for the culprit and spied it upon the mantelpiece: a clock that showed its inner workings.

"Let me be frank with you…" The reverend rested his hands on his stomach, forming an arch with his fingers. "I'm beginning to think that what we have here is almost a feud, a vendetta, between you and Pamela. Like any feud, it's impossible to trace what started the problem and who's to blame. Do you understand?"

"A feud?" she said, faintly.

"I told you that if you started a witch hunt–"

"That I would become the hunted. Yes, you did say that. But this isn't a witch hunt. This is simply an acknowledgement of the past, of what happened to me.

Calling it a feud is wrong. That's like saying that the Jews were partly to blame for the Holocaust, that women are feuding with men when they're raped by them."

"Oh dear, it's barely breakfast and we're already on to the Holocaust and rape," the reverend said, rising. "Coffee?"

He shuffled off to the kitchen, muttering to himself.

Beth looked around the room. She couldn't get this old man to see her viewpoint, to accept her truth. What was the barrier? Was it that he refused to think of Pammy as a sinner, of anyone as a sinner? Or was it that he didn't believe what she was telling him? There was only one way to find out.

When the reverend returned, he was carrying a tray of coffee and croissants, and a little tissue paper parcel which he handed to her. Inside the parcel was the mood ring.

"From the prison," he said. "Please take it. It belongs to you."

She sighed resignedly, slipping the ring onto her finger. There was just no getting away from it.

"I'm guessing you've had nothing to eat," he said. His manner was so congenial, so fatherly, so utterly out of synch with the turmoil she was feeling. "Do have a croissant. They're rather good."

Her stomach rumbled at the sight of food. She reached for a croissant. The reverend nodded at her, encouragingly.

"Reverend..." she said. "There's something I need to ask you, so I'm just going to come out with it...Pamela abused me. Do you believe me?"

He lifted his head to the sky as he ate, nibbling, eyes fixed upwards as though there were a fascinating object there. "In the last days of her life," he said, "Pamela told me that she never harmed anyone."

Beth stared at him. "So how did she account for me?"

"Do you really want to know, my dear?"

"Yes." She put the croissant down and braced herself, her hands clenched.

"You were abused by your biological mother, were you not?"

"Yes," said Beth.

"Pamela said that when you arrived with her you were already damaged. You started to make up stories about Pamela abusing you in order to get attention."

"Oh!" Beth gasped, clasping her hands to her mouth.

It was what she had expected: what her therapist and doctors would have said; what the other four were thinking yesterday with their depressed, accusing eyes. And yet it was still a shock. She stood up. "I can't stay any longer."

She thought of the last time she had done this, had risen promptly from his company at the prison table – of how regretful he had looked. He didn't look regretful now. He seemed content with the situation, with the way that he had wrapped things up.

"I know what happened," she said. "No one can rewrite my truth, not even God."

He smiled, rising slowly to his feet. "Interesting

that you should bring Him into it. I thought you didn't believe in Him."

From the moment he had first spoken to her on the phone, there had been judgement in his voice. And now it finally made sense why. If this was a feud, then he was on Pammy's side. Because Pammy believed.

"I have to get back to my family," she said.

"Of course," he said, drawing his dressing gown more tightly around him and nodding graciously.

"You know…It's funny," she said, a thought occurring to her. "But if Pamela carries no blame, then why did she beg my forgiveness?"

"No one said she was blameless," he said, sternly. "You have misunderstood. She served time in prison for neglect. And as for forgiveness…" He raised both eyebrows and clasped his hands together. "She was humble enough to confess she had let you down, that she did nothing to help you."

"Humble?" said Beth. "Ha!" She got her sunglasses out her handbag and pushed them onto her forehead to hold back her hair. "I feel sorry for you, Reverend. I'm not going to stand here and knock your God, but on this occasion He's clouded your view — because you're backing the wrong side."

"And you say this isn't a feud," he said, with the ghostliest of smiles on his lips.

Beth reached for the front door handle, desperate for fresh air to greet her on the other side. "I'm going to finish what I started," she said.

He laughed softly. "It won't get you anywhere. If it's forgiveness you're after, then you won't find it this way."

"Who said anything about forgiveness?" she said. "That was you. And her. Not me."

"Oh?"

"I apologise if I haven't done things your way, but I'm not religious. I don't want to feel righteous. I just want to heal."

"The church—"

"No, Reverend." She held up her hand. "The church can't. This is where you and I part ways. I need to follow another path to healing, away from you and Pammy."

"Ah, but it's not that simple, my dear," he replied, holding out her hand to shake it farewell. "You can't walk away that easily."

"Why ever not?" she said.

"Because of her will," he said. "She's left you everything."

Elias hadn't meant to make a fuss at the preschool. He deeply regretted it. He had been trying to navigate himself, to assess the lay of the land. It caused a terrible kafuffle and he'd had to keep a low profile since then, as the police were hovering. His father had taught him to respect authority, so unlike some members of the Order, he did not fear or resent the police – mostly because he had nothing to hide. His life was clean, as befitted the life of a true Ovate. A key requisite for a Healer was purity.

Angel and Skye were sunbathing. He had managed to lever them out of their stale cabin with the promise of hearing the first cuckoo of spring. This was a falsehood. The cuckoos would already have arrived along the south coast headlands a month ago.

> *In April come I will*
> *In May I sing all day*
> *In June I change my tune*
> *In July I prepare to fly*
> *In August away I must.*

But the girls didn't know this and they were delighted. He referred to them both as girls because they were so young; Skye only sixteen years older than her daughter, Angel, the mute puffy-eyed thirteen-year-old with candyfloss hair. Angel could not have been more aptly named, as though Skye had known, even then, that her daughter would remain utterly defenceless for the rest of her life.

Skye and Angel. Could there be two more cloud-like individuals on earth? He glanced at them lying out in the sunshine, wondering whether he should have roped them down lest they might float away. Their white limbs reflected the sun. They didn't embrace the heat, but lay stiffly as though they had expired in it.

They had liked hearing the cuckoo though, first one of the year or not. Skye said her grandma had told her that when you hear the first cuckoo of spring you should run in a circle three times for good fortune. Angel tried this and tripped over. She didn't laugh, but clasped her hand to her mouth and wiggled her head and opened her eyes wide to indicate merriment. Her mother laughed for her. She had a nervous laugh like a doorbell afraid to wake up the residents.

Then they lay back down together like two wooden clothes pegs.

He recalled the second time he had met them, not long ago at the winter solstice at the Castlerigg stone circle in Cumbria. It was a cold night, snowing in fact, but Elias couldn't remember a more colourful and potent celebration, and he had attended hundreds of druid festivals over the past forty years. There was a large bonfire ablaze; they all held hands around the fire, a candle in their spare hand. The snow began to fall more heavily and the wind got up, yet their candles miraculously remained lit. It wasn't unusual as Elias had witnessed this countless times before, and yet there was an energy at Castlerigg that night that he hadn't felt before.

As he moved amongst his fellows, recognising most people, stopping to greet them, drink mead, star-gaze, he suddenly recognised a face amongst the crowds. It was Skye. She was holding a younger girl's hand: Angel. And he knew instantly that it was Angel responsible for the remarkable energy that night.

The first time he met Skye was in the same spot thirteen years before at the same solstice, when she took part in a baby-naming ceremony for her newborn child. The Chief Druid had blessed Angel, but predicted a world of silence for her. It was written in the clouds, he said. He was sorry. Skye wept upon hearing this prophecy. She was new to the Order, vulnerable, having run away from home to have her baby. Elias regretted that people came to them when they were lost, and yet it was the way he himself had found his people, and thousands before him.

Skye had packed up and left like everyone else after

the solstice thirteen years ago, leaving Castlerigg just as they had found it. He didn't think any more of her and her child. He didn't look out for them at festivals. He did not give them a thought.

Until he saw them again that snowy night and detected that Angel had a special aura. He had only sensed it in one soul before: his beloved Malachi.

He was much aggrieved to learn that evening that the Chief Druid's omen had manifested itself. Angel was mute.

Skye recognised Elias too. She approached, Angel at her side, and asked him whether he might consider helping heal her daughter. She had heard of his reputation as a great Ovate.

He was not sure that he could help but he could not refuse Angel, with her pale blue eyes that spoke for her. And so he took them under his somewhat dusty wing; Skye as his daughter, Angel as his granddaughter. He began to study Angel, hoping for a solution to her affliction. As of yet, nothing had worked – no potion, ointment or balm. And yet he remained hopeful, in accordance with his position in the Order, and his faith.

"Shame we weren't this way sooner," he said. Angel raised her head an inch from her sunbathing position to listen. "Could have crowned you the Cuckoo Princess."

"The whatty?" said Skye, putting her hand to her eyes and squinting.

"It's a ceremony in Wiltshire. They crown a princess in honour of the cuckoo's return."

"Sweet," said Skye, lying back down.

"Quite," he said.

The cuckoo called again. Elias tugged at his beard, lost in thought. In some southern rivers, the cuckoos called the salmon upstream.

Sure enough, there was a splash behind him. By the time he turned, there was just a circle of dilating ripples on the surface of the water. But he knew that it was the salmon – that it was leaving him now, because he was at his journey's end.

It was the most manipulative thing Pammy could have done. To beg Beth's forgiveness, to win the reverend over with lies and religious talk, and then to bequeath Beth the biggest possible gift, as though stamping the matter with ink that read *case closed*. By making Beth the sole benefactor of her will, she was saying that Pamela Lazenby was a good person; that Beth Trelawney was the one that was all chewed up inside.

Beth laughed on her way back to Bath. Pammy was still trying to control everything, even in death. If this was supposed to change the final verdict then she had wasted her money.

When Beth got home, she stood for a moment in the kitchen doorway surveying the scene. No one had noticed her yet. Danny was lying on the sofa, whistling to the radio; Brett was playing *red twain, blue twain, who will win the wace?* Erland was sautéing something smoky, his jeans slung low on his hips, a tea towel over his shoulder; and Rosie was perched on a chair with her coat on and her overnight bag at her feet. Evidently she had had enough.

"Mama!" said Brett, running to her.

"Yo, Mum," said Erland, raising a wooden spoon in greeting.

"Howdy," said Danny.

"Oh, thank goodness," said Rosie.

Beth didn't enquire as to what the problem was. Her mother-in-law barely saw Brett, since Jacko's new girlfriend had arrived. Perhaps she was anticipating new grandchildren, so was pulling away now to avoid awkward scenes in the future. Whatever it was, she didn't help them often. So Beth didn't feel inclined to ask what was wrong. The boys couldn't have been that bad.

Beth waved goodbye to Rosie, then asked the boys to join her at the kitchen table. "But I can't leave my roux," said Erland. "It's at a critical stage."

"By the way…just to warn you…" said Danny. "Erland set fire to the lounge curtains."

"What?"

Erland coloured up. "Singed is a more accurate term," he said. He was concentrating on stirring his roux. "Needs a dash more pepper," he said.

"What were you doing with fire in the lounge?"

"Chemistry homework, Mum."

She sighed. "Okay. I'll take a look later. Everyone's okay though, yes?"

"All present and correct," said Danny. She glanced at him. He was noticeably more cheerful than when she had left him. She wondered why.

"Where was Rosie at the time?"

"Watching EastEnders," said Erland. "Don't be cross. It was a crucial episode."

Beth made a mental note not to ask Rosie to baby-sit again. She had her sights set elsewhere now.

"So I had an interesting trip…" she said.

"Yeah?" said Erland.

"Yes. Pammy left us Yew Tree Cottage, her stables and fifteen acres of land. About £600,000."

She waited for their reaction. Erland dropped his spoon, roux splattering on the floor tiles.

"Why the hell would she do that?" Danny said, folding his arms unnaturally high. He did this when he was really cross.

"Who cares?" said Erland, abandoning his roux to join them. "This is amazing."

"*I* care," said Danny. "Feels like bad money to me."

"Bad money?" said Erland. "What's that?"

"It means it comes from a bad source. It'll bring us nothing but bad luck. Trust me. We should nail this thing from the start and refuse the money." Danny stuck out his chin argumentatively.

Erland was staring at him in disbelief. "Are you nuts? You need to get out more. A broken leg isn't an excuse. Bad money! It's just paper. It's not good or bad. It doesn't have a personality." He flicked his long fringe out of his eyes. "Next you'll be telling me that your knife tried to attack your fork at dinner because it'd just had some bad news from the spoon."

"No, you got that wrong – it's my knife that'll try to attack you, you numbskulled loser."

"Hush now," said Beth, holding up her hand. "I agree, Danny."

"You do?" he said, staring at her as though such a

thing were impossible.

"Yes. I was repulsed at first too. Downright horrified. But then I thought – that money could pay for all of you to go to university. It could–"

"Oh, here we go…I knew you wouldn't agree."

"Hear me out, Danny…It could safeguard your futures."

"There's nothing safe about it," said Danny. "You won't change my mind."

"But there's not just you to consider. There's Brett."

Brett stopped what he was doing and came to her side. He always took hearing his name as a call to action. He climbed onto her lap, snuggling into her. He smelt of milk and marmite. The bottoms of his socks were filthy where he had run up and down the garden path again without shoes. She had missed him.

"You're young, Dan," she said. "You think purely from an emotional point of view. And that's okay because that's what I…what we all…love about you." He was rolling his eyes. "But as you get older you think about other things. You realise that sometimes you have to be sensible."

"Sensible," Danny said, smirking. "That's right. Except…" he said, leaning forward towards her, "This isn't sensible. This binds you forever with the person that you hate."

"I'm bound to her anyway, Danny," she said. "The last twenty-four hours have made that apparent." She kissed the top of Brett's head, pressing his curls to her lips, inhaling the scent of his hair. "We don't have to act yet.

We can think about it until we know whether to keep it — what we could spend it on if we did."

"Would it help if I wrote you a list?" said Erland.

That night, when her vision came to her, Beth was ready.

She peered forward through the shadows to the side of the wardrobe. The girl didn't like bright lights and space, but darkness, corners, shadows.

Beth sat up in bed, her pillows plumped behind her and reached her hand out.

"Please, come here!" she whispered, mindful not to wake Brett.

The child didn't need coaxing. She stepped forward, compliantly. Beth knelt up to greet her. She tapped the side of the bed. "Come join me."

The child perched on the edge of the bed. Beth would have liked to have changed her, washed her, combed her ratty hair, but knew that was a job for someone else in another realm.

The child stared at her with her forlorn eyes. She reminded Beth of someone. Perhaps herself, how she must have looked in Pengilly — neglected, unloved. Except that Beth was much darker, swarthier, and this child was fair, ashen.

"What's your name?" Beth whispered. "Are you here to help me heal? Because I think you are. What is it that you are here to show me?"

The child did not, could not reply. A vision was a vision — bound only to illuminate the eyes, not the ears. Beth sighed with frustration. Brett turned over heavily, his mattress bouncing. She rose to check he was asleep before returning to the child, who had vanished.

They had the most colossal row last night; well, *she* had the row. It was mostly on her own. A midnight diatribe. All the neighbours must have heard.

It was so humiliating, and frustrating. Her own parents had fought every day of her childhood in Dublin. The effects had been wearing, debilitating, like battery acid being slowly infiltrated into your cornflakes, until one day you discovered that your insides were rotten. She had sworn not to raise her children the same way, but here she was doing exactly the same thing – causing her girls to cower, flinch and weep underneath their bed covers.

She had been worried about him all day. He said he was popping out for a few hours after lunch. Admittedly, she hadn't asked him where he was going; she assumed Homebase or B&Q. They made scones for tea and set a place for him, and he hadn't shown up. Sarah kept trying his mobile, pouting when it went straight to voicemail. She didn't realise and kept responding to his message as though it were him answering.

'Daddy!' she said, brightening. 'Hello, Daddy!' It made Clare's heart heavy to witness.

Until Sasha plucked the phone away and slammed it down. 'That's not him, you dummy.' Then Sarah started to cry and Clare gave her a cuddle, stroking her hair, telling her a story about Floppy Bear. It was Clare who knew all these little details about the girls' lives. Not him.

She had no idea where he was, and she hated him

for it.

He had come home so late, she was about to ring the police. She was lying in bed, rigid with worry, mobile in hand. The front door slammed shut and she heard him stumbling up the hallway. He tripped over the girls' Wellington boots; she had left them underneath the radiator to dry. He was cursing.

She rose, grabbing a cardigan and went out, squinting at the bright kitchen light.

He was stood, swaying, making himself an incongruously large salami sandwich. As she demanded an explanation, he sat down on the kitchen stool with his chunk of bread, margarine smeared around his mouth, and began to chew, smiling.

The smile incensed her. "What the frick is so funny?"

"You don't know where I've been, do you?" he said, his smile developing into a low chuckle.

She folded her arms. "Enlighten me."

"You really don't know what today was?"

She was too enraged to play a guessing game.

"That says it all," he said, staggering to the bin to toss his sandwich out – too drunk to finish it. "That says it *all*." He turned to her, pointing, his eyes bloodshot and swimming with alcohol. She could smell the beer on his breath. She closed her eyes, repulsed. "Champions League Final. Chelsea, Barcelona."

"You mean to tell me that this…" She moved her hand in a circular gesture in the air. "This is about *Chelsea?*"

He took a step closer to her. "Don't you want to know the score?"

She despised him more at that moment than she thought humanly possible. "Go to hell," she said.

"Well, since you asked...Chelsea, two: Lampard, thirty-four minutes, Torres, thirty-six minutes. Second half, Barcelona equalised. Both Messi. Chelsea won on penalties." He gazed into the distance, his face lit with bliss. "Just like Danny predicted."

"You what?"

"My lad," he said. "He was spot on." His eyelids twitched as though he was about to fall asleep standing up.

"Wait a minute," she said, shaking him. He was not going to deliver this news and then go unconscious. "Your son? When did you speak to *him*?"

His eyes snapped open. "Lunch," he said. "During the week. We had panini. On my bench."

"Bench?" she said. "What bench?" She shivered, drawing her cardigan around her. "For God's sake," she hissed, trying to keep her voice down. "What the hell are you talking about?"

He sat on the edge of the sofa and folded his arms, smiling unpleasantly. "Why didn't you tell me about all the times he called?"

"All the times?" she said. "He called once. Twice, most."

"So, why not tell me?"

"Look," she said, holding her hands up. "I forgot, Peter, okay? I forgot. Honest to God, it's not as if I don't have enough to remember as it is. We have two children living here, in case you hadn't noticed. I have other things to do than play secretary to that shitty little teenager."

He shook his head. "Listen to yourself, Clare.

When did you become so nasty?"

His tone was so patronising, so demeaning. She felt her jaw clench. She thought of the girls lying upstairs in bed in their Minnie Mouse nighties; of how little regard he appeared to have for them; of how careless he was with them.

"You've no idea, have you?" she shouted. "You've no frickin' idea how busy my life is, how much I have to organise, how much I have to cope with."

"Oh, here we go again," he said.

"Here we go again?" she shouted. "Are you having a laugh?"

"You work because you want to, Clare. And you've got a cleaner. And the girls are always with Bernice. So what's your bloody problem?"

It was the mention of Bernice that did it – that skinny-jean clad bimbo with her vacant eyes. She thought of Bernice in her pink pumps, with her tight T-shirts and push-up bras.

And then she ran at him.

"I hate you!" she screamed. She glimpsed his startled face as she pushed him, catching him off-guard. He toppled backwards, landing woodenly onto the floor, like a mannequin.

There was an awful thud. She didn't dare look over the side of the sofa at him.

She clasped her hand to her mouth. She hadn't meant to push him.

What would he do? Was he all right?

She wanted to laugh hysterically. Or run out the door. She would run barefoot through the streets, across the city, across the sea to Dublin. Mum and Dad would be there. They hated each other, but were good to her. They would take her in and would look after her. She didn't have to stay here any more with this…this… She didn't know what to call him.

Was he alive?

He rose solemnly and straightened his shirt, as though it mattered. The sofa stood between them. "I'm going to visit them," he said, looking sober all of a sudden. "I've fixed a date. I'm visiting my sons on their mum's birthday."

She felt her shoulders sag as the air and energy left her. She glanced at the clock. It was half past twelve. She was exhausted. Her throat was raw from shouting, her limbs were heavy, her head was throbbing.

"If you see that bitch," she said, "then you'll never see our children again."

"As you wish," he said, and turned away.

She noticed for the first time that he was wearing his Chelsea shirt and scarf. He must have gone out wearing them. She hadn't noticed.

She waited to see whether he would commandeer the bedroom. He did. Within minutes, the lights were out and the house fell silent.

She went upstairs and slipped into the twins' bedroom. They were both breathing heavily. If their sleep had been disturbed, it was only transiently.

She sighed in relief. The pony carousel nightlight was twirling. Childhood was so pretty, so pastel, so unrealistic. It smelt of milk, Haribo sweets and Savlon.

She got into bed next to Sasha, putting her arm

around her waist, feeling the warmth of her little girl's body, drawing the Barbie cover to their chins.

Lying here, it was easy to find sleep, easy to sleep like a seven-year-old, whisked and teased into sleep, watching the ponies dance on the ceiling.

The third child

April Morgan hadn't found it painful when she had her tongue pierced; she enjoyed it. She used a technique whereby she pretended that something didn't hurt, so it didn't. It was all about perception. She used the same technique when she went out with boring men and pretended to find them interesting. Secretly, she was sucking on her tongue stud and rolling her eyes, but to them she was smiling. She used the same technique to pretend that her job cleaning out rabbit hutches was fulfilling and didn't stink of rotten straw and poo pellets. She used the technique whenever someone asked her what her parents did for a living, or how many brothers or sisters she had, so that she could feel nothing as she replied. She had used the technique so often that she really did feel nothing now.

And she lied. She told people that her mum was an air hostess, that her dad was the pilot and they met on a long haul between Heathrow and Johannesburg.

She lied about absolutely everything all the time. And the real kick was that nobody ever noticed.

EIGHT

Danny was sat at his usual spot at the attic window, when he saw the barge appear. He immediately snatched up his binoculars. There was such an intricate design painted on the side of the boat, it looked at first glance as though it were an uprooted tree floating along the canal. The entire barge was embellished with the branches of the tree, like a mythical beanstalk run wild.

What sort of tree was it? He peered at the design. It was a yew. Most unusual.

There didn't appear to be anybody on the boat. It was drifting along on its own.

And then it stopped, right at the bottom of their garden.

Danny's heart quickened. There was a symbol above one of the windows: a vertical line with four horizontal lines through it. He had seen it somewhere before.

He pulled his compendium out from under the

floorboards and tore through it to the section on Ogham, the secret druid tree language. Years ago, Danny had carefully transcribed the symbols of the tree language into his book.

There it was. The symbol on the barge was *yew* in Ogham.

He sat for a moment on the floor, thinking. The yew was the druid symbol of reincarnation and eternity. It was most associated with the Ovates – the healers.

It was early Sunday morning. The house was quiet. He closed the compendium and returned to the window, easing it open. There was no breeze to freshen his face. It was a still, heady day.

Why had the barge stopped at the bottom of their garden? Was it going to moor there? He focussed his binoculars upon one of the windows. He saw a flash of something light beyond – hair perhaps, or a pillow. It was hard to tell. And then suddenly there was a pale face at the window staring up at him – a face surrounded by a cascade of sunlit hair, like a halo.

Danny gasped, letting his binoculars drop onto his chest, and stepped back. He stumbled onto his bed and sat there, stunned.

When he looked out again, there was a bearded man stood on the deck of the barge, dressed all in white, gazing up the garden to Lilyvale.

Oh, God. What had he done?

"Dan?" There was a knock at his door. "You up? Can I come in?"

Danny's eye fell upon his compendium and the removed floorboard lying in the middle of the room.

"Wait!" But his mum was coming in. He couldn't move quickly enough.

She glanced at the hole in the floor without interest.

"Everything all right?" she said. "How's your leg today?" He tried to bend to put the compendium back. "Here, let me help you. Does this go here?"

She put the book back into the floor and helped him lay the floorboard in place. Talk about ruining the mystique.

"So seeing as it's a nice day, do you think you'd be up for –?"

"Mum. There's a man…" He was beginning to feel faint. He put his hand to his forehead. He was burning up.

"A man? What man?"

She was about to laugh, but then he saw her make the connection.

"The stalker? Where is he?" she whispered, glancing about her, as though he were under the bed.

He pointed to the window. She looked out. "He doesn't look like much of a stalker, I have to say…What on earth?…Are they allowed to moor there? I'll go have a word with them."

"Them?" said Danny, feebly. He joined her at the window. There were three of them now: the tall man in white, and two women – one of them the halo-headed girl. "I have to tell you something." He hobbled after her.

"Not now, Dan. I'm must ask them to move on before they get too settled. We can't have them there. Who do they think they are? Bloody hippies. Just pitching

141

up in our garden!"

She was setting off down the narrow stairs. He couldn't possibly keep up with her on his crutches.

"Mum!" he shouted. "Stop and listen!"

She stopped outside her bedroom and turned to look at him. He caught up with her, placing his hand on her arm. "Don't go out there yet. I need a moment to think." He was out of breath.

"About what?" She narrowed her eyes at him. "What's going on?"

He swallowed hard. "I did a Hoodoo spell."

"A what?"

"A potent spell."

"And why would you do such a thing?" She raised an eyebrow.

"For you. To bring love to you."

"Love." She said this word as impassively as though saying *dough*.

He nodded. "Well, specifically…Peter."

"Peter." Still like saying *dough*.

"Yes."

"I see." He looked down at the carpet. "And what does this have to do with the hippy crew outside?" she said.

"They're druids," he said.

His mother's look of utter blankness was spoilt by a thumping sound on the back door. There was no knocker or doorbell there, as no one ever came around that way. Unless you were a man dressed in white who had just sailed in on a druid barge.

There were three loud heavy knocks at the door.

"That'll be them," Danny said, his eyes widening

dramatically.

Beth got Brett settled with a bowl of Rice Krispies before answering the door. She wanted time to think about how to handle this. She thought cheerful breeziness was the best way forward.

By the time she swung open the door she was wearing her best smile. But there was no one there. She stepped outside and looked about the garden.

She was on her way back to the kitchen when the three knocks came again. She turned about heel and went back, no longer wearing her smile.

"For goodness sake!" she said, pulling open the heavy door. Brett was at her side, spoon in hand, a mouthful of cereal. "Oh!"

The man in white was looming in the doorway. He wasn't entirely in white – there was a makeshift belt of green rope at his waist, and he wore an embroidered green hat. His hair flowed past his shoulders; his beard was white and pointy. He might perhaps once have been handsome, but age and bad dress sense had run amok, rendering him dignified-looking at most. It wasn't easy to look dignified wearing a white smock and barefooted, so she gave him some credit for that.

He bowed his head a long way down, demonstrating surprising agility.

"Good morrow," he said. She suppressed a smile. As he straightened himself, a waft of aroma escaped from him: lavender, sandalwood. Musty hippy smells.

He extended his hand to her. "Elias Underwood, at your service," he said.

As he smiled, his eyes sparkled, and in them – such dark eyes, within such a white setting – she recognised something familiar.

"Funny man!" said Brett, pointing his spoon at him, before padding off to the kitchen.

The old man was standing completely still, his hands by his side, eyes locked upon her. He looked vaguely puzzled.

Danny had been hovering behind her. Now he joined her at the door. "Everything all right?" he said.

"Ah!" the man, exclaimed, holding out his hands in greeting. "*Now* I understand!"

At this inappropriate display of familiarity towards her son, Beth's sense of congeniality disappeared.

"This is private property," she said. "What do you mean by mooring at the bottom of our garden? If you don't move off immediately, I'll call the police."

She felt Danny stiffen next to her in anticipation of the reply.

"You have every right to consider this vexatious," the old man said. "I shall not trouble you for more than a moment of your time." He spoke methodically, deliberately, as though enjoying the sound of each word.

"What is it that you want?" she said.

The man looked past her to Danny, enquiringly. "It is I who might ask the same question," he said. "For it is *you* who summoned *me*, is it not?"

Beth glanced at Danny. He had blanched.

"You don't have to answer that, Danny," she said, putting her hand across him, protectively.

"It's okay," Danny said, removing her arm and

straightening his chest in a manly gesture. "One of the conditions of magic is that you have to face the consequences. I summoned you here and I...um...fully accept the consequences. So...bring it on." And he bent his head as though the old man was about to decapitate him with a sword.

"What are you doing, Danny?" Beth said, grabbing him by his collar to pull him up.

"Highly commendable attitude, young man. Hoodoo candle spell, was it?"

"Yep, that's the one," said Danny. "I was a bit dubious, it being my first time and everything, but I soon–"

"Excuse me," said Beth, her hands on her hips. "But we are *not* having this conversation."

"Oh?" said the old man, his mouth retaining the sound and the shape of 'O' for longer than necessary. Beth found him deeply irritating, in the few minutes that she had been acquainted with him. She glanced beyond him to the two girls clutching at each other at the bottom of the garden, gazing about them as though seeing daylight for the first time. For goodness sake.

"Now you listen here!" she said, angrily. "I don't know what you want, but I suggest you leave before I really lose my temper."

"Do you not see it for yourself?" he said. "I had hoped that you would."

He looked down, his dark eyes upon her. He really was tall for an old man.

"See what?" she said, feigning incomprehension.

But a feeling was coming upon her, creeping up like a nasty spirit through the whispering grass.

He smiled, pressing his hands together and bowing again.

"That I am your father," he said.

It wasn't the easiest cup of coffee she had hosted and certainly wasn't a typical social gathering in the houses along their street. Elias refused to be seated on the sofa, choosing to sit cross-legged on the floor near the fireplace – *always be near an element*, he said to Danny, who nodded profusely. He requested a cup of hot water, which he sprinkled with something before drinking. The two girls requested the same, looking to their master for his magic sprinkles before drinking.

The girls were odd in the extreme, sat huddled together on the floor some distance from the old man but within arm's reach should they need him. Beth didn't want to ask why they were travelling with this old man. It seemed creepy.

An old red setter was lying outside in the sunshine on the back porch. Elias said the dog didn't need anything except a bowl of water. Nor did it need tying up. It wouldn't stray; its instincts were too strong. Beth knew nothing of animals or their instincts, so said no more on the subject.

"The familial similarity," Elias was saying, "is remarkable."

"He's right," said Danny, looking at his mum and Elias in turn. "You do look alike...I have to say, it's awesome to meet you, Elias – a real live druid. Fancy that, Mum. My granddad is a druid. That would explain a lot, eh?"

At this, Erland tutted and left the room. "Gotta go move my bishop, Mum," he muttered, gesturing with his thumb that he was returning to his computer. He lolloped off, his feet appearing comically big in his oversized trainers.

"So one of my grandsons is a mystic, and one a chess fiend?" said Elias, with amusement.

"Yes, they couldn't be more different," said Beth.

"Well, I'm not so sure…" said Elias. "Chess is associated with the Freemasons, and shares some similarities with Tarot cards. There are those who believe that chess, with its shades of light and dark, represents man's struggle with good and evil, in our eternal quest for–"

"I was told you were a gypsy," said Beth, cutting him off.

"By whom?"

Beth shrugged. "General hear say."

"Ah. Well, I suppose gypsy is a crude term for how those Cornish folk might have seen me. I was nomadic, mysterious. Gypsies have always had an association with the occult, but upon a far lesser level than other sectors due to the lack of written text. Rather a shame….You are disappointed?" Elias said.

"What," said Beth, "that you're a…a what instead?"

"An Ovate."

"Disappointment would suggest that I had been expecting something," she said. "Whereas I have had no expectations about you ever in my life."

An awkward silence fell upon the room. Elias nodded peacefully, as though oblivious to any tension.

Beth took a sip of coffee and eyed the two girls again. Upon inspection, she deciphered that one was older than the other.

Danny was also attracted to that side of the room, Beth noticed. The younger girl was rather pretty, in a startled yet vague sort of way – as though she had just been affronted by something but didn't know what.

"What's your name?" he said, to the girl. Two dots of pink appeared on the girl's cheeks. She shook her head profusely.

The older woman held up one finger and kept it there in the air. "No words," she said.

"Oh," said Danny, looking in confusion at his mum, who looked at Elias.

"Mute," he said, simply.

They all looked down at their cups.

"Magnificent house," said Elias. "Wonderful aura. I admire your taste."

Beth put her cup down impatiently. "So you just decided after forty years to sail in on a barge and tell me you like my curtains?"

"Angel, Skye," said Elias. "Perhaps you would care to take a stroll around the garden? Ask Ruby to stretch her legs with you."

The two girls rose and drifted from the room, like two oversized dust balls. Beth could feel Danny's eyes upon the girl as she moved – upon her slender delicate form.

Don't even think about it, she thought.

"You are angry," said Elias.

Danny moved to the corner of the room to occupy

his bean bag. He picked up his supporter's magazine as a prop, but Beth knew he had every intention of listening in.

"Did you know I existed?" she asked.

Elias shook his head. "I'm afraid not."

"So I'm supposed to believe that you responded to some voodoo–"

"Hoodoo," murmured Danny.

"…That you came here because of a spell?"

"For a non-believer, it may be hard to accept…" Elias said, stroking his beard. "I had a little help with navigation from the salmon. Otherwise–"

"The salmon," she said. "Oh, of course."

Danny sniggered.

"How well did you know my mum?" she said.

He turned his dark eyes upon her. They were unnervingly like hers.

"Vivi?" he said. "We were in constant company for the best part of two years."

"So what happened?"

He rose to the window, his form eclipsing the light. He turned his back to her to look outside, so she could not see his expression.

"We parted ways. I did not know she was with child. I heard some years later that she had passed away. I was most aggrieved, but not shocked. She was weak, your poor mother. A lost soul…"

Beth put her empty coffee cup down, a lump forming in her throat. Suddenly this old man appeared more potent, more authoritative. She gazed at his white back – at the blank canvas. He had information. He could be of use.

There came from outside the sound of a dog barking and laughter. Beth rose to join Elias at the window and watched the two girls running in the grass. The dog was chasing them. The girls were laughing, but only one made a sound. Away from prying eyes, from close company, they were different – like ghosts let out of a bottle.

"I have been attempting to care for those two," Elias said. "Finding a cure for Angel's muteness has become my life's purpose."

He turned to Beth. "It is recompense for Vivi. I failed to save her. I was too young." He watched the girls again, a thin smile upon his face. "There are those who join the Order as a last resort to acquire strength, but the Order cannot provide them with it. And then the sands of time run out."

There was a flutter of paper as Danny turned the pages of his magazine. She had forgotten he was there. She wasn't sure how appropriate the conversation was for him – how much he could even hear of it.

She leaned in towards Elias, her voice low. "Am I like her? A lost soul?"

She wanted to retract the words the moment she said them, regretting opening herself to a stranger. But he pressed his hand upon her arm and held it there, forcibly yet gently. She saw in that moment that he was benevolent – no more a threat to anyone than the old dog was.

"Your son's Hoodoo spell summoned a father," he said, glancing at Danny. "And the universe sent me. Your need for a father was evidently greater."

He took her hand. She looked away, suddenly self-conscious about her proximity to this odd figure. His hand was leathery, weather-beaten.

He was staring at her hand; he raised it closer to his eyes. "You are wearing your mother's ring!" he exclaimed.

She glanced down at the mood ring. She hadn't taken it off since the reverend had given it to her. "You knew Pammy?" she said.

"Pammy?" he said. "No – Vivien. That's Vivi's ring."

She felt utterly confused. "It was Pammy's."

"I don't know a Pammy." They stared at each other. "Look inside the ring. You will see the symbol of ido."

"The symbol of what?"

"Ido," said Danny. He had crossed the room and was hopping about on his crutches behind them. "It means *yew*. Yews are a big deal to druids; trees in general, actually…"

Beth wasn't listening. Sure enough, there inside the ring was a minuscule symbol. She hadn't noticed it there before – hadn't been looking for it.

"This was Vivien's ring?" she said. "How could that be so?"

Beth must have arrived at the cottage wearing the ring. She had called herself Princess. It wasn't Pammy's ring, and Princess wasn't Pammy's nickname for her.

What else had she got wrong?

"I want you to tell me everything you know," she said suddenly, insistently. "About my mother – about my past."

He clasped his hands together and bowed, humbly.

"As you wish," he replied.

"You must stay for lunch. And supper," she said. "Stay a few days. However long you like. However long it takes."

"Naturally," he said, bowing even lower. He really was supple.

"Wicked!" said Danny, punching the air. "A real live druid for tea!"

"I will inform Skye and Angel," said Elias, withdrawing from the room, with a flap of his white tunic.

He was just stooping to pass through the front door when Beth caught up with him. "One last thing," she said. "You didn't say what an Ovate actually is."

He smiled. "A healer."

Clare booked a babysitter and a window seat at the Bengal Brasserie for the night before Peter's trip to Bath. It was his favourite Indian restaurant. She wore her low-cut dress, bought a new lipstick, straightened her hair with tongs and wore her tummy tuck knickers, but kept her tone slightly gruff to avert alarm. She had made up with him after their big row, had apologised for her hysteria, had approved the trip to Bath, and now this meal. She couldn't insult his intelligence. Hence the gruffness. Anything other than gruff would raise suspicion.

They had come straight from parents' evening. It was a mood dampener and her hair had frizzed on the journey, but at least the twins had received a lustrous report. The young teacher had a disconcerting lazy eye, and fancied Peter. Lots of mothers and teaching staff fancied her husband, she noticed – handsome men in good shape with hair being somewhat a scarcity in the playground. The teacher directed all her attention to Peter – although with the lazy eye, it was hard to tell where she was looking. Why did they send these women into schools with silly surnames, hair lips, lazy eyes? They were sitting ducks behind that desk.

She was pleased to hear that Sasha was doing better, although she deemed school reports worthless; sycophantic attempts to reassure parents that their child was cleverer than everyone else – so clever that they were a pompous ass whom everyone hated. But not to worry because all the children were pompous asses, so they all hated each other and *no one* stood out. Which was marvellous and ironic because they all called their children names such as Rafferty and Blue to make them unique, and all that happened was everyone else had a unique name too. Bring back Sharon and Tracy, she thought.

Her mind was rambling. She was nervous. She had to still her hand upon her wine glass. He would notice.

The report was meaningless. Clare wasn't going to place her trust in the school anyhow; she had just hired a home tutor. She wasn't a Tiger Mum as such. She just expected her daughters to do well. So a tutor was starting next week, home coaching Sasha (might as well do Sarah at the same time) in all the key areas. Bernice would be put out. Clare was cutting her after school hours dramatically. The silly girl would pout, sulk, go buy herself another pair of pink pumps and would get over it. And if she didn't, then good riddance.

Peter was quiet tonight. He was always quiet. She

wondered what he was thinking about – what went on beyond those hooded eyes. She had found the hooded thing irresistible in the early years: enigmatic, masculine. Now she found it annoying, closed, incommunicative. Sad, in one who had once been such a gusher.

He still liked to gush sometimes, but only about sport. Upon all other matters he was silent. Yet, she couldn't loathe him tonight – not before completing her mission. So she reached out to touch him, asking him about his day. He didn't reply. He was looking at the menu.

Tommy hadn't questioned her this morning. It was his most endearing and most lethal quality: lack of moral obligation. The youngest of her five older brothers, he had always been as flighty as flour: solid when you put him together with something else – a science lab, a rock band, a girl whom he loved – but insubstantial when singled out for examination. He had been singled out for some time, running a pharmacy in Camden Town. The pharmacy was on a dingy street in a dingy area; the sort of place where she expected to find a back room with a swinging light bulb, a boxing ring, a dog fighting pit. Instead she found Tommy, as hyperactive and twitchy as ever. He gave her what she wanted and sent her on her way. It was a blessing how little he cared about doing the right thing.

The pill sat in her pocket. An innocent thing like an aspirin. Small, chalky, easily dissolvable, almost impossible to trace. Slowly dispersing into the stomach's lining, lying dormant for twelve hours before striking. Something fizzy like lager was perfect for disguising it. Peter had politely asked her if she would prefer him to share a bottle of red wine with her, but she had steered him back to a bottle of lager.

Perfect. Now she just needed him to be distracted. Not easy in one so unattainable.

And then she had some good fortune. Just after the poppadoms arrived, Peter's attention was diverted to the foyer. He was watching who had arrived. It was their next-door neighbour, shaking rain from his umbrella.

She dropped the pill into the lager, feeling her back break out into a light sweat. She wiped her top lip. Peter was still watching the man, frowning, as he tried to work out where he had see him before. Any moment now, he would turn to ask her. She was watching the effervescent pill fizzing its way through the drink to the bottom of the glass; a frothy minuscule bomb of destruction that made one final bid towards glory before giving up, its bubbles joining the head of the beer.

All gone.

"Who is that?"

"It's our next-door neighbour," she said.

"Ah." He nodded. He was no longer interested. He picked listlessly at a poppadom before taking a long drink of lager.

Thank you, she thought, looking at the man. Funny how someone could change a life, facilitate a misdemeanour without even realising. She surveyed the man with curiosity. Perhaps he was aware of his ability – of his eerily well-judged timing. He looked simple enough – rather uncomplicated, unassuming. Rather attractive.

He was on his own, she was pleased to see. No, someone had joined him. A tall brunette in jeans and knee-length boots. So he had a lover, or an associate. Did associates wear jeans? Definitely a lover. They brushed their lips together before reading the menus.

She felt a pang of jealousy. How ridiculous. She barely knew the man. Perhaps she was jealous of their intimacy, at how natural and effortless it was.

She wouldn't look at them any more.

Oh good, here was her Chicken Korma.

NINE

June arrived with a gust of warmth and an explosion of colour. The leaves on the trees had doubled in quantity, thickened and widened, deepening into a green so lush that it assaulted the eyes. The canal path was laden with undergrowth, the air scented with the creamy smell of meadowsweet. Brett had discovered the burdock that grew at the bottom of their garden – how its seeds stuck to the back of clothes. Elias walked around with an array of burdock on his back, holding Brett under his arm like a cushion.

The two girls had been living in the spare room for the past fortnight. Elias had opted to remain on the barge. The girls whispered around Lilyvale, their feminine outlines floating down the corridors. They brought a curious sense of gentility and femininity to the house – so curious that Beth began to wonder whether her life had been hitherto female.

Beth hadn't craved daughters. She had only known

girls to be complicated, demanding, needy to the point of grabbing. At Pammy's, the girls who arrived at the 'safe house' were competition – vying for Pammy's attention, for Beth's clothes, begging to look through the shells that she had collected down on the beach, or to go through Pammy's jewellery box and play with the rainbow hued beads. She had to fight girls to defend the little that she had. The boys that arrived were different. They didn't really want anything. With the boys, she had to refrain from not being needy herself – to not kick them to provoke them into talking to her, not force them to look at her collection of shells. They mostly wanted to climb the tree in the garden, drink milk and watch Crackerjack on Fridays.

Skye and Angel weren't competitive or demanding, that Beth could see. They sat cross-legged on the bed, brushing each other's hair. Their pursuits were imbued with childishness. Angel liked to make paper fortune-tellers – the sort where each flap was numbered and opened to say *a stranger with dark eyes will proposition you* or *kiss me now!* Except that Angel's fortunes were more innocent: *it will snow*. And they liked to practise ballet, their hands pressed to the bedroom wall.

Beth would glance into their open door as she passed, feeling a pang of something – of what? Envy perhaps, evoked by the display of maternal love. Angel was absorbed in her shells and her mother's head was bent next to hers, devotedly.

The one similarity between the girls' hobbies and Beth's childhood pursuits was the shell collection. Angel kept a collection of shells in a shoe box that she carted around with her. She decorated the shells with doodles; not glittery insipid designs, but intricate designs in black pen, that meant something and nothing. Beth wondered at the detail in those designs – at the hours of work, at the misplaced devotion. She would have liked to examine one in more detail – to hold a shell in her hand and turn it round and round – but Angel was highly protective over her collection. Not even Danny was allowed near.

Angel liked to look at Danny. Whenever he was caught in something like his supporters' magazine or *Home and Away*, she watched him. She would be sat at the kitchen table doing an embroidery or designing a shell, when she would look up at Danny and keep her eye upon him. Beth couldn't read the look exactly; Angel was too guarded, too cagey, but she could tell that it was based upon a form of admiration. Danny, with his sporting prowess, had never been short of admirers. Seeing him temporarily disabled, slothful, missionless, was not seeing him in his best light, and yet he was handsome enough to carry off a pair of crutches with aplomb. He was just like his father. Women would adore him because of his ability to understand them.

As much as Angel liked to look at Danny, so Danny liked to talk to Angel. In a way, her muteness counteracted his inability to stop talking. He liked to tell Angel what he thought about everything, sensing in her a captive audience. He was extra-talkative because of his own captivity, and she literally couldn't get a word in.

Angel, for all her immaturity, could see in Danny what her mother, Skye, feared she could see. Beth didn't know Skye's story – why she had run away from home so young – but guessed it wasn't a happy one. There was a sadness that pulled the corners of Skye's mouth down, as though it had been stitched too tight. She had little to say for herself, other than to speak for Angel as required. She seemed to exist purely as her daughter's keeper, a careful hand upon her arm, a gentle pulling back on her shoulder should she stray too far.

Bizarrely, Skye was shorter than Angel. Skye, a fully grown woman, had been stunted, prematurely thrust into adulthood, cut off at her prime. Angel was still blossoming. Without words, her growth was going into her limbs, sending her upwards. Whoever her father was, he had something spirited within him because Angel had something defiant in her, in the cut of her chin and the shape of her rinsed out-blue eyes that made Beth think there was more to her than first impressions suggested.

Still, she was mind occupation for Danny. His cast would be off in two weeks and he would be back at school. It would do him good to get back to normal – to mix with normal people again. There seemed little hope of this ever being the case for Angel, who appeared to have had an abnormal upbringing in the extreme: one solstice after another, a barefoot traveller, an apprentice in star-gazing at best. Beth would ask Skye about school-work. Possibly she could tutor the child whilst she stayed here – a bit of English literature, if her mother permitted it.

With this in mind, Beth lent Angel her copy of *Alice in Wonderland* – a book she had stolen from school. It still bore the *Pengilly Primary* stamp inside the cover, as testimony to her crime. She hadn't felt the slightest bit guilty, and didn't to this day. Children without the money to buy books couldn't be blamed for sneaking them home down the back of their pants. It was a hot, uncomfortable walk home, during which she had more than paid her penance.

Angel read the book in one long sitting at the bottom of the garden underneath the palm tree. Encouraged, Beth wrote her some questions to answer about the story. Angel completed the exercise surprisingly well. So Beth did the same with *Huckleberry Finn* and *Pride and Prejudice*. She was impressed with Angel's analytical responses, but Skye's mouth pulled tighter, and the assignments were stopped.

Beth's birthday fell on a Saturday. Danny was in a festive mood. There were balloons tied to door handles, Bob Marley was playing – it was a hot day – and Danny was wearing his favourite Hawaiian shorts. He told Beth to wear something nice, so she put on a dusky pink summer dress and a squirt of perfume. It was all rather over the top for her birthday, she thought.

She eyed the proceedings from upstairs as she got dressed. The patio table had been set for lunch: champagne bucket, glinting cutlery, Ketchup bottle. There was even a rose in a vase in the centre of the table…which was set for two, she noticed.

Then she caught sight of the Chelsea napkins and her heart lurched with realisation: Peter!

What was Danny doing? Had he arranged for Peter to come? He was shouting up the stairs that dinner was about to be served. The doorbell was ringing. Oh, goodness – was that Peter?

She could hear voices at the door. She listened, holding her hand to her chest. The voices had stopped.

The door slammed. There was the sound of a moped outside.

Danny had ordered pizza.

Was Peter really coming? What would he think of her now? He used to say she was beautiful. Was she still beautiful?

She started down the stairs and then stopped.

What was she doing? This wasn't a date. Peter was *married*. Even if it was him coming, Danny just wanted his parents to talk, to be in the same location for once. Beauty didn't come into it.

She quickly returned to her room, took her dress off, put on a pair of jeans and a sky blue T-shirt, and ran back downstairs.

Peter moaned and lifted his head from the bucket. He had to make that phone call. He couldn't leave it another moment.

He glanced at his watch. Jesus. He should have been there by now. Where was his mobile? He normally kept it on his bedside cabinet. What had he done with it?

His stomach lurched. He had nothing left to give. He was weak, his stomach spasming, his eyes burning.

He held his head in his hands and moaned again.

Gradually, he made his way downstairs holding onto the banister. His legs were heavy. What in God's name was wrong with him? He couldn't find the cordless phone. It wasn't on its stand. Nothing in their house was ever where it should be, dammit.

"Clare?" He called for her, even though he knew

she wasn't there.

She thought he was going to Bath, so she had taken the girls ice-skating with friends. He pictured the girls going round the outskirts of the rink, shaking their heads, unwilling to take the plunge and skate. Pointless. An expensive, pointless outing.

"Oh, no." He moved forward quickly and tore the lid off the bin and retched into it. Nothing. He was all in. Or all out, rather. He stood hugging the bin for a moment, before shuddering and moving to the sofa.

Maybe he should see a doctor. He had never felt this way before. It was a Saturday. No one would see him till Monday.

He found the phone by accident, hearing it beep as he sat on it. That was one good thing. He dialled weakly, pressing the phone to his ear, hoping that he would not be sick in the process.

Danny picked up. "Dad?"

This was a new thing: he used to call him Peter. It seemed more poignant in the present circumstances. He closed his eyes. "Where are you, Dad?"

He couldn't answer right away – wanted to wait a few moments before letting the lad down.

"Are you near 'cos I'm about to serve up lunch? I can hold on a few more–"

"Danny," he said. "I'm not coming." He heard Danny's quick intake of breath, and his heart sank with regret. "I'm sorry."

"What d'you mean you're not coming? Where are you?"

"At home."

"Home?"

Peter nodded, aware how pointless it was to nod over the phone.

"What are you doing there?"

"I've got food poisoning." He shivered. He felt so cold. He clenched his fist with the effort of speaking. "I had a bad curry last night."

"A bad curry." Danny's voice was laden with disbelief.

Peter could have wept with frustration. He didn't even believe his own excuse. "I'm sorry." It sounded weak, but he was too frail to emphasise his words, to prove them, to rationalise them.

"You're bang out of order," said Danny. "If you weren't coming, you should have given me notice. Bailing on us at the last minute is–"

"I'm not bailing. I'm–"

"Just answer this: did you have your train ticket booked?"

Peter paused. "No," he said, cautiously. "But that's not because I wasn't intending to come. I rarely book anything in adv–"

"Thought so," said Danny. "You spineless moron."

Peter groaned.

"Mum isn't even into you any more, you loser. She's dating someone else. He's got a Ferrari. And he's Portuguese. And I've got a granddad now – a proper granddad who's staying with us and he's a druid and everything. And you know what?"

"What?" said Peter. His heart was beating so fast it

felt like it was skipping beats. It was trying to fight something – an infection, the poison in his body. He couldn't get warm. He reached for a blanket, pulling it over his knees.

"You can stay up there with your stupid head wife and your stupid head kids. Don't bother ringing here again. I mean it, Peter. You can piss right off."

Danny hung up.

Peter listened to the dialling tone, not bothering to move. He sat like that until his heart raced so quickly that he fainted clean away with the phone still pressed against his ear.

Clare knew it wasn't her finest hour. Raised Catholic, she was familiar with guilt – the way it gnawed away inside until confession, but since becoming a mum it was much easier to validate her decisions. As a child, she only had herself to blame if she stood on a snail shell or used a red spider to draw with on the school wall; the guilt had been unbearable. As a parent, she shooed unpleasant feelings away with a flick of her hand: *oh, that? I did it for my girls.*

So whilst it was unpleasant and unfortunate that Peter was at home retching – only for a few more hours apparently – it was a necessary measure to protect her children. It was a small sacrifice for something that would preserve their family more than Peter would ever realise or appreciate. He needed to cut the cord with the Trelawneys. They were high maintenance and *she* would use him and throw him away again. Just like before. If Clare ever had to defend her decision to him at a later date – not that she ever would – she would say that she had been protecting him.

The call came exactly as predicted.

Just as well she had taken the liberty of pilfering his mobile phone. She pulled it from her pocket as it rang, putting a finger in her other ear to listen.

"Hello?" She prodded Sasha forward so she couldn't listen in. "Go skate!" she whispered.

Sarah was stood a few yards on around the rink, holding on to the side, chatting to her friend as though she didn't have skating boots on and was standing bored in the playground.

She couldn't really hear. "Is that Beth?" she said, wincing at having to say the name.

"Yes...Can I have a word with Peter, please?"

"I'll call him over....Peter! Oh, dear...he's just skated off. He can't hear me. It's so noisy in here. Peter!"

"He's skating?"

"Well, yes, of course. We're on a family outing at the skate rink...Is everything okay?"

The phone went dead. Clare smiled.

Not her finest hour, but it was pretty damned close.

"Danny, please open the door." Beth stared at the white paint on the door.

"Go away." She could tell from his muffled voice that he was lying face down on the pillow.

"You should have told me what you were planning. I would have told you not to bother – that it was never going to work."

"I went all the way to London to ask him."

"You did?...When?" She was shocked. Danny never used to keep secrets. London? "Let me in," she said, banging on the door.

She waited. There was the sound of crutches scratching the floorboards as he crossed the room. The door opened slowly.

He hadn't been crying, she was relieved to see. He just looked shorter – deflated, pressed down.

"London?" She perched on his bed.

He shrugged. "You were at the funeral."

"You can't just take off without telling me, Danny. You're only fourteen. I'm responsible for you at all times. Do you understand?"

She joined him at the window. The girls were sat with Elias on a hessian blanket on the lawn, doing some sort of druid class, tatty leather books spread out around them.

She was beginning to think that mothering Skye-style wasn't so crazy after all: that withdrawing your children from society was the only way to ensure none of this sort of mess happened.

"Your father's a good man," she said. "He's solid, dependable. But he's got his own family now and he needs to be solid, dependable with them – not us. He's..." She couldn't bring herself to tell him about the skating. "I suspect that he's under great pressure from his wife."

"Who cares?" Danny said. "I'm over him. I don't want to see him again...I told him that you're seeing a Portuguese guy with a Ferrari."

Beth laughed. "Portuguese?" she said.

"I was thinking of José Mourinho," he said, shrugging.

She went out to the garden and sat down at the table, looking at Danny's efforts. She lifted the single rose to her nose and smelt it, sadness twisting through her.

She glanced up. Danny was watching her, so she turned her face to happy and beckoned him down. He withdrew from the window.

She wondered what had really happened today, whether Peter had decided not to come because it was too much hassle, or because his wife had threatened him.

Beth had only met his wife once. They had been accidentally seated on the same table at a wedding; a social faux-pas which Clare compensated for by engaging another couple in conversation the entire meal, leaving Beth to wriggle uncomfortably alone.

Clare, with her breezy demeanour, her angular cheeks, her light Irish accent, had treated Beth with mathematical precision: a turn of the heel, an air kiss to the left, a shift of her shawl onto her shoulder. She appeared to have so little problem with Beth, that Beth wondered what it was that she was trying to cover up.

In Beth's limited experience, if you could find similarities between yourself and your partner's ex, then it was more bearable: 'well, he went for someone like me, after all'. But when you were total opposites, it stuck in the throat like a chicken bone. Clare and Beth could not be more different to look at. Which meant that one of them had strayed very far from being Peter's type. Which of them was it?

"Expecting company?" said Elias. His class was

over. He had stacked his books into a leaning tower and folded his hessian carpet. He was methodical and neat, despite his living arrangements.

"I've been stood up," she said, smiling wryly. "Care to join me for a glass?" She poured champagne into Peter's glass and motioned for her father to take his seat.

"Thank you," said Elias. "Many happy returns. Thirty-nine today…So who was the foolish man?"

"Danny and Erland's father."

"Ah," he said, lifting the glass to his lips. He was wearing lilac – a strange colour on an old man, but not unpleasant. His hair was tied back in a ponytail, his feet characteristically bare, yet manicured. "You are in love with him."

Her cheeks coloured. She put the rose back into the vase. "I thought perhaps so. But not now. I…I don't like rejection."

"Who does?…And talking of which…I hope you do not associate rejection with me, Beth."

She gazed at him, wondering where his comment had originated from. "Why would I?"

"Because I have not been a part of your life."

"But you didn't know I existed. How could you?"

"Quite," said Elias.

Skye and Angel were practising ballet in the garden, one hand on the fence. It didn't exactly look text book, but they were eerily impressive at the same time: synchronised, soundless, frail. Like ballerinas, they barely ate, Beth had noticed. Little scraps of food, like Victorian ladies scared of appearing greedy.

"You have told me about Pammy. Yet you have

barely spoken about your mother," Elias said. "Are you ready to do so yet?"

"No," she said.

Beth was ready, but she wasn't sure that he was. Whilst in her mother's care, she had broken her collar bone and her wrist. She had been hungry, smelly and cold. Her father would be horrified, overcome with guilt, and he didn't seem to deserve either.

"I will wait for you to tell me," he said, sombrely.

Beth watched a large dragonfly cross the garden, its jerky movements both graceful and sporadic.

"You know…your son, Danny, has a gift," said Elias. "The Hoodoo spell that he performed requires great strength of spirit."

Beth folded her arms stiffly. "I don't believe in magic."

"Ah, but I think you *do*. You just haven't come to terms with it yet – with the spirits who share the air around you."

Beth looked at him uneasily. What was he referring to?

The dragonfly came boldly near to them, hovering above the table, interested in the rose. "The female Emperor," said Elias. "Green. Rather splendid"

There was a banging on the window upstairs. Brett had woken from his nap.

"I'd best go round up the troops for lunch," said Beth.

Elias blew the dust off his hurricane lamp. He

didn't use it often, preferring bare candlelight, but tonight it was windy and although the barge was well-sealed the draught still squeezed through.

It had been such a long time since he had craved human company that at first he didn't recognise the sensation. He had Ruby – who was curled on her old rug at the foot of his bed – for another heartbeat; he had his books, for another voice; his lamp, for illumination. And yet…it all felt suddenly shallow, void.

He picked up his father's silver watch, clutching it in his palm. For the first time in decades, he felt that lamps, dogs, books, did not – could not – replace the feelings that he had felt for his father; his feelings for Malachi; his feelings for Vivi.

He had only included Malachi and his father in his audit of painful memories. Vivi – owner of the third grimoire in the cloth sack that he lay with each night – had remained shut out of his mind, of his life story. He hadn't opened her grimoire in nearly forty years, because his memory of Vivi was muddied by other feelings besides grief. When he thought of her, he thought of regret, cowardice, betrayal.

He put his father's watch back into the sack and reached for the third grimoire.

He sat with it closed on his lap, watching the flames from the hurricane lamp grow and fall on the cabin wall – grow and fall.

If he opened the grimoire, he would have to go down another route, an unplanned route. This was different than going upstream. It was going cross-country – traversing the land along a haphazard path with no navigational tools to hand.

He opened a small wooden box, removed the seven oak leaves and laid them in a circle before him. He stood the lamp in the centre of the circle and closed his eyes.

Dear Universe, illuminate my mind with knowledge so that my soul may forever be true.

He stared at the flame, then selected a leaf.

It was the bear.

In all the years, he had never encountered this mighty beast, had never selected it. He had been living the life of a coward – sheltering from human contact, immersing himself in nature without living like a man.

Now he had to emulate the most revered of animals. In the bear, one married inner strength with perception – power with sensitivity, without weakening.

So he opened the grimoire and the first thing he encountered was the lock of baby hair that he had hidden there thirty-nine years ago today.

The child joined Beth most nights. She could not reply – was as incapable of doing so as the mute Angel – but still Beth asked her night after night: "What are you? Who are you? Are you here to help me?"

The child normally waited until Beth was in bed, but tonight she appeared whilst Beth was undressing.

Beth noticed immediately that there was something different about her – that the child was looking furtive, anxious. "Come," Beth said. "Come closer."

The child didn't move. She had her hands behind

her back.

Beth glanced over at Brett. He was asleep, undisturbed.

"What have you got there?" she said. "Please. Show me."

The child looked uncertain and then stepped slowly forward, holding out her hand.

Beth thought of her first sighting of the child at Sacré-Couer – that she had held her hand out then, had been doing it ever since. She had been trying to show Beth something from the very start.

Beth approached across the floorboards, her heart thumping. Then she gasped, holding her hand to her mouth to prevent herself from screaming.

The child was clutching a fistful of bloody teeth.

"Oh my goodness," Beth whispered. "Who did this to you?"

And then she made the connection.

TEN

Vivi was seventeen when Elias first saw her at Pentruthen bay. She was sat on a farm gate wearing a cherry-patterned dress, her auburn hair in pigtails, kicking her feet against the wooden slats. His eyes were still clouded with grief at losing Malachi; he had been travelling non-stop for twenty days, his feet were blistered, his mouth parched, and Vivi was his crock of gold at the rainbow's end.

Her parents were Cumbrian farmers. They were, by Vivi's accounts, generous, God-loving, interested in sheep ailments and pig-rearing. Some of their furthest reaching land bordered with Castlerigg, the stone circle. Vivi, who found farming tedious in the extreme, sneaked out in a homespun cardigan to the winter solstice of 1971 and never returned.

She had been a member of the Order for a year when Elias met her. Pentruthen attracted druids because it lay at the end of a major ley line through the south west. It was an insignificant town – shabby, forgotten – so the druids were able to set up camp on the outskirts with little interference from the locals.

Vivi belonged to this camp. She had a small white tent which she slept in – allegedly naked – alone, preferring solitude to the company of her fellows. Her personality was extrovert in the extreme, yet she kept herself pointedly separate. She was a coveted jewel; royal almost. Her regality coated her in intrigue, made her untouchable, highly desirable to the males, unpopular with the females. She was, Elias suspected, intensely lonely.

Vivi took nothing seriously. She didn't study druid lore, or learn to write in Ogham, or adopt a skill such as he had with neldoracht. It frustrated him – her inability to take anything to heart. Except him, she would say. She had taken him to heart. Wasn't that enough?

She was pretty, intoxicating, with her freckled skin and addictive laugh. He tried to keep up with her – with her energy, her will o' the wisp soul – but found that he was heavy in comparison, weighted down with analysis and introspection. It was the reason they argued endlessly: *you're a boring old git*, she would shout at him. *And you're heading for disaster*, he shouted back.

Funny how words delivered with careless anger were often the most premonitory. She would give him two fingers back, light another roll-up and head off through the grass with a bottle of mead.

She had a birth mark on her right cheek: a dark circle. The mark of Satan, she used to say. It upset Elias, who pressed the mark lightly with his finger, kissed it. *You won't rub it off*, she would say. *You can't make me who I'm not.*

I wouldn't dream of it, he would reply. But he did. He dreamed that Vivi was a salmon, jumping upstream, changing the course of her life, changing the course of her fate. He dreamed of the salmon more than any other living thing, yearning for its appearance in his oak leaves – yearning to summon its power. Yet the salmon never came and Vivi never changed her course.

He began to see in her eyes the eyes of Malachi. She became malnourished, as Malachi had. Her shoulders spiked, her eyes hollowed. Her laugh became empty. She used morphine and mescaline. There were others like her in the camp, encouraging her, feeding her the drugs. Elias despised them – got into fights with the other users; brawls that higher members of the Order had to intervene in, that he was chastised for. Any more such outbursts and he would have to leave the camp.

He begged Vivi to leave with him. They would return to his hometown in Sussex. He was beginning to crave the life of his father – the placid dignified life of a Fraternal Druid. A silver watch on a chain, a personalised blazer, a fountain pen.

Vivi laughed at such an idea. The more she laughed, the more Elias planned his route home.

When she fell pregnant, he beseeched her to return to her parents in Cumbria. But Vivi refused and made him vow never to contact them.

He knew the child was his, as Vivi was faithful. But the pregnancy made her wilder, even less steady. Fear was her governing emotion – not a desire to protect her unborn child, but fear of being responsible, fear of being chained down.

On the night the child was born, Vivi told him that she hated him – that he had become her parent, not her friend or lover, that his eyes were laden with judgement and resentment, that she did not want him near her for another moment.

He summoned the power of his seven oak leaves and saw with surprise that the salmon had finally come. But it was not for Vivi. It was for him.

He crept into the little white tent whilst Vivi slept and clipped a lock of hair from his daughter's head. Then he stole Vivi's grimoire and set off under the stars, following the clouds as Malachi had taught him.

Elias rose at dawn the morning after the bear appeared, meditated for an hour, fed Ruby, dressed unhurriedly and made his way to the house, his legs swishing against the blades of dewy grass.

He threw a pebble up to Beth's window until she drew back the curtains.

"Come," he motioned to her.

He sat her on his hessian blanket underneath the palm tree and showed her the grimoire, the lock of her hair, told her all he knew of Vivi – all he knew of her own birth.

She sat with her hands clasped on her lap, motionless. There were no tears, no hysterics. He nodded in respect, and with gratitude. He had been spared. She watched the grass moving in the wind. She looked up at the palm tree leaves swaying. She looked anywhere but at him.

"It's all right," she said, at last. She placed her hand on his knee. "It was a long time ago."

He felt relief sweep through him, but her control unnerved him. He searched her face for signs of fraudulence, but she appeared to be telling the truth. Perhaps her anger had been focussed in another direction for so long that it was impossible to reroute it now.

"Did Vivien harm you?" he asked. "It is important that I understand what happened."

"I was so little," she said. "I don't remember most of it."

"But you were injured whilst in her care?"

"Yes."

"Ah!" He hung his head, sorrow burning him so greatly he felt it sting the sockets of his eyes. He had failed his child, his only child.

"Am I like her?" she asked, her voice small as though trapped in a jar.

He looked upwards to contemplate the answer, knowing that insight could not come whilst examining one's feet. He had hoped that she would not ask him this question and now she had and he had nothing prepared.

"I must confess," he replied, "I do not find you to be like your mother at all. There are few physical similarities between you and even fewer cerebral ones that I have witnessed. There is, in fact, only one similarity that I can see."

"Which is?" Beth said, turning her eyes upon him at last. She looked tired and vulnerable.

"Your mother was a loner. I sense the same in you – an intention to be alone."

"Oh…I see." She looked down, despondent. "But I don't want to be alone…" she said, stating it like a child's simple request.

He imagined her momentarily as an infant on his knee – her little hand upon his giant hand, her trust placed in him. Sorrow burnt through him again and he swallowed, trying to digest regret. The most excruciatingly inaccessible place in the world of man – as opposed to the world of nature which did not heed it in the slightest – was the past.

"I want to be loved," the child at his side said. *His* child.

"You want to be loved. Yes," he replied. "And I am a healer. Allow me to heal you. Allow me to undo some of the pain that I inflicted upon you."

"You didn't inflict it."

"That is kind of you to say, but my actions resulted in your pain. I will never forgive myself."

Their eyes met. She wanted to display some act of kindness – he saw her hand twitch towards him, before dropping again.

She was proud. She had inherited it from the Underwoods, from the old Fraternal Druid with the silver watch. Had Vivi lived, she would have been startled to see that she had produced an offspring so stoical, so serious. The gene pool was a deep and curious thing indeed.

"We need to follow a different path," he said. "The one you have explored has reached a dead end."

"Not necessarily," she said, running her hand along the hessian blanket, stroking it absently. "What if there was another child?" She sat up straight suddenly, looking at him intently. "A sixth child whom nobody knew about? Someone whom Pammy hurt and then hid?"

"What makes you think that?" he said, narrowing

his eyes at her. He knew there was someone she wasn't telling him about – a spirit at Lilyvale whose presence she had not announced. When would she be brave enough to confess it to him?

"Just a hunch," she said.

"Quite."

A light came on in the lounge. One of the boys was watching television. A blue light flickered behind the curtains.

"I cannot help but feel drawn to Yew Tree Cottage," he said. "There is something about this matter that pulls everything there. And now that the property is yours, it feels even stronger. Let us start there."

"Doing what?" she asked.

He stood up and clapped his hands. "A house clearing! Let us disturb the spirits there, unravel their secrets. And once the calm has descended, the truth will step up to greet us."

"I'm not sure that I understand."

"You will, in time," he said. "Pammy has given you this cottage. Let's find out why."

They stopped at the back door.

"Thank you," she said.

"What for?"

"For telling me the truth."

They found Peter unconscious on the kitchen floor. The girls began to scream. Clare dropped to her knees and took his pulse. It was fast, strong. She thought for a moment. The girls were jumping up and down.

"Daddy! Daddy! Call an ambulance, Mummy! Call it now!"

"Be quiet!" she shouted at them. "For heaven's sake! Shut up!" Which just made them cry and scream even more. She snatched up the cordless phone and pounded upstairs with it, into the bathroom and slammed the door. She sat down on the edge of the bath and dialled. "Tommy!" she hissed into the phone. "What in God's name was in that pill? He's unconscious!"

"Calm down, sis. Say that again."

She heard Tommy inhale. He was smoking pot. The little idiot. "Peter's out cold," she said. Her brother paused a long while before replying. "*Tommy!*"

"I was just wondering whether he's one of those types. One in half a million."

"What types? What you talking about?" She eyed the bathroom door nervously, worried the girls might enter. She had to be quick.

"Some people have an adverse reaction. It attacks the nervous system. It's pretty rare. It's unlikely that–"

"Why didn't you mention this before?"

He inhaled. She could hear that he was smiling. She wanted to kill him. "Because I didn't think that it was for your husband now, did I?"

"Well, who did you think it was for?"

"I dunno. For you, I guess. Thought you might be using it to lose weight, or something. I knew *you* wouldn't have a reaction to it. I used to slip them in your tea when you were a kid, when you were pissin' me off." He chuckled, a low intoxicated laugh.

She stared at the door. The girls were clambering

up the stairs.

"Mummy? Mummy!"

"Oh, Lord. What'll I do?"

"You phone for an ambulance. That's what you do."

"But I *can't*," she whispered. "What if they find out what I did?"

He chuckled again. "Fancy slipping your old man a pill. That's hilarious, sis."

"Stop laughing!" she said. "Help me. What'll I do?"

"I told you. Call 999. Better an angry husband than a dead one."

She hung up.

"Mummy?" The door opened. Sasha and Sarah stood there, still holding the Calypso lollies that she had bought them on the way back from the ice rink. The lollies had melted in their tubes and were dripping onto the carpet.

"Take those down to the kitchen now!" she shouted at them.

"Is the ambulance coming?" said Sarah.

"*Now*, I said!"

Sarah jolted in shock at her mother's anger and burst into tears. Clare followed them downstairs, pushing her daughter's back to move faster. She dialled the emergency services.

The girls sat down on the sofa, glued together, both snivelling.

"Five minutes," Clare said. "They'll be here in five minutes."

It was actually sixteen minutes. She timed it.

Sixteen minutes of listening to two girls whimpering. She would have put the television on to distract them, but she didn't want the ambulance men arriving to find the kids sat watching The Saddle Club with Daddy passed out on the kitchen floor. It didn't seem right.

So they waited, Clare tapping her foot impatiently, scrolling through her mobile phone for information on medication to induce vomiting. Bulimics were evidently a big fan of the *ill pill*. There were chat rooms and forums saturated with ill pill tips; *I've lost six pounds this week and my stupid mother hasn't even noticed!* According to a pharmaceutical website there were dozens of different types of these pills, all intended for hospital use only. How thousands of bulimic teenage girls got hold of them was anyone's guess. How a chef at the Bengal Brasserie got hold of them and dropped one into the food was also anyone's guess, but it had happened…

The paramedics were not excessively worried. Peter's vitals were reassuring, they said. They would take him in, so that the doctors could explore further. She could stay if she wished, because of the children, or they could follow them. They couldn't take the children in the ambulance. Clare wanted to follow them.

The paramedics lifted Peter outside. She eyed the lifeless shape underneath the blue blanket on the stretcher.

As they opened the front door, she was surprised by the burst of hot air. It was a warm summer's day. Her arms were cold; she was cold all over. It's the shock, one of the paramedics said. Would she be all right driving? Was there anyone else who could give her a lift?

Their next-door neighbour was throwing wine

bottles into his recycling bin – the glass chinking aggressively; wine that he had shared with that tall brunette. He had seen the ambulance outside, had heard the conversation. He would be happy to drive her, he said.

She bit her lip in reply. Anyone was insured to drive their car. It was a possibility. She looked at her daughters, holding hands in the doorway, their clown-mouths stained orange with ice lolly. They looked comic and petrified at the same time.

The paramedics kicked the ramp up and closed the doors on Peter. They would leave her to it and see her there shortly.

The neighbour said it really wouldn't be a problem. He would just go lock up. He was wearing a T-shirt that said Old Men Rule. He didn't seem old enough to be wearing it.

They had to walk a few minutes down the road to their car. It was always hard to find parking on Saturdays, she said, for want of something to say.

They had parked – at rather a bad angle, she could see now – outside a fish and chip shop. She strapped the girls into their booster seats. The man sat down beside her, his muscular arms twisting the wheel. She caught a waft of aftershave: oddly sweet, feminine almost. He was the sort of man who liked to put one arm around the passenger seat when he reversed, which he did now; the sort of man who sat with his legs spread, his arms thrown out on either side of the settee.

She kept her eyes ahead of her, felt herself stiffen. The girls hadn't said a word. They were at an age where men other than their father were utterly repugnant.

He left them at the hospital. She was adamant that they would get a taxi back. He said he would drop the car key into her later.

She wasn't really listening to him. She wanted to find Peter. She thanked him and hurried through the hospital, clutching her daughters' hands.

"Is Daddy going to die?" asked Sasha.

"Don't be stupid," said Clare. "Why would you say something like that?"

Sasha began to cry, as they raced along. "I'm not stupid," she wailed. Oh, Lord. Clare didn't have time for the dyslexia crisis now. "I'm not stupid, Mummy!"

They reached Peter's ward. It had a sleepy lunchtime feel to it. Someone was eating something hot and beefy behind a curtain – a school meal smell that made Clare's stomach turn. A nurse was stood at the counter writing notes.

"I'm here to see my husband, Peter Freeman," Clare said.

The nurse smiled knowingly. She appeared to have all the time in the world – not as though she was in a London hospital on the weekend.

"Ah, you must be Beth," she said, putting her pen down.

Clare started upon hearing the name.

"What an ordeal for you all," the nurse said, misreading Clare's look of shock. "And for you two little ones," she said, looking in consternation at the girls. "He just came round," she said, lowering her voice to Clare. "He's a bit foggy, but he's been asking for you constantly."

Danny found it impossible not to think about Angel. Every moment of the day, he thought about her – about how her beauty was translucent, how her silence was inspirational. She had been sent to him to teach him how serene wordlessness could be – how less was more, how he should shut the hell up.

Her muteness fascinated him, compelled him to draw near, to analyse her every gesture, to watch the little blue vein on her forehead intensify when she was asked a question that she could not, would not, answer. She kept a notebook in her tunic pocket, which she wrote upon – not frantic movements in a rush to communicate, but considered delicate writing that twirled and flounced. She only wrote a few words, perhaps because she couldn't be bothered to write long paragraphs. Or perhaps because she didn't have much to say.

Danny didn't see her muteness as a handicap or a flaw, but as an ability – a superhuman power. He wanted to kiss her, to catch whatever it was that she had, to become similarly afflicted – albeit to a lesser extent. He wanted to still speak, but to acquire a discipline that capped his words. And *why* didn't Angel speak? Was she born that way, or had something happened? Was it harrowing, or did she enjoy the power that her silence gave her? She seemed calm about it, perfectly happy in fact. Maybe she *could* speak, but chose not to. All these things, he longed to ask her. All these words always cramming into his mind. Did Angel think in words still? Or was her brain one long flat line, a communicational nightmare?

Since breaking his leg, he had been doing the odd morning at school. Short bursts of learning, the doctor said. Which meant that he had every afternoon free.

Of an afternoon, Angel normally sat underneath the palm tree on Elias' rug with her mother beside her, like an Edwardian chaperone. Had Danny also been Edwardian, he might have approached Skye to ask permission to court her daughter. Instead he engineered a walk along the canal to collect Brett from preschool, arranging for Skye to stay with his mum and learn how to bake gingerbread.

Skye was of a cantankerous nature, but Danny had discovered that she was eager to learn how to cook. And so it was that he managed to separate Angel from her guardian, in order to kiss her lightly on the lips next to the rosebay willowherb on the verge of the canal.

As soon as he had done it, he regretted it. She looked at him with disbelief and confusion, holding her hand to her lips. He felt as though he had kissed a child. He hobbled off on his crutches, feeling shameful. His mum would go nuts if she found out. *Her* mum would go nuts. It was a bit like kissing a family member. What had he been thinking? It was going to be all awkward now. Oh Jeez.

The next day, Skye wanted to learn how to make scones. Angel wanted to tag along with him to collect Brett, *for the fresh air*, she wrote to her mother. So Danny found himself hobbling along the canal again with her. When they passed the spot where he had kissed her yesterday, he eyed it regretfully. But she grabbed at his arm with surprising strength, went on tiptoe and kissed him. Right there by the rosebay willowherb, as though it were the appointed place for illicit meetings. She kissed him for what felt like a whole minute – not because the time dragged and he wanted it over, but because she kissed him as though she had waited her whole life to do so. Perhaps she had. She pulled away, wiped her mouth on her tunic sleeve and then did something unAngel-like: she grinned at him. She got her notebook out and wrote something. She held it out for him: *NICE!*

After that, there was treacle tart, strawberry cheesecake, lemon meringue pie, smoked mackerel quiche and Cornish pasties. The days merged into one – an array of homemade food being demonstrated in the kitchen, and kisses being demonstrated along the canal.

Until the day came for Danny to have his cast removed. He didn't want it to go. Taking the cast off meant going back to school full-time. It meant an end to holding Angel's hand along the canal, to kissing her, to staring into her eyes that grew bluer on sunnier days and greyer under the clouds.

When his cast came off, he held his leg out in front of him as though it were a butcher's prized loin.

What am I supposed to do now? he thought.

His mum rubbed his arm proudly. Her eyes were saying *we did it, Dan! It's all over.* His heart was saying *it's all over* too, but for a different reason. He didn't tell his mum why he felt so miserable, but nor could he hide his misery from her. He was like an apprentice who had only learned half his craft: the art of not telling anyone anything, but not the art of how to hide the fact that you weren't telling anyone anything. His mum knew he was being secretive. Truly secretive people didn't give their secrecy away.

"I'll drop you straight off at school, Dan," his mum said, as they walked to the hospital car park. "I thought this is what you were waiting for. So why the long face?"

"Because it's geography this afternoon," he replied.

It wasn't a lie. He found geography tedious.

He spent the afternoon thinking about Angel. He hoped that he was never asked what a rain shadow was and why the Gobi Desert in Central Asia had one, because he wouldn't have a clue. He spent so long contemplating Angel in geography, he began to wonder whether he would even be able to find his way home.

He did find his way home, but he walked lethargically, his rucksack slung over his shoulder. He normally raced along the back streets on his Silverfox Demon, upon which he was a king – jumping pavements, jolting down steps, traversing streams. Today, bikeless, fresh-legged from his cast, he was weighted with thought. The world felt more intense – the colours brighter, the light almost stinging his eyes. Was this what it felt like to be in love? He had no idea. Maybe it was withdrawal from his pain relief medication.

Angel. What had he thought about before her? His father? Pah. That wasn't going to happen any more. What Peter had done was unforgivable. Besides, Danny had a grandfather now. Elias was literally a grand father – a father whom Danny could look up to, admire and emulate. Never in his life had such a figure existed, and now he had appeared and had brought Angel with him.

Elias was here because of the Hoodoo spell, Danny was sure. He was the father they all needed. Not weak-willed Peter. Not macho Jacko. But eloquent, analytical, mystical Elias. Had Danny made a list of desired qualities in a hero, it would have been a close match to Elias' skill set.

The old man had made a living entirely from the earth, by farming it, labouring upon it, carving its produce. He told Danny that in the early years he had worked on farms, wherever the opportunities were – Yorkshire, Sussex, Cumbria, even the Hebrides. He had never been abroad, only ever staying in the British Isles. He wanted for nothing, survived on little, saved his money in a swag bag buried in the forest. He had never used a bank or signed on the dole. As far as he was concerned, he didn't exist as an accounted for citizen, but as a free spirit.

When Elias had begun to feel jaded from labour – twenty years ago – he bought the barge with his savings, converting part of it into an art studio of sorts. He floated about, gathering suitable materials for his work. Rich people loved his wood carvings. He depicted tree spirits, sprites. His favourite was *Elka, the Free*, which was secured to the front of his boat. He made enough money to live on, and to put by for his future. Living humbly was the secret to his happiness, he told Danny.

Danny wasn't about to run away to druid camp, but he was drawn to his grandfather – to his enterprising spirit, to his freedom. If it weren't for Danny's football ambitions – for his love of money, control, adoration and social status – he would chuck it all in and join the barge crew. But it wasn't long till next season and now that his cast was off he would have to work hard on his fitness. Angel was important, Angel was everything, but she wasn't football. She wasn't Chelsea.

THE BURNT LOTUS

And it was then, as he opened the front door to Lilyvale and saw that his mum had scrubbed and polished his football boots and had set them on a large card that said *Welcome back, Dan!* that he remembered exactly what he had thought about before Angel had come along.

The fourth child

Rowan Grimshaw was a well-known D.J. in Poole. He didn't kid himself that he had made it big time, although there was a season in Ibiza when he thought he was about to take things to the next level, but it hadn't happened. He had returned to the Lounge Lizard in Poole, where he continued to spin records for locals, tourists and merchant navy men, whilst winking at the ladies in lycra.

No two nights were the same and yet it was all beginning to bore him. He worked out every morning at the same gym – doing the same amount of bench presses, discussing the best techniques and protein mixes with the lads. Then he went for a run along the quay towards Sand Banks, sat on the wall to catch his breath and throw stones at the gulls on the way back, before lunching at the same café, getting a few hours kip, and preparing for the night ahead. He wore the same clothes all the time – a muscle vest, camouflage combat trousers and Doc Marten boots.

To the untrained eye, he looked like a womaniser whose best friend would be a rottweiler.

No one guessed that by his bedside was a book of Tennyson poetry, that he could recite Wilfred Owen's *Anthem for Doomed Youth* by heart.

ELEVEN

With Danny out of his cast, they could make the trip to Pengilly. Elias didn't want to leave Skye and Angel, so they all went – including Ruby, the red setter. One of Elias's friends was lending them a Volkswagen camper van. Beth wasn't sure that the van looked safe, but apparently the friend was a mechanic. The V.W. smelt of patchouli and sandalwood inside. "I've cleaned it out, mind," said the friend, grinning, his front tooth gold-capped. "Got rid of the smokes."

Beth didn't ask what sort of smokes he meant. She just paid him generously for his efforts. He had one of those anxious faces that looked as though money was sparse. He kept looking up at Lilyvale and rubbing his hands together. "Wow...Wow..."

"He's probably working out how to break in whilst we're away," said Danny.

They set off in the morning sunshine. "This is so cool," said Erland. "I've always wanted to do a trip to the sea in a V.W. Very Beach Boys." Erland was wearing a diamond-print tank top and a shirt done up to the neck. He looked like an old man. Beth smiled to herself.

"Beach Boys?" said Danny. "Who listens to them any more? You're so retro and not in a cool way."

"Hush up, boys," said Beth. "I need to concentrate. I've never driven one of these before."

"Mummy crash! Mummy crash!" said Brett, in delight.

"Quiet!" said Elias, holding up his finger solemnly. "One must never speak of ill events."

Elias could do that, Beth noted – say a few words and the place fell silent. Perhaps it was his age, or the beard.

She was feeling peculiarly happy. The van contained everyone she loved – including this latest strange addition to her life: her father. She was beginning to feel stirrings of affection toward him – a desire to hug him, protect him, tell him that she would care for him in his old age. But there was a barrier – the knowledge that he hadn't done this for her. She wanted him to make the first move on any declarations of feelings. He was the one who had walked out on her, after all.

She glanced in the rear view mirror. Danny looked as though he was considering Angel's legs. She was wearing shorts today and faded pink baseball boots. It was the first time Beth had seen Angel's legs. It looked like the first time daylight had seen them too; they were unreasonably white. Angel's mother was squashed next to her, her brow furrowed. Skye always seemed perturbed, but more so lately. Beth guessed that it was because of the new romance.

Danny, for all his efforts to disguise it, was plainly in love. Angel made no effort to disguise the fact that she felt the same way. She reached for his arm all the time to tap him, to draw attention to whatever it was that she was writing down. He would nod in agreement, smile, tap her leg in approval. They had developed their own efficient way of communicating quickly, one which curbed Danny's love of words. Out of sensitivity, he was speaking less.

Beth found their courtship touching. But she wondered what would happen when the time came for Elias to leave. It wouldn't be long before he would be slipping that rope off the mooring station and drifting off again. She sensed that this was the reason for Skye's concern also. Skye wouldn't be worried for her daughter's safety or modesty; Danny came across too well. She would be worried about breaking her daughter's heart, on top of whatever traumas in life it had already endured.

Angel was tapping Danny's leg. She handed him her pad. Danny nodded. "Peachy," he said.

"'Scuse me whilst I puke," said Erland, pulling on his headset.

Beth turned the radio on. Roy Orbison was singing *In Dreams*. It was one of her favourite songs. She drummed her hand on the steering wheel. They were going to the sea. Her father was at her side. Her sons were at her back. She felt the same as Erland – she had always wanted to do this too.

By the time the van pulled up outside Ivy Cottage, Beth's happiness had worn off. Elias didn't have a driving license so she had driven all the way herself. She was tired.

She pulled the heavy door open and stepped down, breathing in the usual damp, dismal Pengilly air. Nothing had changed. Why would it?

"Is this the place?" said Danny, hopping down behind her. He put his hand on her shoulder. There might be a gap between them, but he still knew when to fill it.

"Yes, Dan," she said.

Erland jumped down beside her. "That our new pile?" he said, taking off his headset and tossing it through the van window onto the back seat. "Cool. Not quite sure why it's worth so much though."

"It's the land as well, Erland. The stables and paddocks."

"Bagsy the room overlooking the sea with the pool table."

"You're such a moron," said Danny.

"Where's Elias?" said Beth, looking all around. He had disappeared. They went round the back of the van.

"Bloody hippies," said Erland.

Elias was sat cross-legged on the stone wall with his back to them, facing the sea, his head bent upwards, his long hair flapping in the wind.

She crossed the road to join him. To her surprise, there was a tear running down his cheek. It dissolved into his beard. He didn't seem upset. Perhaps it was the wind in his eyes.

She felt instinctively that she shouldn't break his trance, his meditation. She turned away, and as she did so he touched her arm.

"It does not feel good, Beth," he said.

"What doesn't?" she said.

"This place. It is full of bad vibrations. We must not linger…" He trailed off.

"Let's get on with it," she said.

Pammy's stables and paddocks were situated on the outskirts of Pengilly, a fifteen minute walk from Yew Tree Cottage. Beth used to kneel in the back of Pammy's truck on the way to the paddock, holding onto the sides, closing her mouth because of the flies. They had to climb a steep hill out of the village, before going along a bumpy track that made Beth's stomach jiggle. Sometimes she giggled and Pammy stared at her in the rear view mirror. The stare wasn't one of reprimand; perhaps it was of curiosity. Sometimes Beth liked to lie down flat in the truck, watching the canopy of trees moving above her with the sunlight flashing through. She clutched a twig in her hand for a sword and imagined that she was a child with the power to move horizontally at speed – on a mission to rescue a magical horse.

The magical horse was Apples. Apples was old. He had grey hairs around his ears and forehead. His face was hollow-looking, with deep indentations above his eyes that made him look forlorn and wise. In the summer he was healthy, but each winter he lost weight. Pammy began rugging him and feeding him extra grain as soon as the nights began to grow chilly.

Beth knew nothing of horses. The horses were Pammy's and nothing of Pammy's was hers – not even her love or kindness. She noticed how attentive her foster mother was to the animals, how tenderly she spoke to them, how she examined their coats, their hooves, their faces for abnormalities. Any threat to the horses' wellbeing was met with alarm; she spared no expense at the vets. Yet this was the same hand that was cruel to Beth. How was that so? Beth didn't want to believe that it was because she was lesser than the horses. Instead, she believed that she was above them, that she was too good for her surroundings – a superhuman princess with magical powers. They could all go take a hike – Pammy, the horses and the posh prigs who rode them.

Pammy ran a riding school, *Pammy's Ponies*. She was never short of rich second-home owners to overcharge. Her customers – down from London for weekends and holidays – were mostly young girls. Beth would sit on the paddock gate, chewing on a blade of grass, eyeing the girls in their beige breeches with their shiny hair. She wasn't allowed to ride the horses. *Not unless you've got the dosh like they have*, Pammy would say, laughing.

The horses were just like those girls – haughty, shiny, disinterested. They flicked at Beth with their tails as she scattered hay in the field, as though she were another annoying fly. She began to hate the horses, but she loved Apples.

Apples was too old to ride. She often found herself stood next to him, watching the others setting off on a riding lesson through a wobbly heat haze, neither of them allowed to join in. When she was told to clean the horses – to sponge their eyes and noses – she dabbed quickly at the other horses, but spent extra time dousing Apples, checking that his ears were pricked up, that his eyes were pale pink and bright.

As she brushed Apples' mane, she whispered

secrets into his ears – about how she would rescue him, about how they would run away together. He seemed to understand; he stamped his foot. But she knew that he didn't have it in him to escape.

Two weeks before Beth ran away, she noticed that Apples was becoming lethargic. He began to hang his head low, seeking out dark corners of the stable.

On the morning that she found him motionless, grief overwhelmed her. She lay with him in the hay, crying tears onto his dull coat.

With Apples gone, there was nothing left to keep her in Pengilly.

"So did you ever come here, Mum?" said Danny, opening the gate. He stood with his hands on his hips, squinting. The meadow was abundant with ox-eye daisies. The stables to their left were shabby, almost derelict. The tin sign, *Pammy's Ponies* was hanging askew.

"Yes," said Beth. She reached for Danny's arm to hold it and they stood there together, watching the daisies nodding their heads.

"She owned all this?"

"And more. There are two paddocks beyond. I've no idea how she came by it. It must have been her family's or her husband's."

"It is beautiful land," said Elias. He was monstrously tall, with Brett on his shoulders, who was grabbing handfuls of his grandfather's hair and holding it out to the sides to see how long it was. "I am surprised. It has a different vibration here to that within the cottage."

Beth considered this. He was right. The cottage

was where Pammy had hurt her. Out here in the meadow, Pammy had been indifferent towards her. Had Beth picked a moment of happiness in Pengilly, it would have been here – out amongst the daisies and the cabbage white butterflies.

She went over to the stables and pulled the hatch up. It was rusty and stiff. Inside, the smell of stale old horse manure was nauseating. There was still straw on the floor, hale bales around the walls, and five empty stalls. She moved forward and then stopped upon hearing a rustling noise. The place would be filled with mice or rats. She stared up at the dark corners, imagining the ghastly spiders dangling there.

She went back outside. Erland was playing Angel some of his music; she was wearing his chunky headphones and was nodding, grinning. Danny was eyeing them disagreeably, as was Skye.

"It is charming," said Elias. "Utterly charming."

Through the trees at the end of the meadow, the sea lay shimmering. Beth gazed at the view and was turning away when she saw something white standing up at the end of the meadow.

"Wait a moment," she said, over her shoulder.

She started forward through the daisies, her hands out flat either side of her to feel their heads bob against her palms. She had done this as a child, in this same spot.

Faster she moved until she came to the white object.

"Oh!" she said, tears filling her eyes.

It was a white cross, set on a mound of earth, overlooking the sea. There were letters painted on the cross – letters that were worn and chipped, but that still said

Apples. Tied to the cross was a small bouquet of flowers. The flowers had rotten and blackened. Pammy must have put them there, perhaps before she went into prison.

Beth looked about her. There were no other crosses. She wondered what had happened to the other horses. Maybe Apples had been Pammy's favourite too.

Beth untied the velvet ribbon that was holding the dead flowers. The ribbon was rotten too. She reached up to her hair and took out the rubber band, letting her hair fall loose. Then she gathered a handful of daises, secured them with the band and attached it to the cross. She closed her eyes for a moment before turning away.

The reverend had left the key under the stone urn on the front doorstep. The urn was heavy – Elias had to lift it for her. Woodlice ran free. Brett caught one and held it up in delight before tossing it onto the lawn.

The pea-green paint-chipped door still needed a kick to open it. Beth had spent her childhood kicking this door. Pammy said that she did it too hard; it just needed a little tap. But Beth liked to boot it – to take her feelings about her living arrangements out on the stupid door.

"Cool," said Erland, reaching for the brass wolf knocker to rattle it. It was stiff and wouldn't budge.

Beth stopped in the doorway, adjusting her sight to the dim light. She half-expected to see Pammy there in her elasticated trousers, cigarette in mouth, skinny gnarly hands on hips. *Not today, thank you*, was Pammy's greeting to her every day after school – her little joke, in pretence that Beth was a door-to-door salesman. Beth had wished she *was* a door-to-door salesman – that she could give a polite retort, retreat and move on to the next house to try her luck there.

Beth looked at the kitchen, her stomach churning – at the bedraggled carpet, the outmoded decor, the shabbiness.

How could the others have been grateful to live here? They must have been lying. It was a hateful, depressing place. Or perhaps she had ideas of grandeur, of being above it all, of being royal – as Pammy suggested?

Was she ungrateful, spoilt? How could she have been spoilt, coming from a heroin den in a council flat not far from here?

"It's horrible, right?" she said to Elias.

He exhaled heavily. "It is hell," he said, nodding solemnly.

"Helly," said Brett, curling his arm around his mother's leg. "Helly, belly, smelly."

Beth felt suddenly overcome. She perched on the corner of the sofa, her arms around her. "I don't know what to do, where to start."

"Upstairs?" said Danny. "Why don't we start in the loft and work down? Presumably we don't have to do it all today?"

"Do all what?" said Elias.

"The house clearing."

Elias laughed. He had a booming laugh – one that he didn't release very often, presumably in case it rattled rafters or scared bats. "We are not doing an actual house clearing, oh foolish ones!"

"We're not?" said Beth.

"Of course not! Where is your trailer, your skip?"

"I've got some bin liners in the van. I was going to

see what was here first."

"Bin liners, pah!" he said. "Leave all that administrative nonsense to the trustees! We're not interested in sofas and silverware. No. We are doing a *spiritual* house clearing."

Beth rolled her eyes. "I might have known."

"To be honest, I'm relieved," said Danny. "There's a lot of crap in here. Can I go kick a ball around outside?"

Elias needed to meditate again before performing the clearing. It couldn't have been easy with Danny booting a ball about, but he seemed to manage it – not even flinching when the ball flew so close to him that it rustled his hair.

Beth sat underneath the old tree that was struck by lightening, with Brett beside her playing leopards in the grass. Erland had gone for a walk along the sea front. Skye and Angel were sat on the front door step. Angel was admiring Danny playing football. She wouldn't have seen him play before. She looked enrapt.

Danny didn't seem aware of her adulation. When he played football – even on his own in long grass – he became entranced. It was this captivation that told Beth that football mattered to him more than anything else in his life. She watched him kneeing the ball and heading it, a look of intent upon his face. It saddened her – the idea that no one would ever be able to compete for his affections, and yet it pleased her also. Just as literature had saved her, so football was Danny's salvation. It was like wearing a bullet-proof vest, having a passion like that – having something that distracted one's attention away from affairs of the heart.

Angel was offering Danny a drink of water from her bottle, like a groupie. Poor child. There was no hope for her – no bullet-proof vest.

When Elias had cleansed his mind of negativity and weakness – as he put it – he went upstairs to purify his body. Beth wasn't sure that he would find anything pure up there, but moments later the upstairs window creaked open and she heard a shower running.

So Pammy had installed a shower. Perhaps this was what the others had been grateful for. There had been no such luxury during her days here. The bath had been small – she sat with her knees buckled up around her, her hair creepily cold and wet on her back, watching the spider that lived on the hot tap. He was always sat there, preventing her from running the hot, his big legs dangling down, as though he were on commission from Pammy as a cost-saving device. *Bugger off,* she would hiss at it. The old man next door shouted this at her when he caught her collecting apples from his garden. They were only windfalls – rotten ones most of them – but still he called round to complain to Pammy, to officially report her as a little bugger. Pammy had defended her, probably because she didn't know that Beth could hear. You mustn't call a child a bugger, said Pammy. Which made Beth smile. Even eight-year-olds were capable of understanding irony.

She hated that spider. She hated the old man next door. She hated Pammy. She hated the horses. She hated the horse riders. She hated the girls who filed into the church on Sundays. She hated everyone in Pengilly.

Most of her childhood was spent exploring feelings of hate and anger. She had fallen asleep at night dreaming up ways of making Pammy explode – of stirring an exploding syrup into her porridge that would shoot her head off; or dynamite-laced Wellingtons that ignited the moment her feet stepped into them. She imagined strapping Pammy to a rocket and sending her into space. She spent her days with her legs squashed up in the constricted aisles of the village library in the non-fiction area in the E section, reading the only book on explosives. The grumpy librarian would hobble past in her scratchy nylon dress. *You'm never right in the head,* she told Beth, tutting.

"I am ready to begin," said Elias, standing before her, his hair wet, his hands clasped around a leather satchel, his head bowed peacefully. He then turned and disappeared inside the cottage.

Beth followed him. He was emptying the contents of his satchel onto the kitchen table, upon which he had spread a white cloth that was covered in strange symbols. It was a peculiar array of items. Beth raised an eyebrow in wonder.

"I prefer to work alone, dear child," he said. "Once I begin, there will be an array of energies whirling around, most of which I am expecting to be negative. You may feel distressed if you remain indoors. Best wait for me yonder."

Yonder. Beth admired Elias' reluctance to modernise his language. Or perhaps it wasn't reluctance but pure ignorance, so removed was he from the real world.

She turned to go, then turned back. "What exactly are you trying to achieve?" she asked.

He was rolling up his sleeves. "Purification," he said.

He raised his hands, his palms facing each other and pressed them closer together and apart again, as though squashing an invisible beach ball.

"Currently all of your experiences are trapped here." He glanced at her. "We will negate them, release them. And so you will begin to heal."

He looked back at his hands, moving them closer together, closing his eyes. "Dear Universe," he said, "grant me the strength to purify this place, to make it sacred once more."

Beth didn't know whether to laugh or be impressed. She went back to the garden. Moments later, Elias followed them out and began to stroke the front door as though it were a beautiful woman.

"Come on," she said to Brett. "Let's go find Erland."

When they returned, Elias was bent over washing his hands in the sea. The tide was out, leaving an array of black seaweed on the pebble beach.

They sat on the wall, watching the old man. He washed his hands for a good five minutes, going up and down his arms repeatedly. When he turned to come back up the beach, he was surprised to see them.

He joined them on the wall. "There was a lot of psychic debris clinging to me," he said.

"Oh," said Beth. "Have you finished?"

"Almost," he said. "Just the bells and then we are done."

"Was there much, you know…bad stuff there?"

He turned his eyes upon her dramatically. "Oh, yes," he said, patting her knee. "Indeed there was. It is a wonder that you ever managed to sleep at night."

"I didn't," she replied.

They waited in the garden whilst Elias rang bells, seemingly in every corner of the cottage. Then there was some loud chanting, followed by the banging of a gong and then he appeared in the garden, looking jubilant.

"The purification process is complete!" he announced, holding out his arms.

Beth and the boys entered the cottage tentatively. Skye and Angel had gone to the shop for lunch supplies.

In the kitchen, Beth gripped Brett's hand protectively. She had never imagined any of her children stepping onto this threshold.

On the table, there was an oak leaf and rose petals floating in a saucer of water, with a candle alight in the centre. The air smelt faintly of roses. The light was bright, cool, fresh feeling.

She immediately let go of Brett's hand. "What have you done to the place?" she said to her father.

He smiled, bending into his habitual bow.

"What you on about, Mum?" said Erland, prodding her.

"He's cleansed the space," said Danny, looking around him in awe. "You can feel it, can't you, Mum?"

"Yes, I can," she admitted. "I don't know what to say."

"You say that you believe in magic now," replied Danny.

"Oh, drop it!" she said, folding her arms.

"Come," said Elias. "Let us not squabble. There is something you should see."

They followed him up the narrow staircase to the landing outside Beth's old bedroom. She poked her head into the room, expecting to be saturated with dread and repulsion, but felt no such sensations.

She felt slightly cheated. Had Elias somehow whitewashed the past? Obliterated history?

She checked her thoughts reprimandingly.

Even if he had, it could only be a good thing.

"So what did you want to show me?" she said.

"Well…" he said. "It was quite extraordinary…Once I had cleansed the space below, I became aware of something beyond my reach – an energy that I had not touched yet. So I followed it and it led me here." He pointed to a hatch in the roof outside Beth's room.

She gazed upwards, open-mouthed, wondering how she had never noticed that square in the roof before – that neat square that had betrayed the presence of a secret room just there, all along.

*Elias' notes on performing a house clearing,
as written down for Danny*

*You will need:
A ceremonial table cloth
A saucer used purely for this occasion only
Rose scented tealights – as pure as possible
Fresh oak leaves
Sea water
A bell
A gong*

1) Begin with a long meditation. Then stroke the front door and move around the house from the bottom upwards, stroking the surfaces gently, picking up the messages that you receive. Do not react – merely absorb.

2) Use the oak leaves, sea water and tealights to make an offering. Keep this in the room as you work.

3) Go around the space a second time, clapping the corners of each room from floor to ceiling. Important: now wash your hands!

4) Starting at the front door, ring a bell and then ring it in each room, near to the wall. Holding it nearest your heart is the most effective method.

5) I always finish by banging a gong and uttering a personal mantra and thank you. Thank you is perhaps the most important utterance of all.

There is more to house clearing than the above. However, you can use this is a guide and adapt it to your personal requirements.

TWELVE

He was sat at a table opposite from her, with a single red rose as the centrepiece. She was wearing a dress – no, a plain T-shirt and jeans. Yet there was nothing plain about her. She was the most beautiful woman that he knew. And working in media, he knew a few – Swedish journalists, Slovakian models sliding in for photo shoots. They had nothing on her. Because, even with age upon her face and grey at her temples, she had a soulfulness that they didn't, couldn't possess – a fiery anger in her eyes that set her face apart from the others.

"Beth," he said, holding his hand to her.

He focussed. There was no black hair. No dark soulfulness. But there was anger in the eyes all right.

"Hello, Peeder," said his wife. It had always annoyed him the way she pronounced his name as *Peeder* with her Irish accent. He closed his eyes and rolled his head away from her. She bent forward, plumping his pillow from under him. "How you feeling?"

The girls were behind her. They stepped forward, shyly, sitting either side of him on the bed.

"Who's Beth, Daddy?" asked Sasha.

"Yes," said Clare. "Who *is* Beth?"

"Don't start," said Peter, keeping his eyes closed. Surely he could have her removed? The doctors were trying to slow his heart rate down. Having her here wasn't going to help.

"Can I do anything for you?" she asked. She was trying to sound helpful, but Peter knew her well enough to know when she was suppressing anger. Inside, she was screaming – loudly.

"You can leave," he said.

He had his eyes still closed, but he felt the twins pull away. They would be surprised at their daddy's rudeness. He had been feeling them pull away for a long time now, ever so subtly gravitating towards their mother. Whether it was of their own free will or due to some magnetic field of her design, he couldn't tell. But it was there all right.

He had managed in the space of fourteen years to lose four children. Maybe he could have another family and start over, this time working out a better strategy. Because he was certain that women had strategies, that they kept a list of rules in their hands, like bad referees who were unwilling to share the rules with the players so that they could chastise and penalise at will, without giving any reason why.

Aside from Beth. She wasn't like that, didn't have a rule book. She was too abstract. It was one of the things he had most loved about her – her reluctance to follow any kind of procedure. If he'd had a chance with anyone, it was rule-less Beth. Yet he had let her down. And now there would be no rose centrepiece, no romantic meeting.

At least he had the photograph.

As soon as Clare and the girls huffed out of the room, he pulled his wallet from the bedside cabinet and released the photograph from its hideout in the broken lining. He was pressing the image to his lips when the doctor arrived with the worst possible news.

He could go home.

Dinner was a sombre affair. He was fully recovered, there were no ill effects from his funny turn – one of those freakish things, the doctor said – quite common in city executives at his time of life, but he had a bad head and a heavy heart. Clare had made his favourite chicken and dumplings, yet it seemed stodgy and chewy in his mouth – making the meal longer and more hard work than he would have liked. It was hot in the house, the twins looked sticky, their faces flushed, their forks limp in their hands. Clare was the only perky one, sat upright upon her seat, a forced smile on her lips.

He had done some thinking upon arriving home. He stood in the shower for a long while, letting the water cascade upon his head. By the time he dried himself off, he had decided to face the fact that his marriage was loveless. This is itself wasn't the crux of the matter, however. The crux was how much he was prepared to put up with for the sake of the children. How little love in one's life was bearable, acceptable? It was a question asked so universally that he felt crass and clichéd for giving it any head space.

The lack of love had revealed itself to him through his lack of guilt. Six months ago, no two months ago, he felt guilty thinking about Beth. Now, she was his only relief. He thought of her constantly, between editing Travel News and monitoring Chelsea's performance, and he felt completely comfortable about doing so. She had become a fantasy film-star, a pretty actress in a soap-opera whom it was safe to fancy because he wasn't likely to meet her in real life.

"So," Clare said, laying down her fork and pouring herself more wine. "How did they account for the pill?"

"Pardon?" said Peter. He was chewing a mouthful of chicken that wouldn't be defeated. His jaw was beginning to ache.

"The pill," she said. She took a neat sip of wine. "How did they account for it? Was it the curry perhaps?"

He put down his knife and fork with a clatter, and stared at her.

"What pill, Clare?" he said.

For the first time in their marriage, Peter saw his wife panic. She looked about her wildly, as though searching for her misplaced rule book.

Elias sat with his back against the yew tree, watching the boys play football, with Ruby flopped out on his lap. He felt the rise and fall of her chest against his legs, and placed his hand on her head lovingly. It wasn't long before he began to feel drowsy himself. The house clearing and the journey here had fatigued him.

He closed his eyes, feeling the comforting

sensation of bark against his body. Of all the trees, the yew was his favourite – the only one to keep its Ancient British name. It was powerful, evergreen, eternal. Even this one, that had been lightening struck, had overcome adversity and was showing signs of recovery.

He thought of the yew in the churchyard in the Sussex village where he had grown up. It would still be there now. They used to pick the berries – snottygogs they called them locally – and pelt them at each other on their way into church. His father was a Christian and a disciplined church-goer. Elias followed sheepishly in his wake, and sat chewing his lip during sermons, deeply unsure. If only he had his father's courage, his unwavering self-belief and faith. His father wouldn't have walked out on a mother and child; he would have stayed and dealt with the problems in store. Had he remained with Vivi that night, he could have cared for Beth – perhaps even kept Vivi alive. What would they be doing now? An odd trio they would have made. But a trio none the less; not a dead person, an abused person and a nomad.

He opened his eyes and gazed at the roof of the cottage, wondering what Beth had found in the attic. She had been a long time. He closed his eyes again, regret overwhelming him. Was there any more uncomfortable sensation known to an old man than regret?

The night he left Vivi at the druid camp, he hitched a lift to the other end of the country to Cumbria. It wasn't hard to find Vivi's farm. He was familiar with the stone circle at Castlerigg. Vivi's parents owned a sprawling amount of farm land nearby.

He had to walk a long way from Castlerigg, but

eventually he came to the well-maintained farm buildings and knocked upon the front door of the house. No one came. He rested on the front step, prising his shoes off. He was unshaven, unkempt, his hair pulled back in a bandana.

The next thing he knew, a man was running across the yard, pointing a gun at him. "Who the hell are you?" shouted the man. A woman came running from the cow shed, wiping her hair from her eyes.

They were gracious enough to offer Elias a meal. He ate sausages and mash as though he had never eaten before. Vivi's parents eyed him suspiciously, seated at the table with him but not eating. They cradled mugs of coffee.

"She has just had a baby," said Elias. "You are grandparents." He expected the mother to blink away tears or turn away, but she continued to stare at him without expression.

"Are they well?" she said.

"Alive and well in Pentruthen Bay, Cornwall," he answered. "At the druid camp. I can give you the details if you would like to visit."

"And why would we do that?" said the father.

Elias shrugged. "To meet your granddaughter? To see your daughter? You could bring them back here, give them a better–"

"A better what?" said the mother. "A better life?"

She rose and went to the sink to wash her cup. From behind, she looked like Vivi – had her girlish form and auburn hair – but the similarity ended there. The mother had nothing of Vivi's appeal. She was thin-lipped, guarded.

Elias turned to the father to assess him. There was more of Vivi about him. He was short with thick hair combed flat – neatly turned out for a farmer. His eyes were bright, his lips more generous, but his expression mirrored his wife's. Elias saw in the man's eyes the light of hope and knew that had he been able to corner him on his own, he might have had a chance of appealing to him. But not with the woman in the room – not with her fixing her eyes upon her husband, as though charming him into submission with some unknown power.

Elias did not understand it, but he was in no position to judge. They were all going to let a young woman down – a young woman who was family. And furthermore they were going to let down a baby, within whom lay their own blood.

There was no point him staying any longer. He could see that there was going to be no compromise.

Just as the front door was closing upon him, the mother spoke. The door wasn't fully open – he could only see part of her face.

"She never wanted us," she said. "Our only child. She never wanted to be here with us, took no interest in our farm."

"She was just a child," said Elias. "Still is. I don't expect many young girls are interested in farming. You can't hold that against–"

"You don't understand," she said, opening the door further. "She rejected us. She looked at me and my husband like we were repulsive to her."

Elias knew that look. He had witnessed it many times, directed at himself. "She's in trouble," he said. "She needs you."

"And you think she's going to take our help do you? After all these years?" She folded her arms. "She doesn't want our help. She never did."

"Perhaps you should try."

"I see," she said, insidiously. "And if you're so keen on helping her, how come you're all the way up here asking us to do it?"

Elias looked down at his broken old boots. He could see the red of his sock poking through. "She doesn't want my help," he said.

"Ha!" she said, pointing. "Gotcha! So you're just as bad! Vivien curled her lip at you, told you she hates you, that you can go to hell, that you can drop dead, did she? Because, sonny, that's what she told me. Last words I ever heard my daughter utter!"

The woman was flushed red, riled. Elias backed away.

"I'm sorry I came," he said.

"Damn right!" she said.

"But you'll regret not helping her," he said. "And so will I."

"Be that as it may," she said, and slammed the door.

Elias left, with so heavy a heart he wondered that he was able to transport it.

As he walked through the fields back to Castlerigg, he had no idea what he was going to do next, where he was going or how he was going to afford to get there.

He looked back at the farm buildings, now a tiny pencil dot on the horizon. Vivi hadn't stood a chance with those people. It was a sick trick of nature planting her there to act out her childhood.

Like most family histories, the vine would ramble and twist but would remain true to its source, connected to its roots.

And so Vivi's daughter would be born hundreds of miles from home in an entirely different spectrum, but true to source – she wouldn't stand a chance either.

Beth pulled the cord to turn on the bare light bulb. The attic room smelt of wood – of raw splintered boards that were lining the rafters as stepping stones. It was unbearably hot and unventilated in the attic. A fat wasp was buzzing along the ceiling. It looked like the queen wasp, but Beth wasn't worried about it. She had larger perils in mind.

Before her, upon the boards, were five green shoe boxes, each one bearing a different label: *Aaron Deakin, Teresa Close, April Morgan, Rowan Grimshaw* and *Beth Trelawney*.

She wasn't surprised by the shoebox filing system. She knew that Pammy was systematic, having watched her meticulous upkeep of the horses, and no one filed a tax return like Pammy could. But she was surprised by the apparent sentiment of it all. It was so unlike Pammy. And yet perhaps it was utterly like her – reducing five children's lives to the size of a pair of trainers each.

As she couldn't face her own shoe-sized history yet, she opened Aaron's. Inside was the fostering paperwork, a photograph presumably of his mother, seven handkerchiefs hand-embroidered with his initials, and a toy tractor with a missing wheel.

It was, Beth guessed, all that Aaron had arrived with. Someone had loved him enough to hand-embroider his handkerchiefs for him – to send him on his way with enough to see him through every day of the week.

Beth closed the lid hurriedly, feeling suddenly as though she were trespassing upon hallowed ground. She looked dubiously at the other sealed boxes. Had their recent meeting been happier, she might have arranged to have the boxes sent to each of them. As it was, she would leave it to the trustees to decide. They might not even go up here. The boxes could remain untouched for eternity, gradually crumbling. If they hadn't mattered until now, they wouldn't matter in the future.

But her own shoe box? She sat with it on her lap, breathing slowly. The wasp was still buzzing over head. She wiped the perspiration from her top lip and untucked her T-shirt from her waist, flapping it loose. She could hear the boys shouting in the garden, the dull thud of the football being booted about.

"Here goes nothing," she said.

Inside was the same fostering paperwork as Aaron's; a violet dress with a black swan motif on the chest that seemed familiar; a comb decorated with sea shells; and a letter addressed to *Miss Bethia Trelawney*.

"Oh, God help me," she said, going to tear the letter open. To her surprise, it was already unsealed.

The letter was from her mother. She looked upwards momentarily.

"Okay...I can do this."

Dearest Bethia,

You are about to leave. I want this letter to go with you. It's not strictly allowed, but I have a way of getting what I want. Except that I'm not getting what I want now. I have begged them not to take you, but they are going ahead. Even I can see that it might do you good to have a break from me.

I don't know when you'll read this. Perhaps later today. It won't mean much, but save it for another day when it may make more sense.

I haven't been good to you. I'm not sure that I even tried to be. I'd like to try now – or soon. If I have hurt you, I didn't mean to. Half the time I don't know what's going on. I'm ashamed and in moments of clarity I know the full horrors of what has taken place, but then it drifts again and I know nothing.

Sorry isn't enough but it is all I can offer at the moment. That and my vow that I will come for you and we will be together again.

When you were born, I called you Bethia because it is Hebrew for daughter of God. In Gaelic, your name means life. So I know you have both God and life in you, and that you are going to be fine because of that.

I left home when I was young – like you, but for different reasons. I took just one thing from my home with me, which I enclose for you now. My mother bought it for me at a fair. It's a worthless ring, but it linked the past to my present and served me well. I would like you to have it – to link your past too – to link you to me. I hope it doesn't rust. I hope when you look at it, you think good things about me.

I promise you Bethia, I will come for you.
Mummy

Beth sat down on the floorboards, looking at the

ring on her finger, guilt twisting inside her. She wasn't able to look at the ring and think good things about her mother. She didn't think anything of her mother – good or bad. Time had protected her by erasing memories. Her early years in Pentruthen were mostly blank, her mother a foggy freckly blur.

You couldn't be angry with a freckly blur. But you could be angry with the person who had stepped in as a replacement, in full three-dimensional glory: Pammy. That Pammy was replacing an equally abusive mother was beside the point, although Vivien had been far less conscious of her actions. Beth had chosen the baddy in her story and it was too late now to recast.

She wondered if she had read the letter as a child, if she had understood the content, if she had taken her mother's promise literally and had waited for her to come – her nose pressed against the glass on rainy days, watching for the flash of her mother's red Mac approaching along the seafront of Pengilly. She could remember the red Mac and her mother's auburn hair – the way the two colours clashed and merged on wet days – but that was all. She remembered nothing else of her days in Pentruthen with her mother. All other memories were of being alone – alone at school, alone on the way home, alone in bed. The only time she was cared for was when she was in hospital having her injuries tended to.

She had never felt sorry for herself. As an orphan, you either self-pitied or lashed out. It was healthier to do the latter because it directed the problem away from herself. Without that anger, she wouldn't have risen through the ranks to university lecturer. As her mother said, it was important to travel with one thing. Years ago, Beth all but tissue-wrapped her fury, and had kept it deep inside her – a secret memento of her own.

She put the lid on the shoebox. She would take it with her. Everything else in the cottage could stay, could rot for all she cared.

She was reaching out for the light cord when the wasp dropped down and flew at her. She ducked. The wasp flew over her head and out through the attic hatch door. She wanted to get out now, to get some fresh air.

She was standing up again when she spotted something green underneath one of the boards. Crawling forwards, she reached underneath the board, trying not to touch the fluffy asbestos. She hooked the object with her nail, dragging it towards her. It moved a short way before becoming wedged. Damn it. She tried to manoeuvre the floorboard. It was too heavy.

"Everything all right, Mum?" Danny's head appeared at the top of the ladder. "We were just wondering about lunch."

"Perfect timing. Help me with this."

Together they moved the board. Underneath, squashed and bashed, was another green shoe box.

"I don't believe it," said Beth, picking it up and blowing the dust off it.

"What is it?" said Danny.

There was a label on the lid, just like the others.

Fleur Wishart, it said.

"So there were six of us," said Beth. "I knew it!"

"Six what?" said Danny. "Tell me! You're scaring me."

She was looking about her anxiously. The room suddenly struck her as being eerily in order. She had never seen an attic so unlikely to invite explorers or to entice anyone to probe about. No cobwebbed chests or intriguing curios.

All swept clean – mopped up.

"My God, Pammy," she said. "What did you do to her?"

THIRTEEN

In her first year at Cambridge, Clare was voted the person most likely to get out of any situation by blagging. It seemed a ridiculous accolade at the time – insulting even – but there were times over the years when her skill had been useful. And never more so than now.

She looked about her, momentarily disarmed.

"The painkiller," she replied. "The pill that the nurse said you took. You know – when you got to the hospital? I wasn't sure what she was getting at, to be honest. I thought perhaps you knew."

She picked up her cutlery and began to slice her chicken.

Peter was still staring at her. "What are you talking about?"

"Oh, forget it," she said, flapping her hand. "It's not important. Just something the nurse was saying. But it obviously doesn't matter. Just enjoy your meal."

To her relief, he picked up his fork and began

prodding at the dumpling again. Like most men, if you bombarded them with words you would soon disinterest them. He went back to his meal, chewing slowly, probably doing a countdown in his head until the next Chelsea game. Only eight weeks until the next season, or something like that. He would know the weeks, days, hours, minutes until kick off.

She thought she had got away with it, but that night he rose from their bed without a word and took his pillow to the spare room. She knew better than to pursue him.

Was this it? The start of marital downfall?

The next night, it wasn't just his pillow that was gone but his watch, his handkerchief and his alarm clock.

During the course of the week, she noticed objects vanishing until their bedroom was left feeling distinctly female. He had even taken the photograph down from the wall of his old school football team – where he was sat on his team mates' shoulders holding a trophy. She didn't care about the photograph – had always objected to it being the first thing that she looked at in the morning – but still…

The girls were beginning to tiptoe around the house in their Hello Kitty pyjamas, cowering around their father in case he shouted at them. Which wasn't fair because he didn't have a history of shouting, but there was something in him that had shifted and which made them mistrust him now. He appeared much bigger than them, all of a sudden, and far stronger.

"Peter," she said, one night over supper. "We need to talk."

"No," he said, bluntly, scraping his leftovers into the recycling caddy. "That's the one thing we don't need to do."

"I see," she said. "So what do you suggest instead? Silence?"

He shrugged moodily. "Why not?"

"Oh, for Christ's sake!" she snapped. "Grow up!"

"Me grow up? That's rich! It's not me running around playing games, manipulating everyone like a spoilt five-year-old!"

"And what's that supposed to mean?" she said.

"Leave it," he said, holding his hand up. "I don't want to fight. Just be–"

"Silent?" she said, bitterly. "Yes, I know what you want. You want me to shut the hell up and bare this misery. Well, I won't! I'll go back to Ireland. That's what I'll do. And I'll take the twins with me! Then see how you like silence! You miserable cheating–"

"Cheating?" he said, drawing near, his interest sparked at last. "How so?"

"Don't think I didn't hear you saying her name."

"Whose name?"

"Oh, don't play games with me, Peter! You know exactly who I mean. Have you been meeting up with her, sneaking around behind my back?"

"Oh, don't be so stupid. You always were paranoid."

He pulled a beer from the fridge, twisted the cap off and took a long drink.

"You know what?" he said, pointing the bottle at her. "I thought I could try again – try to patch things up, but it's impossible, Clare. *You're* impossible."

"Then get lost!" She shouted at him. "Just get out

of –." She broke off.

Sasha and Sarah were stood in the doorway holding hands.

"We don't want to live here any more, Mummy," Sarah blurted out.

Clare cried herself to sleep. It wasn't even Friday yet. It was only Thursday. She had peaked too soon.

When Friday came, she didn't have any tears left. She didn't have anything to do. She felt panic prickling her skin. Perhaps she could go and see Tommy. No. He was a useless eejit.

And then she heard a noise. Someone was banging next door – a nail going into the wall perhaps.

She ran upstairs and changed her top from a rugby T-shirt to a tight top that lay flat on her body like a leotard. She pulled on her most flattering jeans, brushed her hair and glossed her lips. A spritz of perfume, and she was back downstairs. She didn't want to think about what she was doing. She didn't glance at the photograph of her happy girls on the mantelpiece on the way out, or her husband's jacket on the coat peg. She just let her feet carry her forwards.

"Hello," she said, as soon as he answered the door. He was holding a hammer in his hand and a nail in his mouth. "Got a day off?"

He plucked the nail from his mouth. "I work from home Fridays." He was wearing a Sex Pistols T-shirt.

"So do I," she said. She plunged her hands into her jean pockets and leaned against the door frame. "I'm in the middle of writing a report. I'm desperate for a mental break, or just someone to talk to really, that's not involved with a tribunal for a middle-aged man making an ageist claim. I think my head's about to explode."

"Well, tribunals aren't really my thing," he said. "But I can make you a cuppa, if that helps. So long as you promise not to explode in my house. I just had the carpets cleaned." So he had a sense of humour.

He led her through to the kitchen. There were Miles Davis prints on the walls. A few obscure surrealist paintings. He was a minimalist, or just male. It was pretty sparse.

"You're in H.R?" he said.

"Someone's got to be," she said. "I don't know why me though. I used to have an imagination. Now I'm all dried up and hopeless."

"Cappuccino? Latte?" He had a fancy Italian coffee maker. She moved forward to admire it. It was black, shiny – she could see her reflection in it. She looked away.

"To be honest, just tea would be nice."

He smiled. Was he laughing at her housewifeyness?

"So how's your husband? Is he okay now?"

"No. He's not okay. Nothing's okay…"

She crossed to the window and looked out. It was the same view as from her back window. She gazed down at her garden. She often sunbathed down there when the children were at school, when the sun made an appearance. She hadn't realised he could see her from here. Had he seen her? Did he even care about it? Who did she think she was? She was a weather-beaten dried-up mother, who couldn't even attract her husband's interest any more.

"I've got tea at home," she said. "Do you know what I really came here for?"

He paused before replying, his hand hovering over the sink as he steeped the tea bag. "Uh…"

She moved behind him. "I just want you to kiss me," she said, startled by her own boldness. It was a Friday. Anything was possible on a Friday nowadays.

There was a creak at the door. In walked the tall brunette. "Everything okay?" she said, flicking her hair.

"Oh sweet mother of Jesus!" said Clare, rushing from the room, down the hallway and out the front door.

She got home and stood with her back to the door, her chest heaving.

What had she been thinking? Was she going insane?

She paced up and down. The panic that had barely touched her earlier was now full-blown. The photographs, personal belongings that she hadn't glanced at before were now looming before her. She was a mother, a wife, a responsible HR director. What in God's name?

She ran back upstairs into the spare room. She would move everything back into the main room. She would make him love her again – would make him see that she was worth far more than Beth, that she was loveable, that there was nothing wrong with her. He would soon see!

But she stopped in the spare room and gasped.

It was empty. She tore through to the bedroom and opened his wardrobe. Empty.

She sat down on the bed. He had gone.

The reverend hadn't heard of Fleur Wishart. He maintained that there were only five foster children – that Pammy had told him so and why would she lie?

"Why indeed?" Beth said.

She was sat at the desk in her study, Fleur Wishart's shoe box on her lap. On the desk in front of her was a large manila envelope containing her paper on the metaphysical poets for Florence University; a courier was due shortly to collect it. Beth had worked through the nights for the past week to complete the paper.

"Were there foster documents in this so-called shoe box?" the reverend said.

Beth rolled her eyes at the phone. Did he think she was making the whole thing up? Why did she always feel as though she had to prove everything to him?

"No, but she's *got* a shoe box, which means she was in Pammy's care at some point."

No reply.

"Pammy probably destroyed the adoption papers," she said. "But there must be records somewhere. Maybe you could ask that friend of yours, the one that helped you before?"

"I've already cashed in that favour. I can't presume to do so again…Besides, I thought you didn't want anything else from me. You were quite clear on the subject at our last meeting."

He had a point. "I'm sorry," she said. "I just don't know who else to discuss this with. And you said at West Marsh that you would help me…Never encourage a stray,

Reverend."

He sighed. "So what exactly are you looking for?"

"The truth." She opened the lid of the shoe box and tipped out the contents again. "What if Pammy concealed Fleur's existence to cover something up – something evil that she did?"

"Evil?" He laughed dryly. "If you look for evil, you'll only encounter grief. Mark my words. This is going to backfire on you. You'll be the one to get burnt."

"But who is there to burn me, Reverend?" she said. "The only person who ever burnt me is now dead."

After the phone conversation, she looked back through Fleur's shoe box. It was fuller than Aaron's and Beth's. It contained a small book called Baby's First Prayers, copyright 1992; a Teletubby toy; a purse containing hair bobbles; a cassette tape of lullabies, and two tiny knitted cardigans in lemon and chalk pink. Fleur was younger than the rest of them – twenty years younger than Beth, she estimated, and was only a baby when she first arrived at the cottage.

As Beth held the lemon cardigan to her cheek, smelling its musty sweetness, she saw the study curtains ripple. The little girl was moving towards her.

"I think this was yours," Beth said, holding out the cardigan to her. "Are you Fleur? What did she do to you?"

The doorbell rang, sending Beth an inch off her chair in fright. It was the courier, come to collect her paper.

Beth was enjoying spending time with Elias. With Danny back at school, they had fallen into the routine of walking Brett to preschool in the morning with Ruby, then sitting in the garden under the palm tree, talking, before going to collect Brett again. Skye and Angel made themselves scarce, sensing that this familial time was sacred. There were many years to account for. Beth told Elias about her life, and he in turn told her of his – of his beliefs, his knowledge, his journey.

Whilst sitting underneath the tree in the hazy morning sunshine, Beth began to sense that her time with her father was restricted – began to think of the limited life of the butterfly again, of how fragile and mortal everything was. And as much as she tried to philosophise about how all good things came to pass…she began to feel an uneasy tugging deep inside her – a warning sensation – the tugging of a rope to sound the bell of melancholy. She knew that her father was about to cut the rope, that he would not fix himself to one point for too long.

So she was not surprised when he turned to her one morning over their customary tray of ginger tea – one of Elias' homespun blends which was unexpectedly palatable – and said, "I am leaving tomorrow for the summer solstice."

"Oh, right," she said, lightly – rather too breezily to be taken seriously.

He hadn't bought it. "You knew I would be departing soon, I trust?"

"Yes, of course," she said, aiming this time for less breeze. "Are you heading for somewhere in particular?"

"The stone circle at Stanton Drew."

"Stanton Drew…Isn't that–?"

"Not far from here, yes."

"Then I will drive you."

"No. I could not," he said, gravely. "I would not take that liberty."

"It's not a liberty. It's a lift. Please," she said. "It's the least I can do."

A canal boat was chugging past, a radio playing onboard. Children in stripy sweaters were stood on deck, talking to each other in German. "Guten tag!" they called to Beth, waving enthusiastically. It was a nice way to travel, Beth thought – to see England from the water. Her father, who had first appeared to her almost as a vagabond, a tramp, was leaving her as a king – a man who had solved the mysteries of life. She could see now what it was that he was striving for – no, had already achieved – and part of her wanted to travel with him.

Love liberates.

She had once seen those words inscribed above the entrance to an art gallery. They had struck her as wonderfully simple words: love liberates.

Love did not bind, constrict, stifle. She had to let Elias go.

She spent the rest of the afternoon steeling herself for the sadness that was as inevitable the next morning as the sun rise. And then something odd happened to delay its arrival: Danny came home from school, heard about the solstice at Stanton Drew and begged Elias to take him along.

"Yes," Elias replied, instantly.

Beth, who was frying eggs, turned in surprise, oil dripping from her spatula. "Now wait a minute…"

"What?" Elias and Danny said in unison.

Beth turned back to the eggs, poking them hesitantly. Was Danny old enough? What would go on exactly? He could end up stripped naked, chanting, stoned, surrounded by hippies in white gowns offering sacrifices, copulating under the moon...

Elias was hypnotically persuasive – the master of signing contracts with his eyes.

"I assure you that Danny will be utterly safe in my care. This is a vital step for him – an initiatory step towards adulthood. To refuse him this, would be to hold him back from an enriching experience."

So that was that.

Beth was dropping them all off in the morning: Danny, Elias, Skye and Angel. The solstice fell over the weekend. Danny wouldn't even miss school.

But as she fried the eggs, watching the whites bubble and spit, she wondered how the experience might change Danny – whether he might enjoy it so much that he would run away from home. They were all runners. It was in their nature to do so. Her mother had run away from Cumbria; her father had run away from Pentruthen Bay; she had run away from Pengilly. What was to stop Danny from doing so? And yet she couldn't keep him locked up in the attic like a trapped bird.

Love liberates. What it didn't mention above the gallery door, was that it also hurt like hell.

"Why don't you want him to go?" Elias asked her later that evening. "What is it that you are afraid of?"

They were sat on the bistro chairs on the patio, sharing a bottle of wine. There were bats in the air, swooping low across the canal, racing through the garden before disappearing beyond. It was a blowy evening. The tree tops lining the opposite bank of the canal were swaying, shaking angry black fists.

Beth looked at her father speculatively, knowing that if there was ever a time to confide in him it was now, yet lacking the courage to divulge the secret that she had hidden so vigilantly.

"I'm worried that he may be susceptible to things, like me."

He nodded. "Things?"

"Yes." She took a long drink of wine and secured a couple olives on a cocktail stick before continuing. "I sometimes see things."

"Go on…"

"A vision." She nibbled an olive.

"I thought as much," he said.

Only Elias could be so unfussy about the subject matter. He was looking beyond her to the canal. He was attracted to water – looked for it over his shoulder, tailed off mid-conversation to check for it, like a mother monitoring her toddler's play at the park. He was never really focussed when water was before him, like having a conversation with a man when the football was on.

"And you understand your vision?" he asked. "You have interpreted it?"

"I think so," she said.

"Then you must follow it to wherever it leads you."

"I'm trying to," she replied. "But the reverend has warned me against doing so. He has predicted sorrow for me," she said. "I don't want sorrow."

"Quite," he replied.

He was watching a bat swooping across the garden. "Do you know, there are seventeen different types of bats in this country?" he said, picking up his wine glass and setting it upon his knee. He was wearing a hessian jumper and his usual white trousers. He seemed older than when he had first joined them, as though the effort of becoming acquainted with them had aged him.

"They dominate our mammal population," he said. "Yet we barely glimpse them." He rubbed his eyes. He didn't wear glasses. He told himself that his eyes could see clearly and evidently they could.

"And so it is with spirits, visions, visitations from other realms. They are always within our reach – all around us like a multitude of nocturnal bats – and yet we barely notice them. You, my child, have merely noticed one."

Beth watched the bats. She would never have thought of it that way – would never have equated her vision with something natural, instinctive. The reverend had made her feel almost ashamed, ungodly in her pursuits.

She couldn't remember having needed someone before in her life, but she looked at her father now longingly, wishing that they could stay together – that he would forever turn her demons into innocent sprites.

"After I return with Danny," her father said, with a sense of timing that was terribly off and yet spot on at the same time, "I must depart."

She nodded. "I know," she said.

Beth placed the covers gently over Brett's shoulders. She crossed to the window to close it, since the wind was chilly, flapping the curtains impatiently like a child tugging his mother's dress.

There was a light in the window of her father's canal boat. She hadn't even been onboard, hadn't inspected his life there. He hadn't offered and she hadn't asked. Perhaps he thought she would judge his humble circumstances, alongside Lilyvale's grandeur. Or perhaps he wanted to keep her separate.

It was strange how easily they had slipped into the child and parent role. He was the teacher; she was the pupil, absorbing his wisdom. And like a pupil she felt unable to make demands – couldn't ask him whether they might meet again. How could she? She had no real claim on him, not after almost forty years of separation.

She gazed at the light on the boat, trying to imagine how her father had felt when Vivien drove him away – how difficult it must have been trying to hang on to her, whilst she was pulling away in the opposite direction. Vivien had shunned his offers of help, in order to raise their child alone. Loneliness was a preferable alternative to his company. How would that have felt to Elias – poor wounded Elias?

It occurred to her, and not for the first time of late, that she had followed in her mother's footsteps without having even realised that there were faints tracks on the path before her. She hadn't known the past, her mother's history, and yet she had still done exactly the same thing. She had also driven her children's father away. They had both shunned support in favour of loneliness. She couldn't say for sure that her mother was lonely, but premature death seemed a lonely ending – a friendless, uncelebrated way to depart the earth.

Beth hadn't examined the choices she had made in life. There were no parents, siblings, grandparents, aunts and uncles to discuss her decisions with – no one to steer her or chew the fat with. She became used to making decisions intuitively, without upheaval or fuss. She had approved her decisions, like a parent blindly supporting a child's every move, regardless of the merit of each step.

Leaving Peter had made sense to her. She hadn't been ready to announce to the universe that she was happy, that she had managed to pull it all together and marry a good man, despite her childhood. She wanted the struggle. She wanted to prove the damage that had been done to her – to wear it like a uniform that said she was an orphan who had overcome adversity. Her anger was raging, and being a single parent had been the best way to demonstrate that. Not that she had considered this so bluntly, so brutally at the time. She had simply followed the flow of the anger, following it right away from Peter.

So here she was, a single parent, demonstrating her rage. Except that the anger had ebbed with each passing year. She had become less tolerant of her old self – less supportive of those decisions, like looking back at a school satchel adorned with *meat is murder* and CND badges from one's comfortable middle-aged armchair and cringing.

The light went out on the barge.

"Good night, Elias," she said, taking this as her cue to end the day also.

She sat down on her bed and reached under the pillow for the photograph of Peter. She had left it in her jeans' pocket after the argument with Danny, and it had gone through the wash. She could only just make out the details of his face now – his brown eyes gazing at the camera earnestly. Soon he would be all faded and gone. The butterfly would die, having lived its one glorious day on earth.

"I shouldn't have left," she said, sitting down on the bed, pressing the photograph to her heart. "What I must have put you through...Forgive me."

She got into bed, her heart laden with sadness.

She wished heartily for Danny to return after the solstice – for him to come back to her – not just in body but in being. She wished for her father to moor at the bottom of the garden always, to teach her all he knew about bats and clouds – for him to not be lonely, running away from sorrow.

And she wished, as she tucked the photograph away underneath the pillow again, that she hadn't left Peter – that there was some magical way of making that good again.

The fifth child

Bethia Trelawney was born on a druid camp. Moments before she arrived the Chief Druid circled the sacred fire sprinkling oil onto the flames, asking Brighid, the goddess and saint, to spread her cloak of protection upon Bethia. The Chief then poured sea water gathered from the ninth wave into the cauldron, urging Manannan, the sea deity, to make the baby's arrival smooth. Then the needles of a silver fir were thrown upon the sacred fire to bless and protect the infant.

Once Bethia was born, she was washed in the sacred cauldron by her father who summoned Brighid's healing spirit to protect the child.

May no Being of this World or the Next harm thee.
May no evil hand disturb thy sleep or wakefulness.
May Brighid's cloak cover and protect thee from henceforth.

There were two shooting stars that night. The Chief Druid recognised this as a prosperous omen. Light in this world and the next; light today and tomorrow; light in day and night.

He touched sacred water upon Bethia's minute crinkled forehead and hoped to high heaven that Bridgid would watch over the child, because her mother was intoxicated and her father had already left.

FOURTEEN

The summer solstice, *Alban Hefin* in Druidry, at Stanton Drew wasn't as big a deal as Danny had expected, mostly because it turned out that Elias was more of a 'hedge-druid', doing things alone, and because no one else in the w-orld had heard of Stanton Drew.

The village was only seven miles from Bath, which meant that he could get home quickly if he pressed the panic button (his mum had raced out to buy him a mobile phone), but it looked as though there would be little to panic about since the two hundred thousand revellers were up the road at Stonehenge instead, leaving the eight others of them at Stanton Drew.

"Hi, I'm Graham, the church curate," said one of the eight, holding out his hand to Danny. He was wearing a knitted cardigan and corduroy trousers.

"Are you allowed here?" said Danny. The man frowned before moving away.

"Danny," said Elias, touching his arm. "You must

understand that there is nothing profane about these proceedings. Many of the Order are deeply religious."

Danny coloured. He was beginning to get bored standing about in the field, waiting for nightfall. Stanton Drew was nothing but a field of massive stones behind a row of farm cottages. The signs clearly indicated that you weren't supposed to camp here, weren't supposed to do anything but look at the stones before moving on. It was private property – the back of the cottages, the ground they were stood on. There were even cow pats amongst the stones. He didn't want to be the one to mention breaking the law though. Druids didn't seem to pay much attention to county council signs. He decided to keep an eye on the horizon for approaching police cars instead.

The longest day was tomorrow, but they had to stay up all night to welcome the rising sun. There were no white cloaks about – just the four of them, plus Graham the curate; a ginger-bearded man called Bartholomew and his life partner who had one of those funny names that sounded like aniseed and was spelt Anais – there was a girl called Anais who sat behind him in maths at school and cleared her throat constantly; plus a bald man dressed in orange who looked like he had his dates wrong and meant to attend the Hare Krishna convention.

The car journey to Stanton Drew had been oddly wordless. His mum drove with white knuckles, her brow knotted. Elias had been deep in a trance all morning, cleansing himself mentally. It was a wonder he had managed to pack. In fact, he appeared to be travelling pretty light. Where were the tents? Angel had braided her hair and was wearing a T-shirt covered in hearts and bird cages that his mum had leant her and which Skye appeared to hate.

Skye had a bad attitude. Every time his mum drew near to Angel, Skye recoiled. She seemed pleased that Beth was staying behind, out of the way. He daren't touch Angel in the car, even though he wanted to squeeze her knee to make her jump. He hoped one of these days he would catch her out and she would scream out – make a sound at last.

He had entered a new phase of finding her silence frustrating. Where before he had sensed enigma in her muteness, he was beginning to find it bland, limiting. And never more so than now, stood with her in a field next to a pile of rocks.

As she dropped them off, his mum lingered, making small talk, but in actuality furtively scanning Graham, Bartholomew, his life partner Anais, and Hare Krishna – exactly as he himself had. Whatever he had felt about his mum over the past year, he felt better about her in that moment. They were the same creatures, he and his mum. One day, it would be better between them.

He was grateful for the mobile phone. He was grateful for the loan of Erland's cub scout tent. He was grateful for his mum's offer to help pitch it, since he didn't really know how. He was grateful for the packed lunch in a non-druid Waitrose carrier bag, and his non-druid Waitrose hamper for supper: pork pies, crusty baps, coca-cola in a special chilled holder, chocolate muffins and mango salad. He even had Harry Potter napkins, which had seemed like a good joke at the time – first thing this morning as his mum ran around as though he was leaving the country – but now seemed ridiculous. He was grateful for the waterproof anorak, the gloves, the winter coat, the thermal leggings, the skins he wore for football, since it would get cold tonight, and for the muscle rub in case his knee ached. And he was grateful for the kiss goodbye, the quick tap on his back jean pocket, the disguised sadness and concern.

He wanted to tell her that it would be all right, that he knew they would be close again – sooner than she thought, perhaps – but he couldn't do it.

So he stood there, hands shoved hard in his pockets, deliberately looking the other way as her red car reversed and took off back down the country lane.

But he could see it out of the corner of his eye. He watched the little line of red above the hedges as it faded into the distance before disappearing.

Then he regretted it. He imagined running as fast as he could. Even if his knee wasn't stiff and he wasn't having physiotherapy, he wouldn't have been able to catch her – not unless he had the super power to cross hedges faster than a horse.

And then he remembered his mobile phone.

He dialled his mum's mobile. "Dan?" she said. "You all right, love?"

Upon hearing her voice, he wanted to cry. He knew it wasn't discreet, or manly, and in fact it was pathetic in the circumstances, but it was him.

And now more than ever he wanted himself back.

"I'm sorry, Mum," he said, turning his back upon his grandfather, upon Angel and her mother, and walking away from them. "I'm sorry I've been an arse."

"It's okay, Danny, sweetheart," she said. "I'm

sorry too."

He wasn't going to hate himself for it. Some men cried. Some really cool men cried. Football players cried all the time. It was part of being alive, of loving the game. So he was a crier. So what?

"I love you, Mum," he said. And he lifted his T-shirt to wipe his tears.

When he turned back, Elias, Skye and Angel were sitting in a circle with the others, holding hands and chanting. Luckily Danny's phone was a trendy one so he sat down hidden in the long grass and checked the scores of the pre-World cup friendlies.

It turned out that the orange man was part of the Hare Krishna movement but was curious about Druidry. So when the fire was lit and everyone was sat around it, and Bartholomew was strumming some sort of ukulele and his life partner was umming to it, Elias told the orange man about the eight points in the druid year – four solar, four lunar. Danny took the opportunity to sneak to his tent to put his football skins on underneath his clothes. His mum was right. By eight o'clock it was chilly, even next to the fire.

He was the only one with a tent. The others had put down groundsheets and woollen blankets in preparation for their night under the stars. They didn't seem to have much food with them either, aside from a few chunks of bread, cheese and bottles of mead. Danny's tent felt like a tuck shop that he kept sneaking off to visit. He wasn't sure what the protocol was about food – was he supposed to share it? None of the others seemed hungry, tired, cold, or in need of the toilet. It was just him: the human one.

That said, his grandfather was cool, solemn, majestic. He could imagine him attending solstices when he was younger – surrounded by hippies, druggies, nutters, and he always remained the same: his face tilted upwards to examine the night sky, his eyes closed in meditation, his focus unwavering. It must have been difficult removing himself, especially when he was younger. But now that he was an old man it was easier to be a hedge druid – to let the brambles roam wild and thick upon him until no one could get through.

Angel was being clingy, tugging on his shirt sleeve every time she scribbled on her notepad. He wanted to tell her that he couldn't see what she had written because it was getting dark, that he was fed up with reading her words. Her allure was diminishing – not only because there was a new girl next to him in physics who told him that she wore only cashmere next to her skin because it was so soft – but because of the impracticality of it all. Angel had no words, no clue about the real world, about cashmere, and she was leaving soon. And the football season was starting eight weeks today with Chelsea versus Hull. Was that fickle? Perhaps. He was fourteen. Fickle *was* fourteen.

Have I done something wrong? she wrote.

Bartholomew's life partner was playing bongo drums now. Danny shook his head at Angel and chewed on a blade of grass. How could he tell her that it was because there was something wrong with *her* – that he wanted her to tell a joke, laugh, sing a song, say hello.

"I'm going for a stroll," he said. Angel wanted to come with him. She jumped up and tugged on his arm. He flicked her away with irritation. She bit her lip and looked at her mother, who had stood up beside her in an instant.

"What is wrong with you?" Skye snapped, the fire dancing upon her face devilishly. This, Danny realised, was the moment that Skye had been waiting for. She looked aggressive, ready to box.

Danny decided to acquiesce. There was no point having a fight here at a druid camp, spoiling his granddad's big night out.

He walked across the field, looking at the stone formations. It was the third largest collection of prehistoric standing stones in the country, according to Elias.

Danny was gazing at them, imagining that they were wedding revellers turned to stone, as the myth went, when Angel tugged on his sleeve again.

Please tell me what's wrong.

She looked so mournful, Danny felt bad. "It's because you're going soon," he offered. "Right after the solstice. There isn't much point."

Her mouth formed what would have sounded like a sad little 'Oh'.

He turned back to the stones.

Maybe we could stay in touch?

"I don't think so," he said. "It's not as if you're online on the barge, is it?" He laughed, not feeling very humorous. He didn't want to put her down. He wanted things to end nicely, to dissolve. For her sake, and for his grandfather's.

How greatly things had changed in only a few weeks. It was his leg that had done it. His inability to move had altered his perspective, had made her silence seem bearable, attractive even. And it probably was, for the right sort of person. But that person wasn't Danny – with all his noise, his words, his heart beating drama.

So he was thinking as he came to a halt in front of one of the megaliths, gazing up at its humbling size. Until a hand slammed down a piece of paper on the stone in front of him.

It's because I'm a mute isn't it.

In an ironic reversal of roles, he found himself without words.

Another piece of paper slammed down.

Tell me the truth!

"No!" said Danny, taking the paper and screwing it up. "You tell me the truth! Tell me why you can't speak! What happened to you?"

Angel was grinding her teeth, her fists clenched. He had never seen her angry before. She was chewing over potential sounds and words – almost turning blue with the frustration of not being able to retaliate.

But she didn't have to because her mother was there to do it for her, stepping out from behind the megalith like a ghoul in waiting.

"Jeez, where did you come from?" said Danny, jumping back in surprise.

"Leave her alone!" Skye shouted, pulling her daughter away from him, back into the folds of her long protective cardigan. "You're not to go near her again!"

"No problem!" Danny shouted back.

The two women set back off towards the fire, Skye hugging Angel so tightly that Angel's feet were almost off the ground.

So Skye was hiding something, Danny thought. It was just as well they were leaving. He didn't want to be responsible for unearthing secrets that were better left buried.

He put his hands in his pockets and leaned back against the stone. Anais was still playing the bongo drums. He knew he should have stayed home and watched Die Hard.

The summer solstice was a precise moment in time, not an evening, or a morning. It occurred at four minutes past five o'clock that year – the year that Danny was sat on a ground sheet, his feet frozen, his eyes heavy, his grandfather's arm around him. Danny never made it to his tent to sleep in the end, but he did share his Waitrose supper.

The sacred fire was still burning. Bartholomew was a Bard in the Order so he told stories and poems all night. Some of them were entertaining. Some of them were not. Anais did not stop banging the bongos, although she hushed up at four minutes past five o'clock when Elias, the most senior druid present, rose to say a blessing. He scattered five healing herbs and magical plants upon the fire as he spoke, naming each one as it burnt to ash: yarrow, mugwort, St. John's wort, vervain and fern.

Danny could not fail to be moved. His grandfather's beard was glowing in the fierce sunlight as the sun rose over the megaliths.

His grandfather believed, like all druids, that everyone and everything was connected, that separateness was an illusion. Danny, at four minutes past five o'clock, felt Elias' belief momentarily as though it were his own.

By the time the fire had burned to ashes and they were packing up to go home, Danny felt more like his old self.

Angel wasn't speaking to him, not that he could really tell. Skye wouldn't even look at him. He wasn't that bothered. He could take or leave the druids really. He was still into magic, but he wasn't going to any more solstices. At some time during the past twenty-four hours shivering and dew-soaked at Stanton Drew, he had decided that he was more into cashmere than hessian.

He shook hands with Bartholomew and Bongo, with Graham the curate, who had said very little all night, and with the orange man who had turned out to be a decent sort of bloke. He was Indian. When he had seen Danny's mango salad, he had asked if he could have a couple slices. As he ate – as though he hadn't eaten all year – he told Danny an Indian story about the origins of the mango. Danny liked the story and decided to write it into his compendium as soon as he got home. It was always nice to take something home with you from a solstice, aside from the gnat bites.

On the longest day of the year, Beth found herself at home alone on a Saturday for the first time in a decade. To make matters worse, the house had been busier than usual for the past month with their unexpected guests, and now the silence had descended with little notice.

She had a brief cry on her drive home from Stanton Drew, partly because Danny had finally come back to her and they were close again, but mostly because she was going home to an empty Lilyvale.

Brett was at Jacko's, and Erland – having realised that he would be home for the weekend underneath his mum's scrutinizing stare – organised a sleepover at his friend's. He packed up his chess set, Star Wars pyjamas and National Geographic magazine, pressed a kiss on his mum's cheek and set off, chewing on a pear, his jeans slung low. Beth let him pretend that he was setting off into the unknown, but she phoned Mrs Matthews immediately and told her to call back in ten minutes if Erland wasn't there; that he would eat anything but spinach and banana; to make sure that he cleaned his teeth, and to take his torch away if he was still reading National Geographic under the covers after nine tonight.

She almost expected Jacko to cancel but he arrived at the appointed time, saying that he would bring Brett back after tea tomorrow. Brett was waiting at the window wearing his best dungarees, holding his red twain and blue twain, Noddy suitcase at his feet. Beth heard single mums talk at the school gate of how they hated their children departing at weekends – hated the idea of them playing families elsewhere, but Beth felt no such thing. She would miss Brett, but spending time with his father was vital. She would do everything she could to protect it, if not just for the sake of recompensing for past mistakes.

What she wasn't expecting though was for Jacko to say, "Come meet Valerie."

"Wah-ler-wee!" shouted Brett.

Beth glanced past Jacko to the car parked in the street. She could see an anxious face at the passenger seat window. Poor Wah-ler-wee. It wasn't easy for her either.

"Of course," she said.

Wah-ler-wee wasn't as young as Beth expected. She had grey hairs at her temples, soft creases around her eyes when she laughed – which she did now. It wasn't a nervous laugh, but a natural one. She was warm-hearted. And very pretty. But where that would have riled Beth only a few weeks prior to now, she sensed that something had shifted. She caught herself actually feeling pleased for Jacko that he had found someone nice. It was most definitely a bonus for them all, since Brett would be spending time with this woman. What did Beth want – for the girlfriend to be ugly and wicked, so that Brett would hate her and wouldn't see his father again therefore? Where was the use in that?

So Beth found herself talking to Wah-ler-wee and enjoying the conversation.

"I'll take good care of your boy," Valerie said, in her Spanish accent, tapping Brett lightly on the head.

"I'm sure you will," said Beth.

She felt fine walking away, back up to the house, but as she closed the front door she felt bereft stood inside quiet Lilyvale.

"I'll work," she said aloud.

Thank God for her work. It had always been her saviour in life, and never more so than now.

She was just beginning to plan the Influence of the Renaissance on English Literature, for Florida International, when the doorbell rang.

It would be Jacko. Brett had forgotten something.

She opened the door to find Reverend Trist stood there in his weekend casuals, a leather satchel slung on his shoulder. Out of his clergy wear, he looked even smaller.

He was wearing a trilby hat, which he tipped cordially to her.

"I have business to attend to at West Marsh," he said. "I thought whilst I was in the area..." He trailed off, glancing past Beth down the hallway as though fishing for an invitation inside.

She obliged. "Cup of tea?" she said.

Seated at the bistro chairs in the garden that she and Elias were fond of sitting upon together, she was aware how much stronger she felt meeting the reverend not only upon her own territory but in a place that felt consecrated by her father's strength of presence.

"I don't think," said the reverend, nibbling on a triangle of shortbread, "that things have worked out between us as well as they might have."

"Given the circumstances, I think we've done rather well," Beth replied.

It wasn't as warm today. The leaves of the trees were barely moving – merely twitching their tips – yet there was an almost autumnal chill to the air.

"I feel that from the outset you thought that I was judging you."

"Weren't you?" she said.

Instead of replying he took another nibble at the shortbread. He was a man who did everything in small measures – from his conservative dress sense, to his conversational tactics.

"It may help you to know," she said, "that my attitude towards you reflects my attitude to the church as a whole. My doubts about you are my doubts about God."

"Well, I'm flattered that you see so much of God in

me," he said, his tone of voice indecipherable. "And there is more of God in you than you realise, Beth."

"Is that why you're here, Reverend?" she said, putting down her cup lightly. "To have one last go at saving my soul? Can you not just accept that I'm not religious? You must meet people like me all the time."

"Ah, but that's just it. I *don't*."

She hoped that he meant that he didn't meet people often, that he didn't get out much. But something was telling her that this wasn't his meaning at all.

"Have you decided what to do with Pamela's legacy?" he asked, without looking at her. "With the paddocks, the cottage?"

"Not yet," she said. "It feels rather like bad money. My eldest son is against us profiting from it."

"It's only bad if you choose to see it that way," he said.

"And we do," she replied.

"I see," he said, picking up his tea cup and saucer. She had dusted off her best china for the reverend: the Royal Albert *New Country Roses*.

"You're quite an enigma, Miss Trelawney," he said. "You can be so receptive, so susceptible, and yet so utterly unreachable at the same time."

"Orphans' prerogative," she said, smiling.

"Hmmph!" He returned her smile.

Were they friends again?

"So…" He reached into his satchel for a notebook. "I said I would help you…" He tore a sheet of paper from the book, which he handed to her.

She read the reverend's neat handwriting. "My

goodness. Where did you get this from?"

"From my acquaintance. The one who you asked me to ask."

She fell quiet, listening to the branches of the palm tree rustling.

"Reverend Trist," she said. "I know we've had our differences, but—"

"Hush," he said, holding up his hand and shaking his head. "No need."

He stayed a while longer. He liked Lilyvale, liked the garden overlooking the canal, the glimpse of the white stone of Bath's town centre through the trees.

As she showed him out, he turned to face her on the doorstep, pressing his Trilby onto his head and tilting it to look up at her.

"You have much to be thankful for," he said. "You had a terrible start in life, but you have turned it around. I greatly admire you for that."

"Thank you," she said.

"Promise me…" His eyes were begging, betraying affection. He cared for her. He clasped her hand. "…When you have found her, Beth – when you have found Fleur – let it go. Turn away."

"Yes," she said. "I promise you. I will."

Fleur Wishart, according to the reverend's notes, was placed on the missing person's register one year after leaving Pamela Lazenby's care in 2002. Fostered by Pammy in 1992, aged six months old, she left Yew Tree Cottage at the age of ten. Allegedly, she ran away and was never seen again, not that a huge search party would have been launched. There was little demand to track down orphans, there being no pining family to encourage and sustain the search.

So another child had run away from Pammy's care, just as Beth had done twenty years before her. Aaron, Teresa, April and Rowan may have been spared – may have been happy at the cottage – but others were not.

The notes could not provide Beth with what she needed to know: Fleur's current whereabouts. Yet they did something even more vital; they gave her the reverend's blessing. Finally her mission was not vengeful or bitter – an anger-fuelled witch hunt – but a search for answers. Finding the truth had never felt so thrilling.

She spent the remainder of the day trying to concentrate on her Renaissance paper, but she kept drifting to the cottage in her mind, imagining the child in the cheesecloth dress – Fleur – sitting at Beth's place at the table, feeding the horses in the paddock, sleeping in Beth's bed.

What had happened between Pammy and Fleur, that had driven Fleur away – had driven her from the face of the earth?

By the time darkness came, Beth couldn't stop thinking about Fleur. She had forgotten that this was her day alone, without company – so full was her mind of people, places and suspicions.

She sat up in bed, eagerly awaiting her friend's arrival, in the hope that tonight was the night when she received another clue that would propel her closer to her goal. But when she didn't arrive, Beth realised that the child would not appear again until it was safe to do so –

that she might not ever appear again. She had done what she came here to do.

The truth was lying just beneath them now, like bone protruding through skin.

She closed her eyes, turning in bed with a tug of the sheets over her shoulder as though someone were hogging them.

"Goodnight, Peter," she murmured.

Excerpt from Danny's compendium

The Origins of the Mango, an Indian legend. As told to me by the Hari Krishna Indian at the summer solstice, Stanton Drew, England.

The daughter of the sun was very beautiful, talented and kind. Everyone loved her. She was married to a powerful king. In short, she was a bit of a babe. But an evil enchantress in the kingdom was jealous and made the girl's life miserable, taunting her all the time.

One day the girl couldn't take any more. To get away from the evil enchantress she dived into a pool, where she turned into a lotus flower. The enchantress was pleased that she'd got rid of the girl. But the king liked to walk around his gardens, admiring his flowers. He spotted the exotic lotus and was transfixed by its beauty. Enraged, the enchantress set fire to the lotus and destroyed it once and for all.

But from the ashes of the burnt lotus, grew a beautiful mango tree. The king was keen to taste this mysterious new fruit. As he picked the mango, it fell to his feet and from its centre appeared his wife. The king was overjoyed to be reunited with his love, and he cherished her forever.

FIFTEEN

Peter grew up in Fulham, in a terrace house two streets from Chelsea's grounds at Stamford Bridge. His parents had five sons, all Chelsea mad – of whom Peter was the youngest and the maddest. The Freemans watched the history of their club from the loft window – witnessed its demise in the 1970's and 80's, its history ripped out as the wooden stands were replaced, and the club's return to glory in the 1990's when the stadium was finally rebuilt. The air around their house was alive with the sound of chanting, horns, applause and anthems; the night sky lit with floodlights.

When it came to knowing where to call home, Peter had no hesitancy in knocking on the door of no. 29, Leap Street.

Clare used to accuse him of secretly wanting to still be at home with his mother. He wasn't a mummy's boy – had left home aged eighteen, albeit to move ten minutes away to university in the city – yet when you had a mum who made excellent beer-soaked sausages and mash, knew the off-side rule better than the ref, and understood precisely when not to make phone calls or to hoover, it was an attractive proposition to pop round for a cup of tea and to peruse the magnetic premiership tables on the fridge door.

The cups of tea had become more infrequent, since Clare found every reason to not visit the Freemans. She resented his proximity to his parents' home, given that her family were in Ireland. He was tired of pointing out that they still managed to spend every Christmas and Easter in Dublin. It was no use. Clare had made up her mind about the Freemans and their insane addiction to Chelsea. The front door of no. 29 was painted blue – matched to the exact Pantone colour reference of the Chelsea strip. His dad had done this as a joke, but Clare saw it as highly ignorant and un-middle class.

Yet Clare's biggest beef wasn't with Chelsea, but with his mum. She didn't actually say as much. She didn't have to. If his mum sent them home with an apple pie, Clare's pout said that it was insulting, that her mother-in-law was suggesting that Clare couldn't bake or didn't know how to feed her family. If his mum didn't procure said pie, Clare's pout said that his mum couldn't be bothered with them any more – not since his eldest brother had sons. Sons who were insanely addicted to Chelsea also.

Clare acted bizarrely at no. 29, on the few times that they visited a year. She dressed up – lipstick, high heels – and put the girls in their best frocks. It wasn't necessary, he told her. Mum wouldn't expect it. But Clare stiffened as she passed through the Chelsea blue door and remained stiff the rest of the hour. It tended to be an hour.

His mum would welcome them in, not reacting to Clare's formal attire. She wasn't much of a talker, his mum, mostly because she had one eye on the telly, especially at five o'clock on a Saturday when the results were coming in. It was rude – Clare's pout said – keeping the television on when you had guests.

"If I'd known you were coming, Pete, I'd have made you a sponge," his mum would say to him out in the kitchen, as he helped her make the teas. He always replied that he was sorry – that he never knew when they were coming, that his wife decided everything. "Shame!" she said. She liked saying this. It was the understatement of the year.

His dad wore his emotions rather more plainly. "That wife of yours needs a stick of dynamite up her a—"

"Now, now," said his mum, holding up her hand. "More tea?"

Peter had been staying with them for the past week. He hadn't slept so well in years and couldn't remember the last time he was so up to date with next season's fixtures. His eldest brother lived only two doors along and it had been nice catching up with him, and the fixtures. Without Clare, he felt as though he was getting to know his family all over, without the burning eyes of judgement upon them.

It was, in short, rather like being ten again.

"She's fine," said his mum. "She'll mellow with old age, Peter." She fixed her eyes upon him. He knew what she was saying: that he was going to be spending his old age with Clare, that it was the right thing to do.

"If I were you," said his dad, steeping his ginger biscuit for a perilously long time in his mug of tea, "I'd forget them girls and go back to your boys. Girls are a right royal pain in the–"

"Nonsense," said his mum. "Peter can't keep starting over. He has a family now…" She turned to him, her head cocked. "Don't s'pose you ever hear from Beth, do you, love? Nice girl."

"Weirdo," said his dad.

Peter reddened. He was spending such a lot of time thinking about Beth, it was a wonder he didn't say her name out loud more often.

His mum caught sight of the change in his skin tone, narrowed her eyes at him and then quickly recovered, setting her expression to neutral.

"Not really, Mum," he replied, sipping his tea. "I saw Danny though."

"You did?" said his mum.

"That the Chelsea fan?" said his dad, sitting upright in his chair and turning to Peter eagerly. "Named after Petrescu? And did you see Erland? After Erland Johnsen? Chelsea's Player of the Year 1995?"

Peter wasn't listening to his dad. He was watching his mum's face darkening as regret passed across it. He wished he hadn't mentioned the boys. He could see his mum's lips working – the questions that she wanted to ask about the grandchildren whom she had never met.

"You should go home to Clare, son," she said, rising. "I must pop the oven on."

She did a lot of baking, his mum. He was beginning to understand why.

She was right, of course. He had to go home. Clare was flawed – manipulative, controlling, but he had married her and had to see it through. Marriage was a job like any other, a responsibility. He would do the right thing. He would go back to them. Perhaps tomorrow. England were in a friendly tonight. And his mum was making slow-baked mackerel in cider for supper.

Sasha was expelled from school for setting light to a girl's hair in the playground. Apparently she had received several written warnings about her deteriorating behaviour, all of which had been removed from her book bag by Bernice, the childminder, in return for Sasha not telling her mum that Bernice smoked Benson & Hedges on the school run.

It didn't take long for Clare to extract this information from her daughter, and to work out who she had got the matches from.

"She actually set light to the child's ponytail," said the headmistress, an uppity woman with yellow teeth.

Clare, who would have been horrified had one of her own children been the victim, was trying to refrain from laughing hysterically.

"Is something amusing you, Mrs Freeman?" said the headmistress. "The parents want to press charges. They are perfectly entitled to."

"Press charges against a seven-year-old?"

"A seven-year-old *arsonist*."

Clare drummed her fingers on the desk. She left an important meeting to come here. Her daughters were waiting outside the door. Any decision that involved Sasha would affect Sarah also, since there was no way she was going to do two school runs – especially since she had just sacked Bernice. The biggest problem they faced now was that the other local primary school had a metal detector on the gate to uncover knives.

The girls would have to go there, just for a few weeks whilst she sorted things out. There was always private school. She could start working Fridays again. It wasn't as if she did anything but cry on Fridays.

The head was wittering on about procedures, about social expectations, about one contaminated apple ruining the rest.

"Are you calling my child a contaminated apple?" said Clare.

"Mrs Freeman," said the head, laying down her pen and folding her arms. She looked like a woman whose patience was due back at the library. "Where is your husband?"

She had tried calling him several times last week. He wouldn't answer his mobile or his work phone to her. So she had decided not to try calling him about Sasha. He would see how it felt to miss this huge event in his daughter's life, since he obviously didn't care about keeping in touch with them.

After the meeting Clare marched the girls to the car, prodding them in the back to move faster.

"But I don't see why I have to leave too," wailed Sarah.

"Because you're Sasha's twin!" said Clare.

"Where's Daddy?" said Sasha, crying. "I want Daddy! I hate you! Everything's going wrong with you.

Why can't we –?"

"Just shut up!" snapped Clare. "I can't think straight! It's not all about you, Sasha! You've got us into this mess, and now I need to find a way to get us out of it. Okay?"

The whole thing was a disaster. The only good thing to come from it was that she had sacked that skinny-jeaned Bernice. Even that wasn't that great though. There would have to be another one just like her, someone else to help with the school run. Still, she would choose someone with chunky thighs this time.

"Why did you do it?" Clare asked, over supper.

They had eaten spaghetti hoops on toast three times this week. The girls didn't seem to mind. They had been off their food since Peter left.

"I know you're upset about Daddy, sweetheart, but setting fire to someone's ponytail?...Is that how I've raised you?"

Sasha looked up earnestly, widening her eyes. "I just wanted to mess her hair up, Mummy. She's so perfect. It isn't fair."

Clare swallowed hard.

There was nothing as sobering as seeing your worst personal traits handed down to your off-spring, as surely as if you had mail ordered it for them.

The man from next door, the architect, called round the following Friday.

Clare was doing the accounts – working out how to get the girls away from Flick Knife Primary, which they were attending temporarily. Her efforts with a paper pad and a calculator only served to demonstrate that she needed to discuss the matter with Peter, to ascertain their financial situation – their situation as a whole.

So she was thinking as she pulled open the front door, to find her next-door-neighbour stood there.

"Is it too early?" he said, holding out a bottle of wine.

"Uh." She was confused. "Where's your girlfriend?" was the first thing she could think of to say.

"Can I come in?" he said.

She opened the door wider by way of saying yes.

"To answer your question…I don't really have girlfriends, per se," he said, following her down the hallway. "I have callers."

"Ladies of the night?" she said, clearing the kitchen table of paper balls and bank statements.

He laughed. "No! I just don't get tied down in relationships. I'm too busy."

"Well, you don't look busy now," she said. "Have a seat."

She scraped a chair out from under the table for him and opened the wine, placing it between them.

"So what are you doing here?" she said, sitting down and eyeing his T-shirt. She didn't understand the logo – something trendy, Japanese.

He took a drink of wine, before pouring another, as though psyching himself up for something.

She began to feel uncomfortable. After all, she knew nothing about him. She eyed her car keys, the door, the nearest window.

"I would have come round sooner but I didn't

know what your situation was. Is your husband…?" He looked about him.

"Hiding under the kitchen sink?" she said. "No. No, he's not."

"Then would you like to go upstairs?" he said. "Or we could go to my place, if it's more appropriate."

She blinked at his boldness. "You don't hang about, do you?" she said.

"I don't believe in wasting time, no."

She took a drink of wine, feeling it chilling, relaxing her insides. What a different way to spend a Friday. How different from a Friday spent in tears at the kitchen table. If Peter could see her now...

"So what's it to be?" he said.

She looked at the man's lips and wondered what it would be like to kiss them. She spied a tuft of chest hair poking out from above his T-shirt and in that instant she felt a giddying wave of excitement.

She raised her chin defiantly and said, "Why the hell not?"

Angel gave Danny her paper fortune-teller as a parting gift and in that moment he knew what the problem was all along: not her muteness but her immaturity.

She moved the fortune-teller in and out, before holding it up to show him its proclamation: *I love you*, it said.

His fringe shot back in surprise. It was the last thing he had expected her to say.

You don't have to say it too, she wrote down.

He was about to give her a quick kiss on the lips as

a gift in return, when her mother entered the room with a rustle of her skirt, glaring at him.

"Oh, will you lighten up?" Danny said, leaving the room.

Upstairs, he lifted the floorboard and pulled out the compendium. He flattened the fortune-teller and placed it gently inside the front cover of his book.

"Goodbye, Angel," he said.

He heard a noise outside so rose to the window. Erland was throwing a ball to Ruby, exercising the old dog's legs before the trip ahead.

Danny wanted his grandfather to stay, but he knew that all the Hoodoo spells in the world couldn't keep him here. Elias had served his purpose – had given their mum, all of them, a sense of history and of belonging that wouldn't disappear with his departure. They knew that Elias was out there now, under their stars and moon. Where before there had been nothing, there was now Elias – this huge presence in the universe. Nothing, not even his death, could ever affect that.

Elias, the nomad, had brought their mother stability, rootedness. She had changed. And the change had brought Danny back to her.

Outside, Erland dropped the ball. Ruby's master was calling her.

Elias' work was done. It was time for him to move on.

There wasn't the flurry of activity that normally occurred during the departure of guests – no wet towels being amassed, no hurried cling-filming of sandwiches for the car journey. Elias didn't want anything and didn't need to pack anything either.

He stood at the back door, legs astride, hands clasped behind his back, Ruby at his side, his barge waiting for him loyally at the bottom of the garden. Skye and Angel were lurking behind him, hesitantly. Something had happened between Danny and Angel. The rose was off the bloom, Beth observed. They were exchanging awkward arm pats, like rival football players at the end of a match.

"See you then," said Danny, before moving away, whistling softly to himself in an attempt to look as though he wasn't the least bit bothered.

"I'd like you to have this," said Beth, handing Angel her copy of *Alice in Wonderland*, the one she had stolen from Pengilly Primary. "If you're ever this way again, you're always welcome to stop by and stay with us."

She looked at the child wistfully, wondering what they might have achieved together had Angel been allowed to learn from her. But Skye was still watching over them, and her penetrative gaze cut loose any ties.

Angel, unbound, drifted away. Together, she and her mother went down to the barge.

"So," said Elias, clapping his hands. "I depart."

Instinctively, Beth picked up Brett, by way of compensation. It was an immeasurable relief to have children to hold.

"I must thank you for the hospitality you have shown me and my travelling companions." He glanced down the garden at the barge. "I am at a loss as to what to do with those two."

"Slave trade?" said Erland.

"You are amusing," said Elias, chuckling. "Alas, I have not got to know you as well as I might have liked."

"Wise move," said Danny. "Most people make the same choice."

"Hush, Danny," said Beth, tutting.

"With your chess abilities, and your analytical and studious nature, Erland, I trust you would have made a fine Ovate."

"Cool," said Erland. "Maybe next time."

"What about me?" said Danny.

"Why, you are a Bard, naturally," said Elias. "An orator."

"And what's that again?" said Danny.

"Verbal diarrhoea," said Erland.

They all laughed, but it was short lived. Night was beginning to fall. Soon the bats would be here and there would be no one to tell Beth about them any more.

"I got you this," said Beth, handing Elias a mobile phone.

"What do I do with it?" he said, holding the mobile on his outstretched palm as one would a grasshopper or butterfly. "Does it require feeding?"

They all laughed again.

"Just plug it in," she said. "I'll pay for it. You just need to answer it when it rings."

"Who will ring it?" he asked.

"Me," she replied, her voice wobbling. She cleared her throat. No tears. It wasn't fair on him. He was a traveller, not a land lubber.

"I have something for you," Elias said, turning to Danny.

There was a cloth sack at his feet. He pulled something out from the sack and handed it to Danny.

"It is Vivi's grimoire – your grandmother's," said Elias. "I have kept it for nearly forty years. I knew this time would come."

Danny turned the pages in astonishment. "It's like my compendium. Wow! It's awesome. Thank you so much!"

Elias bowed his habitual bow.

"Keep at it, son. You have a talent for magic. It is in the Trelawney blood. And this…" he said, addressing Beth, "is for you, my child."

From the sack, he pulled something that glinted in the light from the lounge window.

"It was Father's," he said. "It stopped the night that he passed away. When I came to Lilyvale, it started again." He pressed it into her hand and closed her fingers around it. "Look after it. It is all I have of him."

He kissed Beth upon her forehead, then Brett, before turning away.

"Come on, Ruby," he said, tapping his leg.

Only when the barge had gone, when Angel had waved her copy of *Alice,* when Elias had bowed one last distant goodbye, when the trail of smoke from their stove had finally disappeared and the wake had settled to calm on the surface of the canal, did Beth unclench her hand, where she found her grandfather's silver watch, ticking softly.

SIXTEEN

Beth pined.

"Just ring him, Mum," said Danny.

He said this so often that she wondered whether he had an ulterior motive. She was bound to enquire about Angel if she spoke to Elias, after all.

"No," she said. "I won't bother him."

She found the walks along the canal the most difficult, walking alongside the meadowsweet on her own, on her way back from dropping off Brett. Nothing seemed the same now. Everywhere she looked, she saw something of Elias. The meadowsweet wasn't just a wild flower but a sacred plant with a perfume so strong it was used to anoint clothes at rituals and ceremonies. Her heart tugged at the sight of each butterfly, each bird, each tree. She kept her grandfather's silver watch with her at all times, comforted by the sensation of its ticking rhythm as though it were a heart beat.

With the boys at school and Brett at preschool, she

wondered at her having coped with such loneliness prior to Elias. What had she done before? The idea of solitude appalled her. She worked outside whenever possible, moving her notes to the bistro table, conversing with Elias sometimes as though he were seated there still.

On days when it was dull and raining, she immersed herself in her work indoors, and in her fruitless detective work to find out what had happened to Fleur Wishart.

The police were unable to help. Fleur had vanished eleven years ago. Not only did they have no record of her, but they had never been given cause to find her. Beth told them she was giving them cause now, but the officer shook his head and said that a hunch wasn't enough to justify spending tax payers' money on.

The child with the missing teeth had stopped visiting her; Beth's anger about Pammy was abating and in its place rose loneliness – it being unfeasible to be fully owned by two emotions at once.

She found herself praying to the universe for a resolution, to find Fleur, to put an end to the past. But nothing happened. Their lives continued without change.

Until one morning when a hand-written envelope arrived in the post. Beth didn't recognise the writing, but had a heavy feeling that whatever lay inside was going to change everything.

She took the letter out to the garden and sat underneath the palm tree with it.

It was a while before she mustered the courage to slide a nail underneath the flap and read the contents.

Inside there was a business card. She tipped the

envelope upside down, shaking it. There was nothing else enclosed.

The card was for a floating hair salon in Bradford-upon-Avon, just along the canal from Bath. The card was highly decorated with miniature flowers.

New! Coming to Bath on Wednesdays, it said at the bottom.

The name of the business' owner was in large writing and yet she read everything else before acknowledging it. When she finally did so, she dropped the card in shock as though it had burnt her.

When Peter got home, he was astounded to see the twins wearing unfamiliar red school sweaters. "Why are–?"

The girls jumped up, pushing their spaghetti hoops to one side.

"Daddy!" They ran at him, pulling on his arms, jumping up and down. "You're back, you're back! Mummy, look! Daddy's back!"

He glanced warily at Clare who had a look on her face that he couldn't translate. He hadn't expected her to jump up and embrace him like the twins, but at least a smile, a word in greeting...

She was keeping her eyes averted, pronging her meal with her fork, a vaporous smile upon her lips.

He was going to have to do all the work. Well, that was fine. On the Tube journey home from work, he had prepared his speech: *I'm really sorry for deserting you. It was wrong. I'm back now and I intend to make every effort to fix things. I...er...* He couldn't say this bit smoothly even during rehearsals. *I…love you. So tell me what I can do to make you happy again.*

Had she ever been happy? Not just with him, but in her whole life?

And then he had to stop himself again because he wasn't even home yet, hadn't made up with her yet, and already he was picking faults with her. He couldn't think like that any more, if this was going to work.

At the Tube exit, he had stepped out into the evening sunshine, determined to achieve the task in hand. On the two minute walk home, he noticed a seagull circling the air above him – one lonely bird on its own, its white wings startlingly clear against the turquoise sky.

Seagulls always reminded him of Beth, as she had grown up on the coast. He liked to fancy when he saw one that it was her, sending him a sign, keeping him company. Tonight, he wondered why this bird was on its own, soaring above suburbia.

Was it a sign from Beth? Was it saying that she was lonely?

As he put his key in the lock, the bird was still circling the air above.

No more, Beth, he thought. *I cannot think of Beth any more.*

So there he was with his wife and her spaghetti hoops, and his bouncing children.

"Can I speak to Mummy alone a minute, girls?" he said.

They obediently shot up to their bedroom, not wishing to impede their parents' reunion in any way.

He knelt down on the kitchen floor by Clare's side

and cleared his throat. "I forgive you," she said, brusquely, setting her green eyes upon him.

He felt anger prickle him instantly. Who was to say that he was about to apologise? Maybe she should be the one apologising? She was presumptuous and…

"Thank you," he said, placing his hand on hers. She was still holding her fork. "Clare, I…er…" He tried to remember his speech.

The doorbell rang. Clare jumped up and let in an odd-looking woman. Odd in that she was heavy, not in build but in motion – moving as though each leg were weighted down with bags of flour. She was also wearing some serious teeth weaponry. She stood, glancing about her, sucking on her braces.

"Peter, this is Bernice's replacement. She's here to discuss the role, if you don't mind."

And Clare turned her back on him, taking the flour bags into the lounge, leaving him stood with his overnight bag at his feet.

In his mind, it had gone a lot differently.

The next day, he was up to speed with the twins' school and childcare arrangements to the point that he was sat in the lobby of The Borough, a fee-paying all girl's school in Hertford. The train commute was wholly manageable. Flour bags would do the journey with them. And money bags was going to pay for it.

Clare's frosty demeanour suggested with little ambiguity that he was welcome to reunite with them, so long as he brought his wallet. Her manner towards him was undeniably polite, cordial, deliberately steering away from all matters controversial or distasteful, as though she was exchanging pleasantries at a business function.

It was rather disturbing. Was this how it was going to be? So long as he paid up, he could live with them and make small talk?

He wasn't going to live like that, couldn't live like that.

So whilst he was waiting for the Head of The Borough, he popped outside to call his mum to ask what she was doing this weekend.

He would make the grand gesture. Clare was always home on Fridays. He would come home from work early to surprise her and off they would set. His mum would look after the twins, whilst he and his wife jetted off to New York. Clare had always wanted to go.

"Mr and Mrs Freeman," said the Head, walking towards them in squeaky shoes. "*Do* come in."

Since leaving Lilyvale, Elias was finding it hard to sleep. He was right to give Beth the silver watch and Danny the grimoire. Yet suddenly he felt bare. With his treasured possessions reduced to his own grimoire and Malachi's, he began to feel as though his life amounted to little. He had always intended it that way and yet…

This potent sense of lacking unsettled him. He drew Ruby nearer to him at night, allowing her to sleep beside him for the first time. He felt animosity towards his former friends: the stars, the clouds, the trees, the birds – the whole shebang – for letting him down, for not sustaining him and sufficing when he needed them to.

He drifted down the Avon and Kennet canal, feeling as though he were going the wrong way. After all, the salmon had turned him upstream, curving his life into a different direction. So he should have been continuing with that new direction, not going with the flow again. Yet he was; flowing onwards, like before.

Skye and Angel were not helping matters. Skye was sporting a permanent zigzag of anger at the bridge of her nose. Her movements were heavy. He could hear her stomping around on the deck, crashing about with plates and cutlery down below. He enquired after her mood, offering to help alleviate her angst with an herbal potion, a story for mind occupation, a walk onshore, but nothing could reach her.

Angel was no better. She sat cross-legged on the decking, braiding her hair, her head bent to read *Alice* again. She had read it at least three times that he knew of. She looked up from time to time to stretch her neck, always wearing the same poignant look of regret and longing.

It was this longing that was fuelling Skye's rage, he supposed.

None of them were the same since anchoring at Lilyvale.

The girls didn't even react when he spotted a kingfisher. He was exuberant, calling to them excitedly to join him, but Angel didn't lift her head from her book, and Skye deliberately looked the other way. A few seconds later the kingfisher took off in a blur of iridescent colour before disappearing.

His time with the girls was coming to an end. Everything felt as though it was ending. He felt sorrow singe his chest bone.

He was so rapt in thought, that he missed the barge entirely. It was Skye who spotted it, had been so transfixed by it that she wasn't able to look away at the kingfisher. She recognised the name instantly, had heard all the conversations at Lilyvale. She asked Elias to pull over for a moment, whilst she hopped onboard the boat. Elias, still preoccupied, glanced at the scissors logo and gleaned that Skye was making enquiries about female things of which he had no interest.

It was only the next day that Skye told him – much to his astonishment – that she had posted a business card to Beth.

Skye had found Fleur Wishart.

Beth drove to Bradford-upon-Avon the next morning. It was a grey non-descript day. The birds sat lethargically upon telegraph wires, waiting for a rainstorm.

She parked in the town car park near the canal and sat, rocking the business card back and forth on the steering wheel.

Fleur Wishart was an uncommon name. She had sounded young on the phone. Beth found it easier, if less honest, to book an appointment in order to win a conversation with her. She would pay the girl for her time.

Fleur Wishart. She was alive, not six foot under at Yew Tree Cottage, or lying underneath the ocean with a brick tied to her foot. Fleur Wishart, the elusive sixth child, was waiting for her just out there on the water.

She remained in her car until the exact time of her

appointment, before walking along the wooden gangway to the barge entrance. The door was open. It was quiet inside, but for the insidious sound of snipping. Beth rapped her knuckles politely on the door and poked her head inside.

The salon was understandably small, but well-lit and organised. It was less rustic than Beth had envisaged, although the steep price she was quoted should have been a clue. This wasn't a hippy set-up, but an upmarket business aiming its sights at the affluent. There were two stylists both with their backs to Beth, cutting hair.

She surveyed the stylists' faces in the mirror. One had punkish facial piercings and scarlet hair cut with a fiercely high fringe. The other was feminine, wearing a floral dress and girlishly long hair loose down her back, which she tossed over her shoulder as she worked.

Fleur.

She set her eyes upon Beth in the mirror and in that moment Beth saw someone else: the child in the cheesecloth dress. There was something there that was distinctly similar. And then it was gone.

"Take a seat," the girl said, smiling charmingly. "I'll be right with you."

Fleur Wishart was the business owner. It was her name brandished everywhere. There were certificates on the walls, dozens of photographs of her cutting hair at what looked like fashion shows and photo shoots. She evidently had done a lot in her young years. And she liked flowers. They were floral designs everywhere – on the walls, on the towels, and fresh flowers at the work stations.

Fleur saw her client out and then turned to Beth.

"So it's just a cut today?" she said, holding her hand to Beth's hair and running it through her fingers.

"Actually," said Beth, flushing, lowering her voice. "This is rather awkward, but…I don't suppose you could step outside for a moment with me? I'll pay you what I was going to pay you for the cut."

Fleur's hand dropped from Beth's hair as though it were live snakes, her eyes instantly closing without actually closing. Where she had been receptive, eager to impress a new client only a moment before, her face was now doll-like, unfeeling.

"Why?" she said.

"I just want a quick chat," said Beth. "If you wouldn't mind."

"What about?" said Fleur, folding her arms tightly around her, by way of self-defence.

Beth recognised Pammy's work when she saw it.

"Pamela Lazenby," she said.

Fleur turned, went to whisper a few words into the red-head's ear, before grabbing a beautiful spearmint shawl and leaving. "It'll cost you forty-five pounds," she said.

"Of course," Beth replied, thinking that despite this girl's enviable elegance, there was no way she would want her near her right now with a pair of sharp scissors.

There was a whitewashed bench next to the canal. On weekends, the canal path was alive with cyclists, tourists, walkers, but today on a quiet Tuesday morning in July there was no one but a pigeon pecking at an abandoned chip.

They sat down on the bench, Fleur sitting as far away as possible. She pulled her shawl around her and fixed her eyes ahead of her.

"How do you know Pammy?" she said.

"She was my foster mum. I know she was yours too," said Beth. "I've been looking for you. There are six of us. I found the others and now I've found you."

"Why were you looking?"

Beth shivered. She wished she was wearing a warm shawl also. Her shoulders were bare and chilly in the morning air.

"Pammy asked me to forgive her. I wanted to know what exactly I needed to forgive, so that I could have a go at it."

"And why would you want to do that?" said Fleur, turning to Beth with a look of bewilderment.

She was, Beth thought, a rather ghostly-looking girl. Her skin was pale and almost transparent, with the veins close to the surface. Yet she was pretty, hauntingly so. Beth wondered whether she had many boyfriends. Certainly men would be interested in her, yet she seemed rather removed from the practicalities of life, as though she would be more interested in dating a medieval knight and since there were few of those around she had given up.

Beth shrugged. "In order to move on."

"Well, I've no intention of moving on," said Fleur, flicking her hair proudly.

"You say that now. You're young. Things may change."

"I highly doubt it."

It occurred to Beth, during these first few minutes of talking to Fleur, that she was looking at herself twenty years ago. The girl, despite her waifishness, was ambitious and angry. Things were much fresher for her – she had been given less time to get over it. Her scars were newer.

She tried to subtly survey Fleur's arms. Fleur's skin was much fairer than hers. As soon as her own arms tanned, her scars appeared – stepping forward to announce themselves: small perfectly formed circles. Fleur's were harder to see, but Beth could just make out the silver marks as the sun caught them, the brandings that proved she belonged to Pammy.

Fleur caught on to what Beth was gazing at and drew her arms underneath her shawl.

"You don't know how important those scars are," said Beth. "They mean that I wasn't the only one – that it wasn't my fault. It wasn't just me. And it means that it did actually happen."

"What are you talking about?" Fleur said. "Of *course* it happened! You think I did this to myself?" She jumped up and held her arms aggressively close to Beth's face.

"Sit back down," Beth said, gently pushing Fleur's arms away. "I understand more than you realise. We've been through the same thing, you and I…That's why I want to help you."

"Help me?" said Fleur, scornfully. "I don't need help! I've cut models' hair, you know." She was still standing up, her hands on her hips. She no longer looked like a delicate maiden, but a petulant schoolgirl. Her lip was curled.

Beth couldn't help herself. She laughed.

Fleur stamped her foot. "You think I'm funny?"

"No," Beth said, shaking her head. "I do not. I'm

impressed with how much you've achieved already. Owning a business isn't a small thing, you know. It's a fantastic achievement. You should be proud."

A solitary seagull circled the air above them, crying softly.

She thought of Peter. He used to say that seagulls reminded him of her when they were apart. He had said that so long ago – twenty years ago, yet still it came to mind.

She felt melancholy, sat there with this stranger who reminded her so much of herself. Fleur was just a child and although Beth knew nothing about her, she could tell that she was rejecting love, was going it alone, was carrying so much anger in her that some days it was hard to breathe. Fleur was just setting out, was about to make the same mistakes that Beth had made. And in twenty years time, she would also be racked with regret.

"As soon as I've got enough money, I'm moving to London to open a designer hair salon called *Fleur's*. There'll be a waiting list for years just for a blow dry. And it'll happen, you know. It's not just talk."

Beth was moved by the girl's passion for her dream. She had a kind soul, Beth sensed. Just a little warped, like a record left out too long in the sunshine. She needed a weight upon her to straighten her out – an anchor, a solid being.

"I don't doubt that you'll fulfil your ambitions, Fleur," she said. "I also moved to London. I'm an academic now. Institutions around the world commission my literary analysis. I'm proud of myself, but I'm terribly lonely."

She looked away, down at her lap. There was a thick trail of glitter on the leg of her jeans; Brett had been playing with glitter glue this morning. You could be surrounded by children – covered with glue and glitter – and still feel lonely, unreached.

"It's not like your life's over. There's plenty of time to meet someone. What are you, like, fifty or something?" said Fleur, sitting back down to Beth – closer this time.

"Something like that," said Beth, smiling.

She gazed at the dark rings under the girl's eyes, and at that moment realised that the similarity between Fleur and the child in the cheesecloth dress was their look of exhaustion.

"You don't sleep well, do you?" said Beth.

Fleur frowned, as though contemplating whether to tell the truth or keep up the act. "I sometimes sleep very well…" she said, flippantly.

"I know what it's like," Beth continued. "You can't bear the dark…"

"Actually, I quite like it when night falls…"

"You don't trust anyone, let alone love anyone. You cry yourself to sleep and the first thing you think when you wake is that you wish you were someone else. Someone with smooth arms without scars. I bet you chose hairdressing because your mission is to make things pretty – perfect again."

Fleur had her hands clasped between her knees, her mouth slightly open. "It's not still like that for you, is it?" she said, after a long pause.

"No." She tapped Fleur's hand reassuringly. "It

gets easier, it really does. To be honest, it was just Pammy's death that—"

"She's dead?" said Fleur. "Wow!" Her eyes glinted devilishly. "I used to fantasise about her dying. And here you are telling me that she's croaked it. I hope it was a horrible slow painful death. Decapitation would have been too kind."

"Stop," said Beth. "I used to think exactly like that, but it's not good for you. You have to let it all go. Love liberates, Fleur. When you feel more love than hate in your heart, you'll be free."

"That's my eleven o'clock," said Fleur, pointing at a blonde lady whose heels were clunking down the barge's gangway.

She stood up, squinting shyly at Beth. They were exactly the same height. "It was nice to meet you. Forget about the forty-five pounds."

"No," said Beth, opening her purse. "I insist…And I always tip."

She pressed the cash into Fleur's hand.

"Let me help you," Beth said.

They had moved to the entrance of the barge. Fleur was eyeing the blonde lady at reception, checking that her punky assistant was seeing to her.

"Pammy left me a lot of money," said Beth, hurriedly. "And I mean a lot. I don't know what to do with it. I don't need it. Why don't you take it?"

Fleur bit her lip. She was still watching the blonde lady, but her head was cocked towards Beth.

"You could use it to set up your business. Somewhere really swish. Just imagine!"

Fleur was imagining it. Her eyes were bright.

"I'll think about it," she said. "I must go."

"Of course." Beth thought quickly. "Do you get a day off, Fleur?"

"Thursdays," she called over her shoulder.

Elias had fallen asleep on his hessian rug, Ruby keeping his bare feet warm, when a sensation washed over him so potently that it stirred his dreams and woke him. He sat up, squinting in the twilight – a blaze of end of day sunshine pouring into his cabin.

He tugged his beard, stroking Ruby's head absently. So Beth had met with Fleur Wishart. He had witnessed it in his sleep. His daughter was at peace. The final piece of the puzzle had clicked satisfyingly into place.

So why the uncomfortable sensation, like a hungry vulture pecking at his insides?

He lit the purple candle and knelt upon the starry rug, where his stone circle was assembled.

Dear Universe, illuminate my mind with knowledge so that my soul may forever be true, he said, before placing his seven oak leaves before him.

The flame of the candle was long. He gazed into its centre, meditating.

Why the unrest? Why the vulture?

He opened his eyes. Nothing had come to him. That had never happened before. What to do now?

He meditated again.

Then slowly he opened his eyes. Nothing needed to come to him – no creature, no visitation of truth –

because it was already here in front of him. The answer had been with him from the beginning.

What was it that was so obvious it failed to meet his eyes?

He looked about him in frustration, before finally staring at the oak leaves.

The seven leaves.

Seven.

Numero, pondera et mensura, he murmured. By number, weight and measure.

It was the deepest belief of his Order. Wren, the druid, had designed St Paul's Cathedral using this principle, had used the number seven to create such sacred geometry that godliness was the result.

If a state of godliness was the desired outcome of a forgiveness quest, then the answer was seven.

He lifted his head upwards, wondering how he would get word to Beth.

She had to know as soon as possible that there were not six of them at all. There were seven.

THE BURNT LOTUS

The sixth child

Fleur Wishart travelled around India when she was eighteen. She spoke to no one unless essential, kept her money and passport in a bag chained to her waist, and travelled lightly so that she could move about unnoticed, unencumbered. Of all the sights that she witnessed, the thing that most struck her was the sight of a pink lotus reaching out of a muddy pond in Dalhousie. She had stared at the lotus for several hours, burning its image into her eyes so that she might always see it. It was still there – beneath her eyelids, ready for her whenever she called for it.

Fleur ate as many lotuses as she could for the remainder of her travels; crunchy roots boiled or fried; leaves used like tortilla wrappers; roasted seeds instead of coffee; petals for soup garnish; tea flavoured with stamens. She picked lotuses, pressing them in tissue paper to preserve them. None of the flowers survived the journey home, but she preserved their remains in a jam jar.

The sacred lotus of India was exquisite yet hardy. It was hermaphroditic, independent. Raised in mud, there were no traces of its rough upbringing on its beautiful body.

To Fleur, it was in every way the most perfect thing that existed on earth.

SEVENTEEN

Clare closed her eyes as she drew on the cigarette, listening to its satisfying crackle. She felt the rush of nicotine to her head and the giddying sensation that followed.

He laughed and took the cigarette back from her. "You're not a smoker," he said.

"I might be," she said, rolling over onto her stomach, pulling the sheets up around her. "Why can't I be?"

She poked him in the ribs. He pushed her hand away and then changed his mind and grabbed it, whilst kissing her firmly. She could taste the cigarette upon his lips, taste the sin and wickedness. It was intoxicating.

The last time she had smoked was on Malahide beach with her gormless boyfriend who somehow managed to blow bubblegum at the same time as kissing her and smoking. She wondered what he was doing now – something multidextrous but brainless, like managing a fruit stall.

She had been thinking a lot about Malahide lately – about her childhood, her parents, her aspirations. She was feeling incredibly young. Affairs did that – brought your youth back, mostly because it was all so fumbly, guilty, naughty: the predominate emotions of her teens, as she recalled.

"I'd better be going," she said, sitting up and grabbing her top.

"Why?" he said, pulling her back down. "There's no rush. Stay a while. I'll put some coffee on."

She considered it. There wasn't much to go home to. The twins had started at The Borough and were playing lacrosse after school today. She had hired a new Bernice, who was stout, plain and annoying – ideally placed to concentrate upon her children's welfare. Work was going well. Peter was…

He was acting as though nothing had happened, as though everything was wonderful between them.

Guilt churned through her. He was trying to make amends and she was lying here. Lying all round, really. Everything was a huge lie.

"I tell you what," she said. "I'll go put the coffee on. You stay here."

"You're an angel."

She smiled tightly, the irony not wasted on her.

In the cool air of the lofty kitchen, she felt strangely as though she were at home but not at home. The room was a replica of her own kitchen, yet how strange it was to be here at midday on a Friday and not at home in her own place, crying at the table, looking for dead sparrows.

She stood at the window, listening to the coffee machine's erratic splutterings, lost in thought.

Suddenly the back door of her house opened and Peter was stood there watering the plants.

She stared at him in horror. What on earth was he doing home?

It happened before she could prevent it.

He turned to water the sunflowers and caught sight of her at the window.

"Oh sweet mother of God," she said, as their eyes met.

Peter attended a breakfast meeting and then bowed out, abandoning his work load until next week. He felt good on the way home, smiling at strangers, giving way to tourists with giant backpacks, not scowling when the doors of the Tube closed on him and he didn't get on and had to wait ten minutes for the next train.

It was going to be hot in London this weekend. The first thing he did when he got home was water the plants to give them a good soaking to see them through.

It was odd that Clare wasn't home. He tried her mobile and left her a message, asking him to call him urgently. There wasn't any rush yet – the flight to JFK wasn't until nine o'clock tonight, but still…He wanted her to have time to pack in a relaxed manner, for them to enjoy the build up, have a glass of champagne in the airport lounge.

He was oddly nervous. He had been preparing in secret all week – ironing his best clothes, stashing them in a holdall in his wardrobe. He was even going to buy her a piece of jewellery, when he considered that maybe she would prefer something from New York to mark the occasion. He wasn't being a moron. He knew they had a lot of wounds to heal, that they probably wouldn't be able to heal most of them. But there was no way that he was going to live a hellish existence. This seemed a sensible way of making the best of things.

Why so nervous though?

He whistled as he filled the watering can, glancing at the clock again.

Where was she? She didn't say that she was going anywhere.

She hadn't said much at all lately. She had withdrawn completely. At first, he thought she was making him work hard as punishment for abandoning her. But the past couple of days he had begun to wonder if there were not more to it. Perhaps that was the course of his nervousness: the sense of unpredictability about the weekend ahead.

When the watering can was full, he lifted it clumsily from the sink, water sloshing all over the floor.

Damn. He would mop it up in a minute.

He unlocked the door and went out into the garden.

He had read once that the feeling of being watched was akin to the powers summoned in black magic and spell-casting. The instinct proved that everyone had psychic abilities and was able to detect negativity.

As he turned to water the sunflowers, the feeling was undeniably strong. It was coming from the window of the house next door. So he looked up.

Reeling in shock, he dropped the can onto the paving stones.

He grappled for the back door handle and dashed through the kitchen, his eyes blind with rage, his heart racing, his brain unable to compose a single thought that made sense.

All he could think was to run next door to smash that bloke's head in. Which was what he would have done, if only he hadn't gone flying over that water on the kitchen floor.

As he lay there in a puddle on the floor, his back throbbing from the fall, his head spinning, his heart heavy, his soul broken, he realised that he had finally reached the end.

Clare opened the front door quietly, her breathing short. She hung her keys up and kicked off her sandals before proceeding down the hallway barefoot.

It was silent. Perhaps he had gone. Just walked out on all the mess. Or perhaps he was crouched somewhere in a dark corner, waiting to attack. He would attack her and then go for her lover.

She walked furtively through the house, her shoulders braced. She was wearing inappropriately ratty denim shorts. Not the best outfit to attempt to defend her honour in.

She was about to run upstairs to change, when she noticed something pinned to the bread board with a vegetable knife.

She entered the kitchen and gasped. He was sat on

the floor with his back to the cupboard where they kept the spirits, a tumbler of whisky in his hand.

"Jesus, you gave me a shock!" she said, clutching her chest.

"I gave *you* a shock," he said.

She pulled the knife out of the board. "Tickets to New York?"

"You and I," he said. "A second honeymoon of sorts. Perhaps you'd like to still go. Take your lover. You've always wanted to go. Don't waste the tickets."

"Don't be so ridiculous," she said.

"I'm serious."

He looked it. His poise was almost eerie.

"Peter..." she said.

He raised his hand. "There's no need, Clare. I understand."

She nearly spluttered in surprise. "You understand?" she said. "Understand what? That I've been sleeping with that guy? That I'm cheap and dishonourable? Is that it? Come on. Tell me what you understand about me. This is your last chance to prove to me that you actually know anything about me."

She was looming over him, hands on hips.

When he didn't reply, she felt like kicking him. Instead, she reached for the bottle, unscrewed it and took a swig, as though she had no dignity left whatsoever.

"Just look at you," he said. His voice was so quiet, she had to strain to listen. "You're so aggressive. So ready to fight at the slightest chance. Well, you don't need to fight me any more. You've won."

"Won what? What exactly is the prize?"

"You tell me."

He poured himself a generous second helping of whisky and ran his fingers through his hair. There was something different about him which she couldn't quite determine. She narrowed her eyes, wondering what he was playing at.

"I'll file for divorce," he said. "We can keep it civil. I'd like official visiting rights, but there's nothing else. I'll help maintain the girls' educational costs and anything else that needs tending to."

"I see," she said.

She was trying to suppress her customary anger — the feeling that she would kill him if she had a weapon to hand.

His demeanour was infuriating. Where was his fight? His male pride? Why didn't he want to know all the messy details? Why wasn't he round there, kicking her lover's door down? Wasn't that what cuckolded men did?

No, she realised. It was what cuckolded men did when they gave a hoot.

Peter's head began to throb half way through the conversation. Not that it was a conversation. He was simply telling her what they were going to do and she was glaring at him with her eyes of fury.

"You're a limp lettuce," she was saying, prodding him with her foot, kicking at him with little sharp movements as though trying to rouse a sleeping bear. "That's your problem."

"My problem," he said, rising slowly, the seat of his trousers still wet, "is that I married you even though I knew you lied about being pregnant."

She opened her mouth to reply and shut it again so quickly that he heard her teeth snap together. She only needed a moment to recover. "Like I said, you're a limp lettuce," she said. "Why else would you have done that, hey? What sane person–?"

"I was flattered that you were so desperate to marry me, all right?" he said. "Now let's stop this because I've got a headache. I'm not going to take the bait, Clare."

He put his glass in the dishwasher, stooping stiffly. His back was sore from his fall. He left the kitchen and as he climbed the stairs, to his surprise a tear trickled from his eye.

He took refuge in the girls' room, looking about the den of pinkness. He wouldn't live with them any more, wouldn't know all the details of their lives.

He clenched his hands into fists and pressed them to his eyes to ward off tears.

"I'm so sorry, Peeder," said Clare, appearing in the doorway. "I'm so sorry about New York. I'm so sorry about cheating." She crossed the carpet towards him, kneeling at his feet. "I didn't mean to cause you so much pain."

"Oh!" he said, his voice brightening. He laughed. "You think I'm crying over you? Good grief, no!"

He pushed past her to leave the room. "And nor is it over the girls, because I intend to keep them in my life no matter what you do to put a wedge between us."

"Then who are you crying over?" she snarled, pursuing him through to their bedroom.

He was looking about for things to pack. He had

only just unpacked from being at his mum's. It wouldn't take long to reassemble his few possessions. He had lost so many of them over the years: his clay Zulu hut from Johannesburg, his Chelsea baseball cap, even his golf clubs. He hadn't noticed them disappearing. He just went to find them from time to time, and they were gone; to the tip, rotting on a landfill, or residing in the corner of a charity shop if Clare was feeling conscientious at the time.

He smirked at his wife in reply to her question. He didn't mean to hurt her so deeply, but he felt the need to finally sting her back.

"No!" she said, shaking her head. "*Don't* say her name! *Don't* say her bleeding name! I swear, I'll kill you if you say it. I'll kill you!"

Her fists were shaking, she was stamping her foot, she was jumping up and down in her tight shorts. Rumpelstiltskin, he thought.

"Beth," he said.

And then he ducked to miss his school football team photograph, which was shuttling through the air towards his head with the force of an Olympic discus.

The photograph smashed against the wall. He pulled the picture from the frame carefully, brushing the shards of glass off. She could clean up the mess, or the cleaner could. He pushed the photograph into his back pocket.

When he turned back to look at her, a change had come over her. She was looking ashen. "I always knew," she said. "I knew all along that you loved her."

Sympathy soared through him. He couldn't leave her like this.

In fairness, he should have told her his intentions – that he wasn't going to be with Beth, that there was too much damage done on that front, that Beth was too mistrustful to ever get past it. But his desire to retaliate was still strong. He couldn't appease her that easily.

Yet he had to offer her something. She looked utterly vanquished.

He gazed at his wife, at her freckled skin, her green eyes, and tried to remember a time when he had loved her. He recalled holding hands with her on Monet's bridge in Giverny – how she wanted to stay there forever, leaning over the side to look at the lilies. That was the memory that he would store, the one that he would rely upon to soften his tone during the troubled times ahead. He still needed her, needed her to comply with his wishes regarding their children.

It was Giverny that enabled him to surrender. He sat down on the bed and rested an arm on her shoulder. "Clare," he said, gently.

She took one look at him and slapped his cheek with all her might.

"I'll be off then..." he said, standing up.

Beth once borrowed a book from Pengilly library about cracking codes. Aged eight – the year she ran away – she became consumed with trying to work out when Pammy hurt her and why. She read the code book in bed by torchlight underneath her scratchy blankets. If she knew when Pammy was going to attack, she could avoid it.

Pammy was a tapper. She was constantly tapping

her cigarette lighter, drumming her nails, jigging her knee up and down. Beth thought there was a meaning in it – a code to decipher.

When the coding idea didn't work, she turned to amateur psychology: a book called *The Way We Think* with a squidgy orange brain on the front.

Then she read in Reader's Digest that people turned to violence as a cry for help, so she offered to mop the floor and hang out the laundry. If Pammy needed help, Beth would help her. On mother's day, she made Pammy a card with pasta stuck to the front and picked her a bunch of wild daffodils from the pony paddock.

Then one hot Sunday afternoon she sat down with Pammy to watch *The Great Escape* and an utterly different solution presented itself to her...

Film Sundays at Pammy's were misty, damp days. The rain lashed down on the Pengilly pavements and then the sun would come out in a blaze, the moisture rising in a sheet of steam. Pengilly was a place of dragons and demons – steam, ash, pain, a chapel opposite with a bell that rang plaintively.

The windows inside Yew Tree Cottage were permanently steamed up on Sundays. It was the one day of the week that Pammy cooked. She called it a roast but nothing was roasted. Cabbage stewed to transparency, sludgy mash, sprouts struggling for survival in a tide of gravy, grey sausages that dissolved in the mouth. Beth was grateful though – especially for the stewed apples and custard, because during the week her meals came from cans. Pammy's larder was devoted to canned meals. When you pulled open the door and the instant light popped on and hummed, the effect was shrine-like. "Choose yourself something nice, Princess," Pammy would say, poking Beth in the back.

Pammy had a tartan shopping trolley, Terry, which she wheeled to the village store on Thursdays to collect her pre-ordered cans. The back wheel wobbled precariously and squeaked, but somehow it kept going. When Beth recently visited the cottage, the trolley was still there by the back door, like a dog waiting for its master to return.

Pammy didn't like talking. When the afternoon film ended on Sundays, she wouldn't turn to Beth and say, *well, that was nice, did you enjoy it?* She just got up slowly, her knees clicking and turned the television set off, leaving Beth staring at the screen with all its nice people and adventures getting smaller until it was a tiny dot that went *puff.* This sensation – of the world departing, of finality and ending – made Beth's stomach churn with aloneness.

Sometimes Beth tried to start a conversation, but Pammy gestured her out of the way with her mop, Cyril. Pammy enjoyed talking to herself more than anyone else – inaudible mutterings that Beth tried to hear but couldn't. There was an unmistakable air of secrecy about Pammy that made Beth want to tie her up and threaten to throw all her cigarettes and cans into the sea if she didn't tell her what it was. For a child with an imagination, the intrigue alone would have been torture enough.

Those cigarettes. Beth hated them more than Pammy. Without them, Pammy wouldn't have been able to hurt her.

In the early days, she just stuck out her arm and took the pain because she deserved it. But the summer of

The Great Escape, she began to fight back. A skinny eight-year-old was no match for Pammy, who was also some kind of martial arts expert, Beth suspected. Perhaps she worked for the government, or was a Russian spy.

Pammy evolved with time, moving up the arms to the shoulders where less people would see. She told Beth that if she ever told anyone she would have her guts for garters – one of her threats which meant nothing to Beth, since she had no idea what a garter was, let alone how her guts would become one.

Beth did tell someone. One soggy Sunday, she crept out to the chapel to seek help. Her shoulder was sore. It was the first time she had entered a church.

It was wonderfully cool inside. There were candles lit, flickering against the shadowy walls. Her eyes widened. All along this marvellous place had been just there! The reverend was in a back room, sat at a desk. He motioned Beth forward. She told him about Pammy, showed him her shoulder. He sat quietly, tapping his pen, becoming visibly angrier. She was enthralled – he was going to go over there and wear *Pammy's* guts for garters himself. That would show her! But to her alarm, he jumped up, grabbed her by the strap of her dress and pushed her back out into the steamy afternoon, telling her never to come into God's Own House again and tell such wicked lies.

She had stood staring at the closed chapel door – banished from its cool interior, before retreating to the bench that overlooked the sea. She watched the sun descending, but didn't feel the day grow chilly. She just swung her legs to and fro, listening to the waves hissing on the pebbled shore.

Pammy adored her horses. She named all her favourite inanimate objects. She was affectionate towards anything that couldn't talk back, so Beth had deduced.

It was the only code that she ever broke about her.

Beth was sitting on the mooring platform, swinging her legs, gazing at the smooth surface of the canal. She was feeling better than she could remember feeling before – lighter, unburdened.

Perhaps this, she thought, was what forgiveness felt like.

She was at the end of the path. With the facts in front of her and no dead bodies at the bottom of the ocean to uncover, there was nothing to stop her from walking away from the past. Apart from one little thing: Fleur.

It mattered immensely to Beth that Fleur realised her goals. If that young woman was a success, if she overcame her troubles then everything would be undone. Their scars would be as meaningless as freckles.

She identified with Fleur. When you came from the same backgrounds, you were prone to comparisons. It was what made school reunions potentially so toxic and what made meeting old university friends sometimes so demoralising. Fleur was Pammy's product, just as Beth was. If Fleur was broken, the whole batch was.

So Fleur had to have the inheritance money.

Danny was fighting her over it. She explained that it was just an idea, that the cottage hadn't been sold so there wasn't even any money yet to give.

She would have to work on him. Perhaps when he met Fleur he would be won over. She was wonderfully easy on the eye.

She would invite Fleur for tea one evening. She could see her here at Lilyvale, floating about by the water.

Perhaps the money might bond them, make them almost family. They shared the same foster mother after all. They didn't have to be in each other's lives, living on top of each other. Just knowing that they both existed, shared the same past and were thriving, would be enough.

The other little girl in Beth's life – the child in the cheesecloth dress – had vanished. She had served her purpose. Which was what? To lead Beth to Fleur, the sixth child?

She would probably never see the child again, would never fully understand her secret. Yet she had found Fleur. And that felt more important now.

She sighed, watching a dragonfly skimming across the still water, and thought of her father. He had brought her peace.

Yes. This was what forgiveness felt like.

The new girl next to him in physics, who only wore cashmere because it was so soft, had to do that because her brain was so soft too. Danny sat opposite her in the school canteen and she said that she ate only green food because it was low in calories. On her plate were peas, celery and a green apple. He immediately scraped back his chair and took his tray to another table, one where people were eating sausages, chips and doughnuts, and wearing polyester.

He hated to admit it, but he missed Angel. When he was with her, she had seemed disconnected, unreal – part of the green food eating club, in a way. Yet now that they were apart, he was beginning to feel as though her world was the only true one; that being on a barge with Elias, star-gazing, cloud-watching, was a far better use of time than sitting through an afternoon of German grammar.

His mum had cheered up since meeting Elias. Not just because it was her father, but because he had opened her eyes to things other than domestic arrangements and literature. He had taught her to look about her – to look outside of herself to the world around her, and she was better for it. She was teetering without him though – edging back towards that cliff that she liked hanging out on.

It was all because of this Fleur woman. Danny didn't like the sound of her. And now his mum was talking about giving all the money to her.

He didn't want the money for himself. He didn't agree with keeping the money, but he could see a better use for it than throwing it all at a floating hairdresser.

One night after dinner, he took his Silverfox Demon out for a ride along the canal. It was important to exercise his legs as much as possible, as the season was beginning in four weeks. Four weeks until he would be under those floodlights again!

It was nine miles to Bradford-on-Avon. He cycled as fast as he could. There were few walkers at this time of evening. He didn't look at the scenery. He put his head down and pedalled fast, his T-shirt sticking to his back, his mouth shut against the dusk-crazy flies.

He came to the barge. It wasn't hard to spot it – the name Fleur Wishart painted on the side, surrounded by lotuses. No wonder Skye had noticed it. It looked like the sort of place Skye and Angel would like – wishy-washy, away with the fairies. Why would anyone want their hair cut by someone who was scared of sharp edges?

He couldn't really see anything. He couldn't get close to the windows to press his nose against the glass, and the front door was bolted.

He was disappointed. What was he expecting though? An interview?

He felt a bit guilty, snooping around. His mum had been here only a few days ago – had been happy to be here, to find a friend, to help her through her past. Happy to use the money for a good cause.

He turned his bike around, facing back the way he came. It wasn't for him to get involved. It was her money, her past, her friend.

Sitting with his foot on the pedal, about to push off, he noticed something out of the corner of his eye. A movement at the window, a flicker at the curtain, and then it was gone. Was someone on the barge, watching him?

He glanced up at the roof of the barge. One big fat crow was stood there, staring at him. The crow opened its beak and began to chatter loudly, still staring at Danny.

"Jeepers creepers," he said, pedalling off, back to Bath.

EIGHTEEN

Elias was pondering an odd cloud formation when Skye came to him and said, "I want a meeting."

"A meeting?" he said, distractedly. The clouds were like giant grey bubbles. He had seen them only once before, hence their name – the lesser-spotted mammatus. It meant one thing: that a heavy thunderstorm was coming. Each bubble contained a vast quantity of water.

"Of course," he said, still gazing upwards. Ruby wouldn't like a storm of that magnitude. She howled at thunder.

"Now?" she said.

When he got downstairs, Skye and Angel were seated at the table, waiting for him. He would have to put the sausages on soon. Spicy bratwurst, his favourite. The girls didn't like them, but Ruby did and was looking so frail the past week that he wanted to perk her up.

"I've called this meeting," said Skye, with disarmingly new authority, "because I want to tell Angel something, with you as my witness."

He bowed his head solemnly. "As you wish." He eyed the kettle on the stove. "Would you mind if I–?" he said, edging towards it.

"I'd rather you didn't," she replied.

"Quite." He took a seat and sat with his hands forming a temple, wondering what on earth could be so important that it interrupted his analysis of the mammatus and his five o'clock cup of camomile.

"I realise that you have dedicated quite some time to finding a cure for Angel," said Skye.

She wasn't twitching or using any props as distraction. She was sat upright, completely still, her eyes fixed upon her daughter in order to detect the first signs of reaction.

"In truth, it's a pointless task…Because it was me." She blew out heavily and dropped her shoulders. "There, I've said it."

"You," said Elias, flatly.

Would she be cross if he at least unwrapped the Bratwurst to let them breathe a little?

"Me." She nodded.

He glanced at Angel, who was trying not to smile. It was the oddest meeting he had ever participated in, and there had been some highly odd gatherings over the years – some involving nudity.

"I've never told you about my roots," Skye said. "My parents were heavily influenced by Aleister Crowley. You'll have heard of him."

"Aye," said Elias. "*The Great Beast.*"

"The very same," said Skye. "Well, my parents

believed in what he preached – that drugs and alcohol were a way to achieve a higher state, a door into a world of magic that couldn't be accessed sober." She shrugged. "That was my world too. Only natural, when I didn't know any different."

"Quite," said Elias.

The Bratwurst seemed out of the picture now. Ruby lifted her head mournfully from her basket in front of the stove, licked her chops and flopped back down. Sorry old girl.

"I was raised amongst travellers, amongst drugs and alcohol. I didn't even know I was expecting a baby…"

Elias raised his hand to reassure her of her acceptance. "You sit amongst friends."

Angel was still smiling. Most unusual. Her hair was braided. She was so innocent and yet appeared less so having met Danny. She had secrets now, little thoughts and longings that made her look away from them often.

"When Angel's silence came to light, I took her to a doctor."

"Oh?" said Elias, turning to look at Skye.

He understood clouds, stars and animals, but not women. Why would she have him do all his research, agonising over a solution, when all along she had withheld information?

"He said that a baby's throat and vocal cords were developed in the uterus. Harmful substances consumed during pregnancy could very well result in muteness." Skye closed her eyes.

Angel pulled her notepad from her dress pocket, scribbled something down and then knocked on the table to get her mother's attention.

It's okay, Mum.

Skye placed her hand on top of her daughter's hand and kept it there.

They remained like that the entire time that Elias fried the Bratwurst. Even Ruby, animated by the aromatic spices, moved more than they did.

That was what Angel was here for, Elias considered. Had she been different, Skye's torture would have been eternal.

But Angel was like her namesake, brought to earth to remind them all how utterly simple forgiveness could be.

That night, the storm came. Elias was a long time finding sleep. The rain was lashing against the barge roof, Ruby was moaning softly at the lightening – too old now for howling. She lay next to him on his bed, a paw over her eyes.

Elias's dreams were mixed – dark long grass blowing wildly, a house on its own on a hill, a rabbit running on its own down the middle of a road.

He thrashed about, restlessly.

Until Brighid, the goddess, stepped forward through the darkness, her magnificent cloak spread out behind her; Brighid, whom he had summoned thirty-nine years ago to protect his new baby.

May no Being of this World or the Next harm thee. May no evil hand disturb thy sleep or wakefulness.

He was just reaching out to Brighid, kneeling before her to enlist her continued support, when she changed into Vivien.

It wasn't the pig-tailed Vivi that he had known in Pentruthen Bay, but a middle-aged woman with flowing grey hair and a brow that was lined with years of anguish and remorse.

Is that you, Vivi?

He got to his feet and reached for her hand. They held hands and she cupped her other hand around his.

Elias, she said. She had changed – grown meek, but dignified. *You must help our child. You must bring him to her. When the first snow falls on the day of Imbolc, he will come. Make it so, Elias. Make it so.*

Vivi, he said. *Please don't go.*

She was fading away.

Come back, Vivi.

Elias woke with a start. To his surprise, his beard was wet. It was a long while since he had been moved to tears.

Moving Ruby gently aside, he reached for his gown. It was four o'clock in the morning. The perfect time to commence.

From his oak trunk, he removed a green candle, oil and a knife. Breathing deeply and peacefully, he began to carve the rune of Gyfu, meaning love and forgiveness. All over the candle, from the bottom upwards he carved the symbol.

The feast of Imbolc would fall on the first day of February. The first snow would fall then and the snowdrops would burst upwards to adorn the earth. It was the time of the growing of the Light, the time when the Child of Light – the sun – would grow stronger again through the Darkness.

As he lit the candle, he sensed a spirit moving towards him through the shadows.

He felt Vivi beside him as he worked.

Together they chanted softly. *May my life be filled with eternal love. May love radiate through me for all the days of my life, from each sun rise to each sun set.*

Brighid was with him too. They held hands around the candle, around the circle of stones. It was Brighid who had protected the sun through winter, so that she could bring it forward to nurture and bless the earth once more.

When the first snow falls on the day of Imbolc, on the first day of the growing Light, he will come.

Together the three of them chanted until the sun rose, setting the earth ablaze.

Beth rose early in a state of excitement. She hurried the boys around the house, chasing them out the door for school. Brett was dressed as a pirate for fancy dress day. She gave him an extra cuddle at the door of preschool and held onto his hand for longer than usual. Today felt monumental, every gesture weighted with importance. She kissed him, smoothed his hair and told him to go chop up some crocodiles.

Erland was doing the high jump later at school sports day, so she and Brett were going to cheer him on. He didn't excel at sport, but his older brother's reputation raised Erland head and shoulders above his peers, as though carried by the hands of invisible fans. And yet he was rather good at the high jump – a burst of energy, a sudden lunge, a flash of long legs and it was over. Danny held the school record for the one hundred and two hundred metres sprint. *No sweat,* he said at breakfast, with a mouthful of Weetabix. Erland meanwhile was struggling to keep his Ready Brek down.

As she drove to Bradford-on-Avon, she thought about the boys' futures. Giving Fleur the money could be seen as prioritising a stranger's needs over her boys'. But she didn't want Pammy's money. And yet…if she had truly forgiven Pammy, surely the money could only be seen as a good thing?

So her thoughts went. In truth she was merely forming arguments in order to solidify the decision that she had already made, a decision that she had made the moment she saw Fleur.

She parked in the car park and ambled to the barge, as she was a few minutes ahead of the time they had agreed upon.

Fleur was hesitant to meet again, which was disappointing. But Beth had pressed on undeterred, gently persuading Fleur to join her for a stroll on her day off.

Taking a seat on the whitewashed bench near the salon, she ran through what they would do. She only had a few hours before collecting Brett. They would walk along the canal to the café with the rainbow-coloured seats outside. There would be just enough time for a coffee, before heading back. Perfect. The sun was even beginning to make an appearance through the clouds.

Where was she? Beth glanced at her watch. Five minutes late.

Beth would have to help Fleur handle the money, to ensure that she invested it wisely. The money would be given with the proviso that it had to be used for setting up the business. Beth wasn't sure if she could legally state that, but she would look into it.

Where on earth was Fleur? She was now fifteen minutes late.

There came the sound of a hairdryer from within the salon.

Beth rose from the bench. They had arranged to meet outside, but Fleur could well be caught up doing something on board.

As she pushed open the salon door, the sun went in. Beth felt a large drop of rain splash onto her shoulder.

As soon as Danny had got home from his cycle ride to Bradford-on-Avon he consulted his grandmother's grimoire, but it told him nothing. She was a bad druid. The grimoire contained nothing but abstract doodles and a few texts in what looked an attempt at writing symbols in Ogham.

Useless. He hid the grimoire back under the floorboards, before deciding to pack it in his rucksack. He would take another look during morning break, in case he had missed something. There was something about that barge – about Fleur, about all of this – that was bugging him.

During chemistry, Danny pulled the grimoire from his bag and sat looking at it on his lap. His teacher was one of those wacky old types who was more interested in talking about the periodic table than wondering whether any of her pupils were listening or even still sat there.

He turned each page carefully, studying the

doodles. His grandmother liked writing poems – bad ones – and using exclamation marks; nearly all her sentences ended with one. Her handwriting was large, uneven, exuberant. How different from his mother's controlled concise style, he thought.

He found what he was looking for at the back of the grimoire.

Vivien, in an apparently rare fit of sobriety and studiousness, had decided to write down as many druid animal lores as possible. There seemed to be no particular order to the list, but it went on for several pages – heavily punctuated with the exclamation mark.

Danny ran his finger down the page: *Fox! Salmon! Bear! Stag! Owl! Rabbit!*

Until he came to: *Crow!*

That was it! The crow that was sat on the barge last night. That was what was bugging him.

He stared at his grandmother's writing, reading it and rereading it until the words blurred on the page.

She was talking to him. Vivi, with her wild exclamations, her random scrawlings, was telling him something across the years. And it was pretty clear.

A crow on the thatch, soon death lifts the latch!

There were two clients sat in the reception, flicking through magazines. They glanced at Beth as she walked in. She brushed raindrops from her shoulders. There was a terrible thunderstorm last night, the worst one she had seen. She had thought about Elias on his barge, wondering if he was safe. Funny that Fleur also worked on a barge. Everything was connected, Elias believed.

"Can I help you?" said the red-haired girl over her shoulder to Beth, whilst leading a client to the sink. Beyond her, a woman dressed in a tight black and white striped dress was cutting hair, her hip dropped to one side. She would be a senior stylist, called something like Siobhan or Geneva.

"I'm here to meet Fleur," said Beth. "Is she here?"

"It's her day off." The girl began to wash her client's hair with a shower head, squinting away from the spray.

"I know, but…"

"Water warm enough for you, ma'am?"

"Perhaps I can wait in your reception then," said Beth. "Seeing as it's raining."

"What? Yeah. Fine." The girl was shampooing now.

Beth sat in the reception, listening to the rain rattling the roof, splattering on the canal water. It was rather soothing. She closed her eyes, thinking that this was the sound her father heard of an evening when a storm came.

When half an hour had passed, Beth rose. She couldn't hang about any longer.

"You still here?" the red-haired girl said, looking at Beth sympathetically. "What was it you wanted again?"

"Fleur," said Beth.

"Because…?"

"We had a business matter to discuss."

"Business…Right." The girl smirked and disappeared behind a bead curtain. Beth watched the beads swaying. Moments later, a kettle began to wheeze.

Siobhan or Geneva strutted out to scribble in the appointments book, jigging her bottom to the radio, tapping her bejewelled nails. Beth eyed her, wondering why Fleur would have chosen to hire her. They seemed so ill-matched.

The girl returned with a mug of tea and sat down at the counter.

"Why did you laugh when I mentioned discussing business with Fleur?" said Beth. She knew it was unfair to push this daft girl, but there was something here that wasn't right.

The girl blushed. "I didn't mean any harm. It's just…" She glanced across the salon to the woman in the stripy dress. "Nothing gets discussed without running it past Kimberley and Keith."

"Is that Kimberley?" said Beth, following the girl's line of vision.

"Yeah."

"And who's Keith?"

"Her brother."

"But Fleur owns the salon?"

The girl almost spat out her mouthful of tea. "She told you that? Yeah, right! Fleur couldn't own a cardigan!"

Beth felt her heart quicken, her blood rise. Her ears were hissing like the sea hitting the sand. She put her hand on the counter to steady herself.

"What about the branding?" she said. "It's her name on the boat. There are photos of her everywhere."

"So? Kimberley liked Fleur's name, liked her look. She's the image, as it were. It's part of the deal."

"The deal?"

"It's weird," said the girl, her eyes gleaming with the anticipation of gossip, "'cos she lives with her brother. He's well into his forties." She lowered her voice. "And he's no looker. I find him a bit creepy, like." She bent closer. "He's got dandruff," she whispered.

"Kimberley lives with him?"

"No. *Fleur!*"

Beth hurried to the address that the girl had given her. She went by foot. Bradford-on-Avon was small. It was the old house with the palm tree in the front garden, right on the high street, the girl said. Beth knew exactly the one she meant. She had driven by before, wondering why a palm tree was plonked outside in such a cramped garden, overshadowing the windows.

She stood outside, wondering the same thing now, wondering what else was blocking the light here – what else was stopping anything inside from growing naturally.

Why was Fleur living with a creepy man and working for that tacky woman?

She ran through their conversation last week. Fleur hadn't said that she owned the business; Beth had. And Fleur hadn't corrected her. Why not?

As she knocked on the door, she found herself looking upwards to the sky – to the God whom she didn't believe in.

Please let her be here. Please let her be here.

The door opened. She felt her shoulders drop with relief.

But it wasn't Fleur.

She knew exactly who it was. "Who the hell are

you?" he said. He was unshaven, gangly, repulsive.

Behind him were several police officers and men in raincoats holding clipboards, crackling radios, briefcases.

"I'm here to see Fleur," Beth said.

"You'll be lucky," he said. He turned his back on her and walked off.

"Can I help you?" said a police officer.

"I'm meant to be meeting Fleur. She didn't show up." She strained her neck to look beyond the officer into the hallway.

"What is your connection with her?"

"We're...We had the same foster mother. Is she—?"

"You'd better come in a moment."

Beth stepped into the front room. It smelt damp. There was no light, no decor to speak of. What sort of place was this? Mouldy, barren.

A man in a long brown coat entered the room. Beth wondered at him wearing such a heavy coat in summer. "Detective Barnes," he said, holding out his hand.

Beth didn't take his hand. She was staring at the only ornament in the room: a photograph of Fleur on the mantelpiece. She moved forward to inspect it. Fleur looked much younger. She was stood in front of a muddy pond. There was a shack in the background. Evidently, she was abroad. She was pointing at the pond, smiling widely. There was something in the water; Beth drew the picture closer to see. She couldn't make it out. Something pink.

She felt a hand on her shoulder. "Madam, Fleur was found unconscious at two o'clock this morning. She passed away at four o'clock. The hospital staff did their best. We're investigating, but it's clear—"

"Can I take this?" she said.

The detective frowned at the photograph in her hands. "That's not my—"

"Take it," said a voice behind him. The gangly man had entered the room.

"Were you expecting this to happen?" she said, approaching him.

"No," he said. Beth eyeballed him – imagined him touching Fleur, crawling over her at night. She wanted to grab him by the throat – shake his neck until it snapped. Fleur was just a child – a vulnerable, abused child.

Her mouth twitched. She inhaled. She thought of Brett in his pirate outfit, of Erland doing high jump, of Danny sprinting. She bolted her knees, clenched her jaw, held herself together for them.

"Was there a note?" she said.

The man blinked rapidly, overcome. The detective answered for him. From his case, he handed Beth a clear plastic wallet. Inside was a piece of paper ripped from a note pad.

Love liberates.

That was all it said.

"Does that mean anything to you?" said the detective.

"I…" She felt her hands tremble. "I think I said something of the sort to her the other day."

"Oh?" said the detective. "Then we need to question you, Mrs…?"

"Miss Trelawney," said Beth. "And question me now. I don't want to be brought in for any questions. Ask me now."

She sat down on the sofa, wishing that her father were beside her.

Beth left the house as the rain stopped. She walked to the car park, not noticing the puddles as she stepped in them, soaking her pumps.

She got into the car and drove back to Bath, her feet squelching on the pedals.

She collected Brett; he was the last child there. She installed him in front of the television and climbed the stairs to her bedroom.

Only when she was safely underneath the bed covers did she allow herself to cry. And it was then that she felt it: the little tugging sensation inside as her heart broke.

NINETEEN

Beth could remember a radio interview she had listened to at university twenty years ago. The lady being interviewed was working with starving children in Africa. On Christmas Day, she had given one of the children a piece of Christmas cake, thinking it a kind gesture. Yet the richness of the food killed the child.

Beth remembered the interview because she had never heard anything so sad.

Until now.

Beth's clumsy financial proposal was the Christmas cake that killed Fleur.

"No, it wasn't," said Danny.

It was a warm Saturday. Beth had pumped up the paddling pool for Brett, who was splashing about with his plastic dinosaurs. Erland was at a friend's house. Danny was lying on the grass, listening to the radio, chewing gum.

"Well, I certainly did something because she quoted me in her suicide note."

He sat up. He pulled his shirt off, his fringe sticking up. It slowly flopped back down, like air out of a cushion. "Mum, she would have done the deed anyway, no matter what you had said."

"How can you possibly say that?"

"Because if someone came up to me and said love liberates, I would say – hey, cool phrase. I like it. I wouldn't think – now I need to go and top myself."

She watched Brett playing, noticing that he was holding a red dinosaur in one hand and a blue one in the other. He liked red and blue. Simple choices. He would always be that way, she would bet. People didn't change.

"I should have found her sooner," she said. "She needed help."

"But you didn't even know she existed until the other day!"

"Yes...I wonder why Pammy covered it up."

"Perhaps she didn't," said Danny, laying his shirt on the grass and lying back down on it. He put his arms behind his head. "Maybe she just forgot. She was probably out of it on morphine at the prison."

"The idea of the money must have scared Fleur to death – literally. She must have been petrified that she wasn't worth it, that she couldn't step up to the task of making something of herself."

He sat up again. "Jeez, Mum – will you listen to yourself? It's not your bloody fault!"

"Shush!" She frowned at him and gestured at Brett, who had stopped splashing and was listening to their conversation.

"Jeez, Mum," said Brett. "Cheese, Mum. Jeezy,

cheesy."

She looked away, at the adjourning countryside, at the hills on the other side of the valley, trying to distract herself. But her mind kept returning to the same thoughts.

The detective had deftly established that her involvement in the case was limited, even given the nature of the suicide note. Fleur had seized upon an idea, he said – an idea that she could just as well have read on the cover of a magazine, as have heard it from Beth, a virtual stranger.

Poor Fleur. Dead, just like that, without a soul in the world to hold her hand, to rescue her. Not like Pammy, with the reverend at her side.

"I hold Pammy accountable," she said, quietly. "Fleur went to her as a baby – putting all her faith in her foster parent. She never knew anything but misery and pain. Pammy did this to her, as sure as if she'd bought the pills and put them to Fleur's lips."

Danny didn't reply. She thought for a moment that he was sleep, but then he spoke.

"No, Mum," he said. "Fleur did it. No one else. Just Fleur. She couldn't heal, couldn't put it behind her. Some people can, some can't. That's all." He shrugged and started chewing again.

She gazed at him – at his perfect form, his tanned muscular limbs. He was so privileged. What did he know of healing, of putting things behind him?

Perhaps more than she realised, she thought.

"Her biological parents might have been nutters," he said. "This might have been her fate, fostered or not. Pammy can't be blamed for everything for all of eternity."

He was right.

But poor sweet Fleur.

Brett climbed out of the pool and onto her lap. She didn't have the heart to shoo him away. She felt the water from his trunks seeping into her skirt. Yet she kissed his forehead and held him, tickling his toes.

"You know what?" she said. "I think Pammy only hurt Fleur and I because out of the six of us, we had the most going for us – the most hope to lose."

"Could be," said Danny. "You'll never know." He flicked away a fly from his chest. "But one thing's for certain…This winter there's one thing you won't be making."

"Oh? And what's that?" she said.

"Christmas cake."

The surprising thing was that Beth's vision returned to her during the week of Fleur's death.

The child crept out from her hiding place behind the wardrobe, startling Beth, who had grown accustomed to stillness again, with nothing sharing the evening air with her except for crane flies and moths.

Beth turned away from the child, told her to go away, to never come back, that it was all over. Yet she just stood there patiently at the bottom of the bed, reaching out her hand.

She finally gave in and rang Elias. She wanted to talk to him about Fleur.

He listened carefully to her account.

"And thus it was written," was all he said in response.

"Oh," she said.

"You are disappointed by my response?" he replied. "I am sorry to hear about that child. But you must not let this tragedy distract you and set you off course. Healing is your goal. You must keep peace at your core. Do you understand?"

"Yes," she said, feeling a pang of guilt. Fleur was to be swept away, just another little autumn leaf that had been shed back to the earth.

"Incidentally, I will be at Stanton Drew for the spring equinox – *the light of the earth* – if Daniel is interested," Elias said.

"I'll mention it to him. I'm not sure if he'll want to go…" She smiled in recollection of Danny's glum account of the solstice. "But does that mean you'll be–?"

"At the bottom of your garden, if you will have us," he replied.

"Of course," she said.

Danny was flapping his arms to get her attention. "Are they coming back?" he whispered.

"Are the girls all right?" asked Beth.

"In perfect health," Elias replied.

"Will they be remaining with you for the time being?" she said.

"For the foreseeable future," he said.

She nodded 'yes' to Danny, who tried not to smile in response.

She was just about to hang up, when she heard Elias calling out her name.

"I almost forgot," he said. "I wanted to tell you something important…There are seven of you. Not six."

Beth felt the old sensation of anxiety stir her. How could there be seven of them? Surely she had found everyone?

Enough. It was over.

"Thank you," she said. "But I'm not interested. As far as I'm concerned, there are six of us – *were* six of us. It's over now."

"Not interested?" said Elias.

"Nothing must send me off course, remember?"

"But that's just it, my child," he said. "Finding the seventh person *is* your course."

It was their first Christmas at Lilyvale. Beth decided to go for a rustic style of decor in honour of absent but ever-present Elias. For the tree and to decorate the walls, she made garlands from felt and gingham. Tiny hessian angels sat on the mantelpieces; felt hearts on ribbon trailed the stairs, and she arranged fairy lights in the fireplaces and around the walls.

She walked alone each morning along the canal path after dropping off Brett, watching her breath before her, trying to ignore her aloneness, busying herself with planning Christmas, with collecting holly and mistletoe from the hedgerows. The canal was eerily still; comforting wisps of chimney smoke escaped above the branches of the lifeless trees reminding her that it was not a barren landscape.

She was aware of each passing season so much more now than before – even more than her days with Apples in Pengilly, when she had spent so much time outdoors. It was due to Elias's teachings. And so she honoured him by collecting as much of his revered mistletoe as possible. *Gather it from oaks on the sixth day of the new moon*, he had told her. Mistletoe had magical healing properties, although it was poisonous. Could something be both, she wondered?

Erland wanted to cook on Christmas Day: Madeira and blueberry duck, followed by pavlova. Beth was just seeing to the drinks. She had made a mild mulled ale, and cinnamon apple punch for the boys.

She sat at the table, looking with satisfaction at the holly and mistletoe, the angels and hearts, the candlelight flickering – and at her three unexpected guests.

It was a last minute arrangement. One phone call was all it took. It had suddenly come to her to invite them, as she was hanging her mistletoe garland on the door.

And now Jacko, his mother and Wah-ler-wee were sat with them, marvelling over Erland's blueberry duck. Except that they didn't call her Wah-ler-wee any more because last week Brett had said her name properly for the first time so now – and forever more – she would be known as Valerie.

They said, in hushed voices later that night as the chill crept in at the open front door, that they would try to make today the start of a new Trelawney-Best tradition.

Valerie nodded enthusiastically and Beth didn't detect any false pretence. It may have just been the mulled ale, which ended up not being as mild as Beth had intended.

As she closed the door, the draft fluttered the mistletoe boughs around the walls. She sighed heavily and went upstairs to bed.

That January, they waited for the snow to come, as forecast, but it only fell in the north of England and in Scotland. The closest it fell to Bath was Nottingham.

It'll come, Danny said.

Deep into winter, she visited Fleur's grave for the first time.

During the run up to the funeral and at the ceremony itself, Kimberley and Keith were nowhere in sight. Their barge had even moved on. Beth helped make the arrangements, paying for as many extras as possible. No one had an opinion on where Fleur should be remembered so Beth chose Bath, in a bespoke spot in the crematorium grounds overlooking a lake – it being the closest she could get to replicating the muddy pool in Fleur's photograph.

The words for the plaque were difficult. She and Danny sat down at the kitchen table and wrote them together:

In loving memory of Fleur Wishart
May you now rest in peace, sweet child

The words seemed crass now, steeped in sentiment. Yet they had felt right at the time.

Still, the sight of the plaque moved her so utterly that she found it hard to breathe. She looked away, watching a kestrel that was hovering over the wild patch of land beyond the chapel.

She knelt down to snip the lawn with a pair of scissors and to polish the brass. Upon doing so, she noticed a pink object lying deep within the grass at the foot of Fleur's plaque. She immediately thought of the pink object lying in the muddy pool – the object that she could never quite make out in the photograph.

She reached forward to pick it up. It was a pink lotus flower – fresh, protected from the winter chill by the overgrown grass. It couldn't have been there long.

She looked about her. There was no one around, but the kestrel.

Was there someone else who knew about Fleur, who knew her story, her delicate history, who wanted to honour her and remember her?

She shook her head sadly, placing the lotus back at the base of the plaque. She began to rub the brass. She would never know.

On the first day of February, Danny was playing on his home ground for Bath Under 16's in an important qualifier for the last sixteen teams for the South-West Premier Cup. The last time he had played the Exeter Colts, he had broken his leg.

He had to go out hard from the start, because they looked to be a fitter squad, but not so hard that he ended up in A&E.

He had spent the night before scanning his grandmother's grimoire for gems of wisdom ahead of the game, something to give him the edge that he needed. It didn't take him long to find it. It turned out that, interpreted correctly, his drunken grandma had some interesting things to say. For example, the first day of February was the feast of Imbolc – the time of the growing of the Light. If it snowed on the feast of Imbolc, things of great beauty occurred.

So if it snowed today, he would win against the Colts.

His mum couldn't come because Brett had chicken pox. Erland was here though. Danny hadn't asked him to come. It was a miracle, but Danny hadn't shown any signs of pleasure about it. He just shot Erland a taciturn glance of acknowledgement, and then offered him a backer to the game on his Silverfox Demon. He'd never offered to do this before. Erland knew how special an invitation it was. But likewise he shot Danny a taciturn glance of acknowledgement back. And so it was agreed.

It was cold. He was wearing training skins underneath his shirt. He glanced upwards as he came out on the pitch, to what sounded like twelve people clapping, thudding their gloves together. It looked like it was going to snow.

Of course, there was a time when snow meant something more...Although none of that stuff mattered now. He couldn't believe that he used to think swallowing snow would make his dad appear. Who cared about that now anyhow? They had all moved on so far.

Elias had taught him that magic wasn't something flippant, random, but something tangible, solid, scientific. Danny had so many questions to ask him when he came for spring equinox next month, things that he had been noting in his compendium.

He had also been compiling a list of things to say in response to Angel, who began writing to him before Christmas, having realised that she could finally go on and on without any comeback from Danny, who couldn't post letters to the barge in return. He would get his revenge when she came to stay.

Erland was seated in the terraces now, waving uncoolly. It was to wind Danny up. Danny did the V's sign back when no one was looking.

The whistle blew. Danny shot forward. Today he was re-enacting the Champion's League final from last summer – Chelsea versus Barcelona. Except that he was going to score quicker than Lampard had. He would skid in front of the V.I.P. box (the chip stand in this case) onto his knees, his fists in the air. The gloved hands would thud appreciatively.

The snow began to fall eleven minutes into the game.

At first, Danny thought he could hear someone whispering to him: *When the first snow falls…*His ears were ringing with the cold. *On the day of Imbolc…*He gave his ear a slap as he booted the ball, looking about him to check that no one *was* whispering to him. *On the first day of the growing Light…*

He looked up at the sky and it was then that he noticed it was snowing. *He will come.*

The coaches began to discuss whether to stop the game. It was a proper blizzard. Danny's hair was soaking. It was refreshing, as well as numbing. He was about to put a goal together, when the whistle blew and the referee shouted at them all to stop – that they would organise a rematch for next week.

Danny left the pitch, his eyes burning with the cold and with disappointment. He put his hands on his hips and bent over, gasping for breath.

When he stood up straight, Erland was in front of

him with a funny look on his face.

"Look," Erland said, pointing.

There were times when Erland looked like a twenty-one-year-old biochemistry graduate, and other times, like now, when he looked like a child about to wet his pants.

Danny followed the trail of Erland's pointing finger. There, amongst the twelve padded supporters, was a thirteenth person talking to the other parents, whom Danny did not at once recognise.

"It's Dad," said Erland, in a voice that sounded as though he'd been caught shop-lifting. "Should we–?"

"Come on," said Danny. "Let's go. I'll grab my kit. Wait for me in the car park."

Erland nodded, still with his eye upon the terraces.

But Peter caught up with them as Danny was wrestling with the lock on his Silverfox Demon. His hands were too numb to work the bolt.

"Hurry up, Dan," said Erland, his skinny knees visibly knocking. "He's coming."

"Hello, lads."

It was too late. Their dad was stood before them.

"It's great to see you," Peter said.

Erland pulled the flaps down on his deer hunter hat, fastening them under his chin to secure himself.

"Oh, leave it out, will you?" said Danny to his father, as he finally managed to work the lock. "Come on, buddy," he then said to Erland, in a manner that suggested that the Trelawney boys always spoke to each other like that.

"How are you?" said Peter.

"In wonderful health," said Erland, politely. "And you?"

Danny nudged him. "Come on, bud. Onto the back." Erland lifted his leg stiffly and climbed behind his brother onto the saddle. "Let's go."

"Boys!" shouted Peter. "Wait! Won't you just listen?"

Danny pedalled ridiculously slowly through the snow, the tyres grinding.

"Wasn't that a bit rude?" said Erland, digging his fingers into Danny's waist. "Mum will be cross."

"Oh, for Pete's sake!" said Danny. "We won't tell her!"

He was panting with the effort of trying to move both himself and his brother forward across the drifts in the car park.

"Just let…me…pedal…"

And at that they wobbled and lurched sideways, flat into the snow.

Peter approached, his shoes crunching. "That was one of the funniest things I've seen in a long while," he said, looking down at them.

"Glad we're a joke to you," said Danny, still lying flat out on the snow. He felt exhausted. He glanced up at his father. What *was* he doing here anyway? "Does your wife know you're here?" he said.

"We're in the middle of a divorce," Peter replied, matter-of-factly.

Danny sat up, feeling the snow saturate his shorts.

His dad held his hand out to him. Danny accepted it and was pulled upwards. Erland got up on his own, still hiding inside his deer hunter hat.

"I've got a job in Bath," said Peter.

"In Bath," said Danny.

"Yes, in Bath."

"Are there jobs in Bath?"

"Apparently. It's for the Herald, the local paper."

"I know what the Herald is," Danny snapped.

Erland cringed, his body recoiling.

"Does mum know?" said Danny.

"No."

"Maybe we should go tell her?" said Erland suddenly, undoing the poppers on his hat.

They put Danny's Silverfox Demon in the back of their dad's estate car. They put the Silverfox Demon in the back of their dad's car on their way back from the club house. They drove home with his bike in the back on his way back from a football match. Things that normal lads did every weekend with their dads. The other lads said things like that all the time – hey Dad, chuck the bike in the back, will you? Chuck it in the back after footy, Dad... These were things that Danny had never had cause to say before. And now, they were doing it.

Neither of them wanted to sit in the front of the car. They sat together in the back, side-by-side; the Trelawney boys. Danny's legs stinging from the cold, Erland's hat still unpopped – the flaps dangling like soppy dog ears.

They sat like that, stiff, like little kids strapped into the back of the car, all the way home.

It was getting dark and the snow was falling in black dots, lit by the weak dusk streetlights, and somewhere along the journey Danny began to believe that the most fantastic thing in the world had just started to happen.

Beth was stood anxiously at the kitchen window watching the snow fall, wondering whether Danny's match would be cancelled, how the boys would get home on his bike, whether she should risk taking the car out.

Danny had left his mobile phone on the table. She turned to look at it, wishing it was safe in his pocket instead of there. Brett was crying softly on his beanbag in the corner of the room where he was trying to rest under a blanket. He was miserable, feverish and itchy with chicken pox.

When the car pulled up, her first thought was that a kind father had brought the boys home. What a relief. She felt gratitude rush through her. What a nice...

She peered closer, rubbing her hands on the window to erase the condensation. It was funny – the man who was opening up the boot, his head bent against the snow storm looked just like Peter. Danny and Erland were laughing, talking to him about something. They were pointing to the house. She wanted to duck, disappear from sight. But it was too late. He was gazing at her – at her form at the window, illuminated by the kitchen light.

And, stood underneath the streetlight as he was, when he turned his face to look at her, she could see quite plainly that it was indeed Peter.

She laughed – a sharp little laugh that wanted to become a cry. She moved to the front door and stood behind it, without opening it.

When Danny and Erland came in, they didn't say a

word. They stripped down to their underpants and hung their clothes on the radiator, before sloping off to the lounge and shutting the door. All that was left of those two boys was a puddle of snow water on the hallway floor.

Which left her and Peter.

She hadn't put the light on. She could just make him out – his silhouette; could hear his quick expectant breath.

"I love you," she said.

She had never uttered those words to anyone but her sons. She didn't feel foolish or vulnerable saying them now. Nothing mattered in that moment – none of the anxious facts; in that moment it was merely about stating the truth.

To her utmost surprise, Peter burst into tears.

"Oh, thank God, Beth!" he said. "Thank God!"

TWENTY

Yew Tree Cottage sold that spring. A property developer bought it to turn into a bed and breakfast, and a riding school.

Beth wanted to see it one last time before the renovators swarmed in. Elias was moored with them for the spring equinox; Skye and Angel were staying in the house as before. So Beth took the opportunity to spare the boys the journey and go alone.

Although not entirely alone.

"Are you sure you don't mind?" She poked her head back through the car window. "I'll only be half an hour."

"I don't mind at all. The match is on." He kissed her on the lips.

She smiled at him and turned to walk along the sea front. Pengilly felt different. Yew Tree Cottage was sporting a bright *Sold* sign; the tree that had been struck by lightening was covered in green buds; the wild garden lawn had been mowed. The air felt lighter, fresher, less oppressive. The sea was grinding relentlessly, hissing against the stones on the shores, but it sounded exhilarating now, not oppressive.

She glanced back over her shoulder, knowing that Peter's eyes would be fixed upon her, watching her leave, even if Chelsea were playing.

She waved before turning into the chapel.

She stood facing the closed door, as she had done thirty years ago – on the day she had been told not to come back to God's Own House again.

Unbolting the door, she pushed it open, her eyes adjusting to the dark. There was the cool air; there were the candles; there was the solace, the refuge against the busyness of the world outside.

"Reverend Trist?" she called out.

He was expecting her. He was sat in the front row of the pews, his head bent in prayer. He stood up to greet her. He was larger here, in his own place – larger in his holy robes, in a sacred setting.

He motioned for her to sit next to him.

"I'm glad you came to say goodbye," he said. "Although I hope this is not our last meeting."

"I hope not too," said Beth.

"I had a call…" he said, tilting his head to look at her enquiringly, his eyes glowing. "…From my friend – the lady who works for Cornwall children's services."

"Oh, yes?" said Beth, fixing her eye upon the stained glass windows.

She thought of the giant mosaic of Jesus at Sacré-Couer, of the Benedictine sisters singing, of the child who had first appeared to her in Paris – whose identity she had never solved. The vision was beginning to wane in strength each time it appeared, a plant that Beth was refusing to water. It was curling, wilting, fading to dust.

"She said they received a colossal donation recently. Anonymously."

"Oh?"

"I don't suppose you had anything to do with that?" he said, nudging her gently.

"Of course not," she said, still gazing upwards.

"I am glad you have found peace, Beth," he said, placing his hand on hers. He cleared his throat, plucking up the courage to ask something outrageous. "I don't wish to pry…but when we met at West Marsh, you hinted that you wanted to find love…I can sense a change in you…Have you found such a thing?"

She laughed. "Yes, Reverend. I believe I have."

"And it is…a successful venture? It is lasting?"

She laughed again. "You are funny…Yes, I believe it's a successful venture. I'm with Danny and Erland's father."

"The one who got away? But what of the wife?"

"She cheated on him," she said.

"As a man of the cloth, I cannot celebrate the breakdown of a holy union. And yet…I did say that I thought it would manifest this way…It brings me great joy to hear that you have found love."

They sat together in the solace of the chapel.

"You know…" he said, his voice lowered as though someone might overhear. "I've been thinking back over Pamela's time with me at West Marsh – the things that she told me of herself… She rarely smiled, I noticed. Do you recall that?"

"She was rather miserable," said Beth, recalling Pammy's strange half-smile – her reluctance to donate a smile to the universe.

"I never gave it much thought, I confess," he said. "And then one day, in the last days of her life, I told her a joke to lift her spirits, and she laughed and laughed. And I noticed that her teeth were false."

Beth thought of all the sludgy, sloppy food that Pammy had served up – her tendency towards mushy, pulpy produce. So that was why.

"The day that she died, I pressed her on the matter," the reverend said, his hand still upon Beth's. "And she cried. That bitter twisted old woman cried..."

He pressed Beth's hand distractedly. "And do you know what she told me? That her father knocked all her front teeth out when she was a child."

Beth froze, the pressure of the reverend's hand seeming suddenly heavy upon her. "And that was why she never smiled," he said.

"Because she was missing her front teeth," Beth said, goosebumps creeping up her arms.

She felt perspiration break out along her hairline, across her back.

"I'd better be going," she said. "Peter's waiting for me outside. But thank you for your time, and for all you have done for me." She pressed a soft kiss onto his cheek. "I hope we meet again."

"We shall," he said, standing to see her out.

And she left – the heavy door shutting firmly closed behind her once more.

The seventh child

Pamela Lazenby was born in Dover in a hotel overlooking the white cliffs, which referred to itself in guide books and on its paint-chipped sign in the front garden, as the last inn in England. The hotel was a shabby place with toilets that creaked and moaned, but her parents made a tidy profit. Pammy was an only child and was used to helping mop floors, mowing the lawn and making the beds for the guests. As there were no siblings or friends to talk to, she befriended the objects that she worked with, and looked forward to seeing them each day: her mop, her secateurs, her mower.

Her mother was always busy with the running of the hotel, and her father liked to gamble. Pammy didn't know what gambling was, but knew it was something to do with horses. She liked horses for this reason and craved one of her own. She was a daddy's girl – loving everything that he loved.

But one day the horses did something bad to her father. He was sat in his armchair, sobbing, saying he had lost everything. Pammy was wearing her green cheesecloth school dress. There was an empty bottle at her father's feet. She didn't know where her mother was. She crept forward.

It's only the horses, she told him. *They wouldn't hurt you, Daddy.*

He didn't give her any warning. He drew back his fist and struck her in the mouth. She held her bloody teeth out to him in her hand in shock. *Daddy! Look what you've done!*

He looked horrified. *Pammy, princess!* he said, trying to get up but sinking back down.

She ran upstairs. It took them days to change her out of her dress, to get her to unclench her hand, to bring her back to life.

When they did – when they changed her clothes, shampooed her hair, bought her a pony and built her a stable – they realised that it hadn't made any difference; that she would never be the same again.

Beth asked Peter to drive her all the way to Treale, the nearest town, to buy it – since there were no florists in Pengilly – and then back again to Pengilly, with it held in tissue paper on her lap as though it were made of brittle sugar.

They walked together through the gates of the churchyard, to the newest headstone and stopped before it.

Peter put his arm around her. There were two seagulls circling the air above them, crying conspiratorially.

She looked out at the white horses in the bay of Pengilly, over her shoulder at Yew Tree Cottage, and at the solid sea-bashed walls of the chapel. She was wearing her mother's ring. She twisted it around on the finger, looking pensively across the coastline to Pentruthen, to the bay where her parents had fallen in love.

And then she knelt at the foot of the grave.

Gently, tenderly, she placed the lotus at the foot of the headstone.

"I forgive you, Pammy," she said.

Peter kept his arm around her as they walked back to the car. The sun was beginning to fade – a burnt orange glow descending, transforming the ugly rooftops of Pengilly.

They set off for home, Peter with one hand on the wheel, the other holding Beth's hand. As they pulled out of Pengilly, they exchanged happy glances, as though they had only just met.

ENJOYED *THE BURNT LOTUS*?

Please write a review of *The Burnt Lotus* at Amazon.co.uk.
All reviews are read by the author and appreciated.
You can also leave comments or just say hello on
Cath Weeks' Facebook page:
www.facebook.com/cath.weeks.1

IN A BOOK CLUB?

Book club discussion notes are available for both
The Burnt Lotus and *The Mood Ring*. To obtain the notes,
contact Cath at www.facebook.com/cath.weeks.1